HIDDEN
PASSIONS

EMMA HOLLY

Hidden Passions

Emma Holly

Discover other exciting Emma Holly titles at: http://www.emmaholly.com

This story is a work of fiction and should be treated as such. It includes sexually explicit content that is only appropriate for adults—and not every adult at that. Those who are offended by more adventurous depictions of sexuality or frank language possibly shouldn't read it. Literary license has been taken in this book. It is not intended to be a sexual manual. Any resemblance to actual places, events, or persons living or dead is either fictitious or coincidental. That said, the author hopes you enjoy this tale!

Hidden Passions is an approximately 74,000-word novel.

ISBN-10: 0988894343

ISBN-13: 978-0-9888943-4-1

cover photo: fotosearch.com

OTHER TITLES BY EMMA HOLLY

CONTENTS

CHAPTER ONE

CHRIS Savoy, weretiger and fireman, hefted a case of sparkling water at the cost of a pleasant strain to his huge shoulders. He'd tended bar for tonight's rooftop party and was now packing up remains. He didn't mind cleanup duty. Their lupine hosts had cleared the rest of the trash, and Chris was no weak kitten. Never mind his gargantuan size as a tiger, in human form he was six-foot-eight of solid muscle and God knew how many pounds. His hair was shining chestnut with brighter streaks of gold. Despite a recent cut, the strands had a tendency to need brushing back. Underneath, the bones of his face looked carved, his eyes a brown that edged into orange. When his tiger rose within him, glints of demon light danced in them.

He frowned as that thought surfaced. His tiger wasn't a demon, just the animal half of him.

"You got this, Chris? We don't mind staying on to help." The question came from Jonah, his immediate subordinate at the fire station. Jonah was nearly as big as Chris, with skin like teak and dark lustrous eyes. He wasn't someone Chris really knew, except in a work sense, where the cat was reliable. Liam—yet another tiger/fireman—stood beside him, as fair-skinned and golden-haired as his crewmate was brown. The pair made a striking couple . . . not that they'd think of themselves that way.

"I got it," Chris confirmed, mentally shaking his head at himself. He was accustomed to keeping secrets, this one especially. "You two go. We're on shift tomorrow, and it's past your bedtime."

"Old men don't need sleep?" Liam joked. Chris outranked him, but the teasing proved the younger man trusted his temper.

"This 'old man' could swing you by the tail on no sleep at all." Chris set the case of water on a handcart, then reached for a box of wine bottles. There wasn't much to pack compared to the supply he'd started with. Tonight's guests had been mostly shifters, and they could put away liquor.

1

"That was a good party," Jonah observed, still lingering. "Considering it was thrown by wolves."

Ah, Chris thought. This was what the terrible twosome's delayed departure was about. Jonah was third in the clan, and Liam was their omega. Jonah was one of their later adds, brought into the clan from another station around the same time as Liam. Despite the power differential, the pair was as close as littermates.

Chris wasn't someone either cat normally hung with outside of work.

"It was a good party," he agreed, settling the second case and straightening.

The roof of the converted warehouse was done up to look like a park: beds of grass, flowers, faerie lights strung between newly planted saplings in competition with the stars. Visibly debating whether to open up about what was bothering him, Liam fidgeted with the front of his dark blue T-shirt. The badge for the Resurrection Fire Department was printed in gray on it.

"That wolf really is alpha to us," he blurted. "That Nate Rivera."

"I warned you he was." Chris's tone was calm and not scolding. "When Evina couldn't force me to shift by herself, he joined his power with hers and got it done."

Evina Mohajit wasn't just Chris's closest friend. She was his station chief and their clan alpha. Recently, Chris had been badly burned while trying to rescue a pair of kids. Afterward, too traumatized to change on his own, Evina and Nate had chivvied him through the process so he could heal. His relief that he wouldn't spend his life disfigured was fresh in his consciousness.

Chris liked being an able-bodied, good-looking were more than he'd realized.

"But . . . they're engaged," Liam objected. "That wolf will be her *husband*."

Tigresses didn't often marry; they were free spirits. Nonetheless, Nate had proposed to Evina at tonight's party, and she'd accepted. The stylish wolf hadn't done the deed half-assed. He'd gone down on one knee and given her a ring, betraying nervousness and dash in equal parts. Privately, Chris found Nate's actions romantic. The chance *he'd* experience anything similar was astronomically remote.

"Evina loves him," he said with a wisp of dryness. "And he'll make a good father to her cubs. She was bound to get over that idiot ex of hers sometime."

"I get that," Liam said, because no one could argue their alpha's ex hadn't appreciated her. "The problem is, what does him being alpha mean to us?"

"Well, it doesn't mean he'll be our boss at work," Chris assured their junior man. "He's a wolf. A cop. He can't do a fireman's job, and I doubt he'd want to."

"What about the rest of the time? You felt his energy. He's as strong as Evina. Is he going to try to boss us in our personal lives?"

"I don't know," Chris said. "But Nate Rivera doesn't strike me as that sort of man."

"Evina wouldn't let him overstep." Jonah almost sounded sure of it.

"No, she wouldn't," Chris agreed. "She respects our boundaries."

"He's not alpha to the wolves," Liam put in. "He's not even his pack's second."

This was an oddity Chris could not explain. Strictly speaking, a wolf shouldn't be anything to a tiger clan. He shrugged philosophically. "This is Resurrection. Magic works the way magic works."

"Doesn't him hooking up with her bug you?" Jonah's dark eyes were watchful, as if he had a stake in Chris being upset. "You're Evina's beta. We always thought, someday, you'd put the moves on her."

Chris couldn't hide his amusement. Jonah and Liam were like kids hoping Mom would marry their soccer coach. Little did they guess how inappropriate the match would be. "Evina and I have never been more than friends."

"But you're great together. All the stations say they wish their first and second functioned as smoothly as you do."

Again, Jonah watched him closely. Shrugging off the effect, Chris clapped him on his thick shoulder. The heat Jonah radiated was typical for shifters. "We'll work it out. Even if Nate weren't alpha, we'd have to adjust to him being in Evina's life. We're used to having her to ourselves. In the meantime, if you have a problem with him, bring it to me. Evina has enough to deal with settling into being a family with him and the cubs."

Jonah held his gaze and then nodded, for which Chris was grateful. If his subordinates had questioned his ability to handle the newcomer, he'd really have been bugged. Authority was a mental game, based as much in belief as muscle to back it up. Chris would go claw-to-claw with anyone he had to, but physical clashes hurt morale, and morale was important in firefighting.

The metropolis where they plied their trade was a "Pocket" city. Located in—but generally invisible to—the human state of New York, Resurrection mixed the mysticism of the land of Faerie with the humans' more stable reality. In a place like this, where a blaze might as easily be magical or mundane, citizens depended on them performing cohesively. *Clear heads, clear hearts, clear spirits* was the RFD motto.

Cool cats knocked down infernos. Hotheads got their fur singed off.

Liam, the young Irish lunk, was as hotheaded a tiger as Chris had on the crew. Luckily, he respected Chris as much as he did their alpha.

"You got it, boss," he said. "If you can stand Rivera, so can we. And as long as he keeps that gay cocksucker away from us, he won't hear any guff from me."

Chris wasn't prepared for this comment. Realizing his jaw had dropped, he shut it. Resurrection's shifters were notoriously macho. For a wolf to come out as Nate's packmate had was rare. Homosexuals existed of course, probably in the same percentage as among mundanes. *Don't ask, don't tell* was a survival tactic Chris was familiar with.

"His pack has accepted him," he advised Liam carefully. "Be smart enough —and polite enough—not to insult him where he or they can hear."

"I mean it," he added when Liam pulled a face. "Forget talk like that not being diplomatic. If you act homophobic, people will think you're gay as well."

Chris saw he'd gotten through. Considering his own situation, the irony of his words didn't escape him. He bumped Liam's shoulder with his fist. "He's just a guy. You can like him or not for who he is."

"He's a guy who sucks dick," Liam said, apparently fixated on this horror.

"You like girls who suck dick," Jonah pointed out, too impish to let it lie.

"That's different," Liam retorted stubbornly.

"Sheesh." Chris didn't attempt to stop his eyes from rolling. "Both of you get out of here. I'd have a more intelligent conversation with a gargoyle."

"Can gargoyles be gay?" Jonah wondered as the pair trailed away toward the door to the roof access.

Chris couldn't decide if Jonah entertaining this possibility was a sign of enlightenment. Then again, how enlightened could Chris claim to be? Like a lot of the city's gays, he was firmly closeted. Jonah and Liam had no idea the number of people they looked up to who were attracted to their own genders. Until they did, they had no reason to change their attitudes. Of course, that their attitudes *would* change wasn't guaranteed. Chris himself wasn't always comfortable with his preference.

Sighing at the dilemma, he returned to stacking leftover bar supplies on the steel handcart. Wolves and tigers had a longstanding and, for the most part, amicable rivalry. Cats comprised the bulk of the RFD, while wolves dominated the police force. Traditionally, firemen were more popular with the public—a fact the RFD didn't let their cop counterparts forget. Grudgingly, Chris gave this particular pack credit for generosity. They'd paid for everything tonight, treating Evina and her tigers like honored guests. Chris had tended bar, and two of their men had pitched in to cook, but other than that all that had been asked of them was that they enjoy themselves.

Freed from Jonah and Liam's distraction, Chris finished packing up quickly. One good shove got the cart's wheels rolling. He was glad Rivera's building had an elevator. Getting this stuff back to his apartment would have been a bear otherwise.

~

Tony Lupone liked to tease his friend and fellow pack member Nate that he should have been the gay one. Nate's slick warehouse conversion loft resembled a spread in a magazine: huge, airy, and almost laughably stylish. It was also laughably neat—at least to someone with Tony's casual outlook on housekeeping.

They were shifters, for goodness sake. A germ or two wouldn't lay them out.

Despite not understanding why it mattered if your guests could eat off the floor, Tony *was* Nate's friend. Before the newly engaged couple took off with the cubs to conk out at Evina's house, Nate had entrusted Tony with ensuring the party wrapped up safely. Tony had organized rides for over-imbibers, supplied the volunteer cleaners with trash bags, and thanked everyone he got a chance to for coming.

This last was more of an ordeal than Nate or probably anyone realized. Tony was the lowest ranking member of his pack. He didn't mind the position and liked to think he had social skills, but the energy of his wolf—a vibe all shifters were sensitive to—didn't automatically command respect. Though charm and humor were good defenses, they couldn't smooth every bump.

They certainly couldn't smooth every bump with macho ass-hats who weren't used to him being out. His pack had grown accustomed to it, or at least weren't shocked anymore. A couple of those stupid cats had actually jerked away when he'd slapped their shoulders, like being gay might be contagious.

Tony snickered to himself as he loaded dirty pots semi-neatly into the second of Nate's two fancy dishwashers. If only gayness *were* contagious. He'd have had fun with a couple of tonight's guests if they'd contracted his "condition."

He undercut his own humor with a sigh. He'd admit to being a teensy bit impulsive. While he'd kept his sexual nature secret for what felt like forever, he couldn't swear he'd totally thought through what being out would be like. Social creature that he was, the aloneness wore on him. He might occasionally have been a short-tempered ass-hat himself when he was in the closet, but at least he'd *belonged.* He'd had no trouble charming women or knowing how to act in a bar. Most shifters could get it up regardless. Their beast halves weren't that damn choosy. That his human half wasn't having fun with his lovers Tony had managed to conceal. Now he barely knew which bars to patronize, much less how to go about hooking up.

He couldn't explain why, but who he hooked up with felt more important now.

Grimacing, he wedged one final pan into the dishwasher. He hadn't had a date in ages, or even a decent flirt. Coming out was uncomfortably like regaining his virginity.

"Stupid," he said aloud and then, "Okay, Nate, where do you keep your spell packs?"

Doing his best to shove his bad mood aside, he began opening drawers and cabinets. The Brownie Hygienics wouldn't work right without their magic soap and, friend or not, Tony wasn't about to scrub that mountain of pots by hand. The drawer to his left held silver, the one to his right a custom-fitted selection of spice bottles. Nate liked to cook, though he'd been banned from doing so tonight, the celebration having been in his honor. He'd closed an important case, somewhat in spite of the rest of the squad, and Adam—their alpha—had come up with the plan for the party as a peace offering. Tony's parents and two of the hulking tigers had supplied the necessary culinary manpower, dirtying every conceivable utensil in the process.

"Damn," Tony said, because he'd slammed a drawer shut and caught his finger. As he stuck it reflexively in his mouth, he realized he was embarrassingly close to tears.

Tony refused to be that big of a pussy. He was only upset because Nate was so happy. The wolf totally deserved to fall in love—and to be loved back by someone as kickass as Evina. Nate was a great guy. Of all the pack, he'd accepted Tony's big announcement the easiest. He'd openly said he liked Tony better now that he was being his real self. He didn't freak when Tony pretended to flirt with him, and he never pulled away. He was still Tony's friend, just like he'd been before.

When Evina agreed to marry him, Nate's aura had lit up like sunrise.

"Fuck," Tony said, the moisture in his eyes having spilled traitorously out.

He *didn't* have a crush on Nate. He wasn't that stupid. He wanted what Nate had: to find someone who was right for him.

Barring that, a sweaty wild one-night stand wouldn't be terrible.

He smiled, straightening with a jerk a moment later. Like all wolves, he had sharp hearing. The freight elevator had just clanked open. The rumble of wheels on concrete warned him someone was approaching. Tony hadn't locked Nate's door. Their pack strolled in and out of each other's houses too often to bother. Hinges creaked as the heavy entrance swung open.

"Hello," a male voice called. "I'm returning the undrunk booze."

Shit, Tony thought. He recognized who it was: the hot-as-hell tiger bartender.

His heart started beating faster, which he really would have preferred it not do. Cats had shifter hearing too. The last thing he needed was one of those stupid felines realizing he had the hots for him.

"Come on in," he said, blowing out a breath as he tried to think calming thoughts. "I'm cleaning up the kitchen."

He was almost braced by the time the cat pushed the loaded handcart into the wide-open living space. He guessed cats *were* snoopy. The gorgeous fireman looked around curiously, his muscle-packed shoulders as broad as a barn door.

"Wow," he said, turning toward the warehouse's tall front windows. "This place is amazing."

The tiger's rear view was amazing—his back, his ass, his strong mile-long legs. Tony was a big guy himself, but this man was a damned giant. He noticed the tiger's jeans were faded in all the right places. Not needing any more inspiration, Tony wrenched his eyes from them.

"Nate has great taste," he said, the words as level as he could make them.

The tiger turned. His expression was as unreadable as an actual cat's. "It's Tony, right?"

"Yes," Tony said. Normally, he was chatty. He ordered himself not to be right then.

The tiger nodded. He didn't introduce himself, though Tony was aware his name was Chris. He'd heard the tiger's coworkers call him that. Tony hadn't precisely been trying to scope him out, but he also knew Chris was Evina's beta and mixed a mean mango martini. He'd smiled a lot at the party—not a loudmouth but easygoing. Someone had mentioned he'd been hospitalized with third-degree burns not too long ago. No trace of them remained . . . or of his earlier good humor. Tony suspected the reason Chris looked so serious now was him.

God forbid a straight guy gave the infamous gay wolf the wrong idea.

Right then, Tony resented his new reality more than he could express.

"You know where I should stash these bottles?" Chris asked.

"I'll take care of them," Tony said, suddenly wanting him out of there. "I know where Nate keeps things."

Chris glanced down at the boxes and rubbed his jaw. When his gaze returned to Tony, it very carefully said nothing. "Your pack left you to clean up by yourself?"

"I'm gay," Tony snapped. "Not infirm."

His own words made his face go hot. To his amazement, they made the tiger smile. "I didn't mean that. I just don't think it's right for me to dump this job on you if everyone else did too."

"Oh," Tony said. "Sorry, I—"

"Forget it," the tiger said easily, apparently unfazed by his snippiness. "You must have had people assume stupid things about you a time or two."

"Yeah," Tony said, relieved he hadn't inadvertently offended someone who was bound to have an impact on Nate's new life. "Nate's storeroom is over there. If you stack the boxes inside, that'll be fine."

"I'll unpack them," the tiger said. "I'm Chris, by the way."

"Tony," he responded automatically, forgetting Chris had said he already knew. "Tony Lupone."

Shutting up, he tried not to blush furiously.

The tiger's mouth curved again. It was a nice expression, hinting at mischief and wry humor—like he'd get any joke anyone told him. Somewhat to Tony's horror, the smile caused his dick to swell.

"I'll get started," Chris said, picking up the first box.

Tony watched him all the way to Nate's storeroom, remembering too late that this was a bad idea. His mouth was dry when he finally looked away, his cock so hard it probably was getting tooth marks from his zipper. Tony wanted to adjust the thing but feared drawing attention. He was lucky Nate's very open kitchen had a big island to hide behind.

The tiger returned for another crate and then disappeared again. From the sound of it, he was filling Nate's wine shelves efficiently. "I heard you organized the work on the roof," he commented from inside.

Tony's mental gears weren't turning over smoothly. "Work?"

"You got a bunch of cops to spend their time off installing the plantings and whatnot."

Whatnot? Evina's big tough second said *whatnot?* Tony shook himself more alert. "My alpha put out the call for volunteers. I just oversaw who turned up."

Chris emerged from the storage room, his smile mischievous again. "I heard you rode herd on them pretty hard."

"Well, Nate *is* particular," Tony said. "He'd have minded if they did a crap job."

The tiger braced straight-armed on the opposite side of the island's black marble top. "You surprised them," he said conversationally. "They didn't expect the low man on your pack's ladder to be so assertive."

"They told you that?"

Chris shrugged his massive shoulders and cracked a grin. "People tell bartenders all sorts of things. To be honest, I wish our omega had your confidence. Shifters tend to rely on bluster when they feel insecure. That's not safe when you're doing a dangerous job."

Tony had a hard time believing Chris's low man really was insecure. The beta's energy was too reassuring for that to be likely.

"Our alpha is no bully," he said aloud. "And my big brother has my back if I need it."

He usually had his back at least. Tony coming out had been an adjustment.

"Rick," Chris said, naming him with no trouble.

Tony's brow furrowed over him knowing that. Then the light bulb flashed. "You're diplomatting me."

Chris lifted one eyebrow. "Diplomatting you?"

"My pack and your clan will be thrown together once Nate marries Evina. You want to make sure we get along. That's why you're being friendly."

"Wouldn't I befriend your alpha if that's what I was up to?"

"I'm the baby," Tony said triumphantly. "You couldn't choose a more endearing route to my alpha's heart than being nice to me. Plus, I'm an easy target."

Chris snorted out a laugh. "An *easy* target. Why do I doubt that?"

"Because you're flattering me."

Still smiling, Chris shook his head. His gaze came to rest steadily on Tony's. His irises were an unusual color, closer to tigerish orange than plain brown. God, he was good-looking, his strong, sculpted features reminding Tony of an antique hero out of Greek myth. Chris looked like he'd grab a bow and aim at a God . . . or maybe seduce one. Lust shocked in fresh waves through his already heated body. Possibly the reaction showed. Chris's face went serious.

"I'm not flattering you," he said.

His voice was a fraction deeper than before, almost as if he were turned on too.

No way, Tony thought. True, his gaydar wasn't perfect; he hadn't had sufficient opportunities to calibrate its dial. This guy, though, read totally straight to him.

"So, uh," Tony said, "if you were a spell pack, where would you be?"

"A spell pack?"

"For the dishwashers. They won't work right without their special soap."

"Ah," Chris responded like the weird moment hadn't happened. "Hold on. I think I saw some in the store room next to the silver polish."

He went to get them, leaving Tony a little sweaty and a lot off balance. Chris came back with the desired items.

"These?" He held them out to Tony. He was on the same side of the island now. He smelled good, like a hot grassy savannah.

"Thanks," Tony said, accepting them.

His throat was scratchy, his answer rough. *Do not blush again,* he ordered. With a minimum of fumbling, probably due more to luck than self-control, he pushed the enchanted soap packs into the proper slots. When he pushed the ON buttons, both Brownie Hygienics purred.

Given how hard his heart was thumping, he doubted the dishwashers' action could mask the sound. Chris still stood beside him, tiger tall, shifter warm, radiating the sweet wild scent that prevented Tony's rigid cock from relaxing. He couldn't force himself to look at the cat. His cock was a fricking flagpole, aching for things Tony—despite being out—hadn't managed to give it yet. If the man beside him looked down . . . if he even moved an inch closer . . .

"Tony," Chris said, as serious as an undertaker. "Are you discreet?"

"Discreet?"

"Do you feel compelled to blab everything you know, or can you keep . . . sensitive information to yourself?"

Tony knew what *discreet* meant. He simply didn't understand why the cat was asking. Reluctantly, he turned his head to his companion.

Chris's eyes had brightened, lemon glints flaring in the orange.

"Why?" Tony asked.

Chris's gaze searched his. Tony realized the other man's breathing had altered. It was shallower now, quicker, and totally sexified.

"Answer the question first," he said.

"I'm a cop," Tony said. "Knowing when to play my cards close to the vest comes with the job."

Chris stared a heartbeat longer. Tony's whole body tingled at what he thought he saw in his face. Maybe getting stuck on cleanup duty was a blessing in disguise.

"I think—" The tiger's Adam's apple jerked as he swallowed. "I think we have mutual interests we could . . . see to together."

Tony's underarms prickled. "You're gay?"

"I'm not out," Chris said hastily. "I can't afford to have people know. My men . . ."

Chris was more imposing than Tony. Older too—to go by his vibe. Even so, Tony abruptly stopped feeling like his junior. "I understand. Shifters can be terrible homophobes. You can trust me not to give you away."

He put his hand on Chris's upper arm. Though the man wasn't flexing, his bicep was hard as steel under the short sleeve of his navy RFD T-shirt. The tiger's self-control broke a bit at the touch. He glanced down Tony's body and licked his lips.

Seeing the flush that crawled up his cheeks made Tony so-not-sorry for giant boner he was sporting.

"Would you . . . want to do it here?" the tiger asked hoarsely.

Tony's grin split his face. "On the kitchen floor, if you want."

Chris laughed, a hint of relief in it. "I *might* last long enough to get you to a bed."

"We'd have to change Nate's sheets after. He really is a neat freak."

Chris let out an extremely sexy growl, took Tony's face in his hands, and slid his tongue deep into his mouth. Every nerve in Tony's body immediately shot off fireworks. He gripped the tiger's muscled back and dove in, sucking, licking, not caring that his canines lengthened right away or that his moan of desire sounded like a dying calf. He'd never kissed a man before. Knowing he was gay was something Tony's body told him without real world experience. He saw he'd underestimated how powerful giving in to his preference was.

Kissing Chris was birthdays and steak and howling at the moon all rolled into one.

Tony guessed the other man didn't mind his enthusiasm. His fangs slid out to clash with Tony's. The cat was grinding their hips together, rubbing and undulating like a stripper. His erection was as thick and solid as Tony's. Tony found this so exciting it took some doing not to come in his underwear.

After a couple insanely nice minutes, Chris broke off and looked at him. To Tony's pleasure, he was panting.

"Don't stop," Tony couldn't help pleading.

Chris's tigerish eyes glowed with pleasure. "You in a hurry?" he teased.

"You're the first man I've kissed."

Chris's hands had been sliding sexily up and down Tony's back. They stopped at his confession. "You're kidding me."

Tony shook his head.

"So you never . . . You never fucked a man? You've never been fucked by one?"

"Please don't tell me this means you'll stop."

Chris blinked, his perplexity obvious. "I'm not planning to stop. I just— I've never been with someone who hasn't done this before."

"I'm pretty sure I don't need flowers."

Chris blinked again and then laughed. "Lube," he said firmly.

Maybe it was strange, but the word made Tony shudder with arousal. "I think . . . Nate . . . probably has some in his bathroom."

Chris's eyebrows went up, but he didn't ask how he knew. He gestured Tony on with one arm. "Lead the way, wolf boy."

This wasn't easy, despite the path being open and free of walls. Twice, Tony nearly lost his footing on Nate's dark floorboards. His crazily surging hormones were running riot through his muscles.

His klutziness seemed to amuse Chris.

"It's all right," he said, catching Tony's elbow the second time. "Once you've done this, you'll see it isn't hard."

"Oh it's hard," Tony joked. "And having a third leg is not helping my balance."

He meant to grin at the tiger over his shoulder. Instead, he tripped on an area rug. This time Chris wasn't quick enough to save him.

"Shit," he laughed, helping him off his knees.

His firm hold made Tony want to melt all over him. Seeing this, Chris's eyes went completely tiger, his irises flaring with golden light. "Don't make me kiss you before we get what we need."

"We're here," Tony panted, feeling ridiculous at being this overcome. He tipped his head toward the bathroom door.

Chris swung it open and went inside. Nate's bath was clean and modern: white subway tile, nickel fixtures, and a square glass-walled shower. Chris searched the medicine cabinet, came up empty, then rummaged in the chest where Nate stored the stuff he didn't want on display.

"Got it," the tiger said, sending a little jar spinning in the air before catching it neatly.

The coordination required for the simple act sparked a zing within Tony's groin. The response was like taking a tiger's measure out in the wild—as if Chris were demonstrating to Tony's beast that his reflexes were healthy. Of course, part of the energy Tony felt was nervous.

They were going to do this.

"Oh God," he murmured beneath his breath.

His companion grinned at him. "Should I promise to be gentle?"

"Um," Tony said, his knees turned to jelly with desire. "Maybe?"

Chris's fangs glinted. "I want you in a bed. I'll wash the damn sheets myself."

Shit, Tony thought, inwardly delighted at the assertive mojo the other man threw off. "Okay," he said, beginning to back toward the nearby corner where Nate's sleeping platform was.

Chris prowled forward at the same pace Tony was retreating. Tony panted harder, and the other man's tigerish grin broadened. Three strides in, Chris peeled his T-shirt over his head. Muscles moved impressively in his arms and chest, and then the shirt was gone.

Tony lost his breath at the athletic upper body Chris had revealed.

"Wow," he said, taking in the tiger's ripped pecs and abs. Like Tony, he was smooth-skinned and tan all over, his ribs and diaphragm going in and out. Sweat glittered like diamonds on his belly.

His erection was a massive ridge pushing out his jeans, leaving Tony in no doubt of his interest.

"You're a monster," he breathed admiringly.

He glanced up in time to watch a shadow flick across Chris's eyes. The darkness vanished a microsecond later, making Tony question if he'd seen it.

"I won't hurt you," Chris said. "You haven't chosen wrong."

Tony hadn't thought he had. Truthfully, he wasn't *always* right about people, but he was pretty good. "Neither have you," he assured, wondering what had darkened the other's mood.

Whatever it was, Chris shook it off. "Good," he said and undid the top button of his strained jeans.

Tony caught his lower lip under his canines.

"Strip," Chris ordered, letting Tony feel his authority.

Happy to obey, Tony pulled off his pink polo shirt, the one he'd worn to get his slightly conservative older brother's goat. Rick loved him, but he preferred Tony's gayness not to be obvious. As his chest appeared, Chris's handsome features flushed gratifyingly. Though Tony wasn't as big as Chris, he knew he had a good body. He posed so the other could admire it.

"Vamp," the tiger accused good-humoredly.

Tony's feet were already bare. He unbuttoned and unzipped his chinos. Preferring not to fall on his ass again, he pushed them carefully down his legs. His boxer briefs were black, their soft Y-front tented by his cock. Tony liked his underwear to fit snugly. To go by the way Chris's gaze dropped and lingered, the stretchy cotton outlined what he had on offer.

"Very nice," he complimented, his glowing eyes rising. "You can leave those on for me to take care of."

"I see you're the bossy type," Tony joked.

Chris stepped up to him. Their chests weren't quite touching but almost. Against his will, his wolf saw this as a threat. Tony took one step back and his calves hit the low mattress. The tiger raised his brows knowingly.

"I *am* your superior," he pointed out.

"Rank-wise," Tony clarified, excited by the other's size and closeness but trying not to yield too much advantage.

With a half-smile Tony thought might be smug, Chris tossed the jar of lube onto the bed. He put his big hands on the bare skin of Tony's waist. The length and hardness of his fingers were shiver inducing. Chris leaned closer.

"Experience-wise too," he whispered hotly in Tony's ear.

Before Tony could make a smart retort, Chris's fangs lightly nipped his earlobe. Thrills streaked helplessly through Tony's nerves. When it came to sex, wolves loved biting, licking, and claw-play. Apparently, big cats were game as well.

Realization rolled happily through him. "I don't have to hold back with you, do I?"

"Not even a little," Chris promised.

The bigger man pushed his chest, just once and not hard. The gentle shove sat Tony on the mattress edge. From there, the tiger's trouser bulge filled his vision—his whole world, it felt like. His undone waist button gapped, the jeans slung low enough to reveal the clouded edge of his pubic hair. Tony didn't know if he was supposed to wait for an invitation, but he couldn't resist feathering his fingertips across the curls.

The tiger sucked in a breath. The ridge behind his stretched zipper was prominent, the swell of his heavy testicles obvious. Tony inhaled, smelled the man's slightly alien feline musk, and every hair on his arms stood up.

Inside his snug black Calvin's, his cock jolted so long it hurt.

He looked up Chris's body to find the man looking down at him. Seen from that angle, the tiger towered as tall as Titan.

"You ever suck a man?" he asked gruffly.

Tony shook his head.

"You want to?"

"Yes," Tony confirmed. "Like I'll die if you don't let me."

The tiger smiled. "No need for it to come to that."

He took hold of his zipper's tab, dragging it carefully down the contours of his erection. His briefs were white, an appealing contrast to his tanned skin.

"Take out my cock," he said.

Tony's blood surged hotly. "You going to tell me everything you want?"

"Why not?" Chris said. "You seem to be enjoying it."

This was true, but Tony still wagged his head. With fingers that shook a little, he spread Chris's jeans wider. Chris let out a grunt as Tony edged both hands into his underwear.

Glancing up, he saw the other man's eyes had closed in anticipation. Liking that, Tony drew his hard-on out of the soft cotton.

That was a heady treat. Everything Tony touched made his hands tingle.

Chris's cock was hot. And smooth. And long enough to give Tony's thumbs a lot of territory to work over.

"Mm," Chris hummed, his hips rocking into the pressure.

With a sense of revelation, Tony dragged his cheek up one side of his hard-on, over the top, and then down the other. Beneath the brush of his lips, Chris's pulse raced faster.

"Don't try to be a porn star," he advised breathlessly. "Just suck what feels comfortable."

"I'll do what I want," Tony contradicted, his entire being zeroed in on what he held. "You worry about yourself."

He dragged the flat of his tongue up Chris's underside.

"God," Chris breathed.

Tony went down on him.

His lips and tongue immediately fell in love. Chris was big, but Tony was blessed with resilient shifter reflexes. This much silky smoothness deserved to be sucked and savored without limit. The curve of Chris's knob against his palate made Tony's mouth water. He took it to the edge of his throat, pulling with his cheeks even as he laved everything in reach. His canines bracketed the shaft but didn't cut either side. The hint of danger seemed to increase Chris's excitement. The tiger moaned, and sweetness washed across his taste buds.

Chris's slit must be welling with arousal.

Tony drew up and went down again, moaning himself with rich pleasure. His spine felt loose, his jaw as relaxed as if someone had shot him with a tranq. Chris's movements were equally languorous. His big hands tangled in Tony's hair, fingers kneading his scalp as his hips gently pushed deeper.

"God, that's good," he groaned, fucking Tony's mouth in slow motion.

Tony found Chris's ball sac and wrapped his palms around it. When he tightened the careful hold, he got more of a response than he intended.

"Shit," Chris hissed. "Pull off. I don't want to come like this."

Tony didn't want to stop, but he dragged his mouth up until it popped off him. He looked up Chris's heaving chest. "I wouldn't mind if you came," he said throatily. "Giving you head is exciting."

Chris's eyes opened, hot gold locking onto Tony's softer green. "*You're* exciting. I want to give you a first time you won't forget."

For a second, Tony completely lost his breath. This man was too much— too sexy, too big and gorgeous, too freaking perfect to be true. He'd had plenty of fantasies about this moment, but none were as good as Chris's reality. He wasn't sure he could speak until he did. "Tell me what to do. I want you to remember too."

Chris's hands still clasped Tony's head. He seemed dazzled, but even as Tony registered this, his expression re-focused. His fingers combed through Tony's dark wavy hair. The soothing stroke ended with a tug firm enough to provoke a jolt of adrenaline.

"Kneel down," the tiger said, not barking the order but self-assured. "Turn around and lay your chest on the bed."

The position stuck Tony's ass in the air. He felt odd about that—self-conscious but excited. Men took each other from the position, buggered each other was the term. Going to his knees behind him, Chris massaged Tony's butt cheeks with strong squeezes. God, that felt good. The barrier of Tony's briefs seemed to help him adjust to the sensation of male fingers. He hoped Chris didn't expect him to last long. He was so cranked up he could have come if he *thought* too hard about Chris's cock.

Chris nudged his knees apart, yet another thrill Tony didn't need. Slowly, gently, Chris pulled the black underwear down his thighs. He stopped dragging when he reached his knees. Tony's legs were probably spread enough, but they were also trapped. Chris's hands returned to his naked rear.

Tony clenched as the cat's palms stroked him.

"This is one fine ass," Chris praised, testing the hard muscles. "I'm going to enjoy fucking it."

Tony moaned, unable to keep the sound inside. Chris bent around him to lick and nip his nape. The sharp little bite felt incredible. Tony shivered, instincts jumping into action that he had absolutely no practice controlling. He wanted to beg Chris to take him, wanted to grovel and whine as he'd never done in his life. This, he thought, was what being submissive meant. This was why he'd never complained about being the pack's last man.

This was what he'd been born for.

Chris growled softly against his neck. "You want this, don't you? You're dying for someone to master you."

Tony panted, his hands curling into fists on the bed covers. Chris reached past his head for the jar of lube. The sound of him unscrewing it was titillating, the quickened rush of Chris's respiration as he scooped out the slippery stuff. Tony's back arched even before Chris's slick hot fingers found his asshole.

"Oh God," he gasped as two of them squeezed in.

Chris's free hand clamped behind Tony's neck to restrain his near-violent writhing. "Tell me if anything I do hurts. If it does, I'll wait until you relax some more."

Robbed of speech, Tony groaned and thrust his butt closer.

Chris let out a raspy laugh. "Okay. I'll take that as a go-ahead."

Tony had never felt anything as good as Chris's big, slightly curved fingers massaging him inside. He'd always resisted letting females play this way, for fear his true desires would betray themselves. Nerves he hadn't known he had were singing. His tight outer reaches itched pleasantly, some hot spot deep within him throbbing out a plea for Chris's lovely stroking to stretch to it.

"I need you," he said when they wouldn't reach. "I need you inside me."

Chris was strong, but Tony got one shoulder far enough off the bed to crane around toward his tormentor. Chris's face was flushed, his features taut with intensity. Caught up in what he was doing, he looked up in surprise at Tony's words.

"You sure?" he asked. "I can get you readier."

Stabs of overexcited pleasure were shooting up Tony's cock. "I'm a little too ready," he confessed.

Chris flashed a very white, very toothy grin. "You want me to take you in this position or face to face?"

"We can do that?" he blurted.

This was a stupid question, apparently. He blushed when Chris chuckled. "Dude, don't you watch porn at all?"

"I was afraid to. I thought what I couldn't have would depress me."

Chris's grin softened. He had smile lines around his eyes that Tony really liked. "You have some lost time to make up for, don't you?"

"Face to face," Tony said, answering his previous question. He hesitated. "Unless you like the other way better."

"I like face to face. I like seeing my partner's expression." His voice had sunk, like he was threatening and teasing Tony at the same time.

"Your partners see yours too," Tony said.

Chris nipped his scruff again, holding the skin for a shivery moment before releasing it. Tony realized the position they were in also had merits.

Chris withdrew from it anyway. "Cats are better at hiding their reactions."

"Uh-huh," Tony responded dreamily. It took a second for him to realize this could be taken as a challenge.

"No," Chris said, reading his response. "Don't try to hide from me. Watching what I do to you is a turn-on for me."

Tony could have said the same but sensed this wouldn't wind Chris's gears. Contrary to some people's claims—i.e., his older brother's—Tony knew when to shut up. Saying nothing, he crawled onto the platform bed and rolled onto his back. Chris finished dragging his boxer briefs off his legs and stood looking down at him.

"You too," Tony said, wagging his toes at him. "I want to ogle that great body."

Smiling faintly, Chris removed the rest of his clothes. He wasn't a showoff like Tony, but he wasn't shy either. He didn't have any reason to be. Firefighting kept weres in shape. Every inch of his thickly muscled body was breathtaking.

Quite a few of those inches thrust out and up from his groin. Tony could have stared at his cock all night: the veins, the flush, the sheen on the head where the skin stretched taut. His balls were drawn up. They swung a little as Chris shifted.

"Can I lube you?" Tony asked breathlessly.

"If you like," Chris said.

Tony didn't care that Chris sounded as if he were about to laugh. He rolled up onto his knees, grabbing the jar of *Tiger!* lubricant on the way. The *Tiger!* factory made condoms too. Due to their champion shifter immune systems, he and Chris wouldn't require those. With a generous scoop warmed between his palms, he lingered over slicking up Chris's erection.

This was nearly as fun as sucking him. Chris closed his eyes while Tony stroked and explored, no emotion on his features apart from periodic grimaces of pleasure. His claim that cats had poker faces wasn't exaggerated. Tony did everything to Chris that he liked himself. Every squeeze was designed to get him—every rub, every upward tug from the tendons of his groin. Pulling out the big guns, Tony rubbed the pads of his thumbs in opposing buffing motions across his glans. At last, the granite cracked. Chris laid his hand over Tony's to stop him.

"That's enough," he said huskily.

Tony grinned like the Cheshire cat.

The beta couldn't let that stand. He put his hands on Tony's shoulders, shoving once to tumble him backwards. "Bend your legs up against your chest."

Tony did as he was asked.

"Wrap your forearms behind your knees."

Too turned on to feel awkward, Tony did that as well.

Chris crawled over him on hands and knees, the grace of his beast apparent in each sinuous motion. His body cast an ominous and exciting heat shadow.

"Pull your legs wider," he demanded.

The order was harsher than before. Tony couldn't help what it did to him. As he obeyed, his breath caught like cotton within his throat.

Seeing this, Chris's manner turned kind of grim. Tony wondered why but didn't ask. The tiger took his own cock in hand. Tipping its stiffness down, he pressed the lubed-up head against Tony's tight entrance. His gaze dropped to watch the place, the sight of them almost joined clearly arousing him.

Do it, Tony thought, unable to speak aloud.

Chris pushed slowly into him.

Tony's neck arched with pleasure. Chris swore, evidently liking the inward glide. The pressure of his entry felt incredible. His cock was thick, breaching Tony's virgin passage bit by bit. Waves of delicious heat spread out from the stretch. Every inch Chris penetrated hummed with sensation, like he was waking Tony's nerves as he went.

"Okay?" Chris gasped after he'd shoved in as far as he could go.

Tony moaned out a *yes.*

His thighs were squashed beneath Chris's substantial weight, his lungs sawing in and out. He felt so good he trembled . . . and wanted so much he didn't know how to ask for it.

A man was inside him. This man. After all those years of nothing but dreaming.

"Open your eyes," Chris said quietly.

Tony opened them. Chris didn't look grim now. His face was intent but calm.

"You feel so good inside me," Tony marveled. "If I'd known, no way could I have held off."

He probably sounded like a twit. Chris's lips slanted. "Nothing quite like taking your first dick."

He was teasing but not meanly. Tony released his thighs and wrapped his calves around Chris's ribs. He guessed that was okay, because Chris brushed a lock of hair off of Tony's forehead. The gesture was tender but casual—no big deal for the man. Tony tried not to think about the other men Chris must have done it to.

"I want the rest," Tony said. "I want you fucking me."

Chris's eyes flashed golden. For a moment, Tony thought the request might have earned him a longer wait. Luckily the cat wasn't in the mood to torture him.

"Okay," he said, shifting to dig in with his knees. "You need anything different from what I do, you only have to say."

Tony wanted exactly what Chris gave him. The cat drew back and thrust in, hard enough that his hipbones slapped Tony's ass. Tony let out a strangled sound. Chris had hit the aching spot he'd been wishing he'd stroke before.

"Again," he said. "Please, God, do that some more."

Chris laughed and did it again and again, until Tony breath whined out with pleasure. He wanted the bliss to go on forever, and he wanted to come right then.

"Hold on," Chris said. "I'm taking this up a notch."

Tony's scalp nearly caught on fire. Chris thrust faster, running over and over what Tony assumed was his prostate gland. "I can't," he said, beginning to twist beneath the barrage of good feelings. "My come's going to explode."

"You can," Chris insisted. "Don't hold your breath like that."

He didn't let up his new more determined pace, his expression as he pounded into him focused but not aggressive. He was going hard to give Tony more pleasure, because he thought Tony could take it. Just in case, Chris's attention stayed on Tony, making sure he kept on enjoying it. Tony couldn't hide that he did—and not just physically. Possibly Chris was being a responsible beta, looking out for a sexual rookie. Regardless, Tony relished being the temporary center of someone's world. His role as the pack's omega sometimes made him an afterthought. Tony certainly wasn't that to Chris. Tony was the reason the tiger's cock was as hard as diamond inside of him. Tony was the reason Chris's whole body was throbbing.

That awareness was almost too exciting. Trying to remember how to breathe, he clutched Chris's back and his claws slid out.

The partial change nicked the tiger's skin.

"Sorry," he panted when Chris reacted with a grunt.

"Nuh," he said, his chest dropping closer, his hips speeding even more. Their flesh slapped together crazily. "That's . . . good for me."

Tony guessed it was. The other man's cock stretched longer, his breath ripped into pieces by excitement.

"Shit," he cursed. "Don't tighten on me like that."

Tony couldn't help it but wasn't able to say so. The other man's fraying control aroused him too much to restrain himself. Desperate to finish it for them both, he slung his leg high around the cat's shoulder.

"Okay," Chris said, working his hand between their bellies. "I'll bring you now."

He gripped Tony's cock and squeezed. His hand was so big he engulfed Tony's erection. His thumb crooked over the sensitive head, his pinkie finding the sexual gland all wolves had at the base of their penises. The dual hot spots jangled, but the fireman didn't stroke or pull like Tony expected. He made a vise instead, moving Tony's lust-stretched skin the little bit it still could over his hard core.

Then he slammed his cock in with all his might.

The force was exactly what Tony's wolf needed. Tony went off like grenades were detonating, his climactic cry ragged. Chris returned the shout a second later, heat and wetness pumping hard into his passage.

Shifters didn't come like mundanes. When they were wound up, they could go multiple times a night. They could also pack half a dozen orgasms into one. That's what seemed to be happening now, both of them grinding, shooting, gasping for air in a frenetic drive to grab for the whole release.

The thing was a breath stealer. Tony couldn't believe the strength of his pleasure. Torrents rolled through him, one after the other. Chris wasn't feeling it any less. Growling like a true beast, he sank his fangs into Tony's shoulder, his claws pricking his butt cheeks. Tony doubted he was treating Chris's barn-door back any more kindly.

The freedom to do this with a partner he truly wanted overwhelmed his emotions. Snarling with a strange mix of pain and ecstasy, he drove his body up his impaler's. His prostate gland spasmed.

"Fuck," Chris gasped, and they shot one final burst of seed together.

The glow that swallowed him afterward was as wonderful as the climax. Giddy, Tony collapsed against the bed, disengaging from Chris in the process. His chest was sticky with his own come, his asshole pulsing with aftershocks. Blood trickled down his shoulder even as Chris's tooth marks healed.

Being mauled by a tiger was sexier than Tony could have imagined.

"Oh man," he said weakly.

Chris tried to hold his weight off Tony but his arms gave out. Tony discovered he had just enough strength to wrap his legs around him.

"I'm squashing you," Chris objected.

Snorting with amusement, Tony patted his sweaty back. "Who do you think you're lying on, cat man?"

Chris mumbled something he couldn't decipher. His head was next to Tony's, face down on the covers. Smiling, Tony lazily stroked his close-cropped hair. The tiger should grow it longer. It was a great color.

"Want a shower?" he offered.

"Too tired," Chris said. He wriggled sideways until his weight was at least half off him. "That was fast. Next time we'll take longer."

Next time, Tony repeated to himself. Warmth spread through his relaxed body, adding a pleasant layer to his bone-deep languor from orgasm. Loving the velvet feel of the tiger's skin, he slid his hand to Chris's nape, cupping the corded column of his neck as his eyelids became too heavy to keep open.

Next time was a nice thing to say, he thought.

~

Chris knew he shouldn't fall asleep where he was but couldn't bring himself to move. The sex they'd had was the most amazing he'd ever experienced. Mind you, he'd had good sex. Sneaking around and not getting it very often tended to whet the appetite. Tonight had been different. Tonight had been euphoric.

Even now his exhausted cock hummed with pleasure. Tony had made him come like Vesuvius. To his dismay, he'd inspired other things as well. Chris liked to dominate bed partners, but as a rule he tried not to bite them. At the least, he didn't approve of drawing blood. He'd done both to Tony, without a hope of resisting. His cat's needs had pushed him to it, which did not sit comfortably. Controlling his primal urges meant quite a lot to Chris. His only consolation was that Tony had scratched him up as well.

He truly wouldn't have guessed he and the young wolf would set off those fireworks.

It was possible Tony's newness to fucking men explained the intensity. He certainly had been into everything Chris did. Actually, he'd been into Chris period. Chris's cock twitched with memory. That blowjob the kid had started off with hadn't been bad at all.

He smiled as his brain spiraled slowly into the black hole of sleep. Tony seemed to be drifting too. His warm hand went limp behind Chris's neck, though it didn't drop completely. He guessed Tony didn't want to let go of his new toy.

Puppy . . . was Chris's too-fond final conscious thought.

CHAPTER TWO

BLACK smoke clung to the ceiling in the apartment's hall as if announcing a coming storm. Company No. 5—Chris and Evina's station—had been called to a four-story residence fire. The serious blaze was at three alarms. Station 12 was venting the roof in hopes of luring the oxygen-greedy fire away from Search and Rescue's route. Most of the building's tenants were huddled in the street.

Chris and his team were hunting down the rest.

Though the fire wasn't magic-fed, it was nasty. Scorching temperatures licked at Chris through his protective gear. Even his feet were sweltering, his spell-strengthened turnout boots transmitting heat from the floor.

If that weren't enough of a challenge, visibility was crap.

Billows of gray mist blocked what light came in from the windows, and the power was out. Swaddled in their big coats and SCBA masks, Chris's men were hulking shadows among the gloom. That is, they were shadows when they were close enough to see. When they weren't, the best way to find each other was by shouting.

"RFD!" Liam bellowed behind Chris. The rookie was checking the right-hand units, leaving the left to Chris. "Call out if you're inside!"

A lock-busting backward kick from Liam's boot followed. Light flickered brighter. The apartment the kid had breached had a pocket of fire inside.

"No life signs, Liam." Evina's calm and weirdly distant voice came through their helmet comms. "Move on to the next unit."

Their chief was watching the fire in her astral form, seeing what they couldn't—and in ways they couldn't—with spirit eyes. Her actual body sat in the station's special sensory-shielded van. Being able to simultaneously astral project and vocalize was an uncommon gift for tigers. Chris had it too, but tonight he was on rescue.

Knowing their boss could only see so much at once, he kicked open the next door on the left side. "RFD!" he bellowed like Liam had. "Call out if you're inside!"

His sharp tiger ears heard nothing: no voices, no heartbeats, just the eerie sigh and crackle of the fire. Part of him wanted to call for hoses, but the resulting super-heated steam would have made further searching impossible. Accustomed to threatening environs, he didn't panic when the flames brightened. His pulse was quicker than normal but steady.

"Nothing," he said for the benefit of the rest, though he couldn't see well enough to tell anyone which unit he'd just cleared.

"Found a live one," came Jonah's voice on the radio. The building's halls formed a *T*. Jonah and Syd were clearing the crossbar on this, the third floor. "We've got no egress nearby. The fire's blocked the next stairwell."

"Backtrack to me and Liam," Chris instructed, suspecting Evina might have to guide the others in the nearly nonexistent visibility. "Station 12 has a ladder at the hall-end window behind us."

Jonah didn't answer but gasped suddenly in shock. "Shit," he said, his voice cracking. "Syd went down. I think he's unconscious."

"Stay calm," Chris advised. "He probably got too hyped and used up his air supply. Can you drag him and carry your victim too?"

"Yes," Jonah said more steadily. "Doing it." Chris heard grunts of effort and then, "Boss, before he dropped, Syd claimed he heard someone moan in the next unit. I think it's the final one on the right."

Chris had to decide quickly. The moan might be nothing. Fire made a lot of sounds, and Syd didn't have as much experience as some at distinguishing them. Evina didn't comment, her attention likely pulled off them to something more important to the big picture. Chris checked his air gauge. Ten minutes remained in his SCBA tank. If the fire didn't get more hairy, he could check it out, no trouble.

"It could be that lady's kids," Liam put in. "The one who screamed like a banshee when we drove up. She said they were on this floor."

Chris remembered. The woman had been hysterical. Parents often were—though sometimes it turned out their kids were safe miles away, and in their terror they'd forgotten.

"All right," he said. "I'll move up to Jonah's position. Jonah, get your victim and Syd to safety. Watch your step. The floor isn't stable in some places."

"Should I finish checking this hall?" Liam asked.

The kid was game as hell but—like Syd—less experienced. "Call out and listen. Do it quick and no more door busting. You hear nothing or anything goes sideways, you hightail it out of here."

Satisfied he'd obey, Chris let his eyes change enough to gain the benefit of his cat's night vision. Though he still saw colors, they were muted.

He picked up the pace as he went forward. He might not have the time he thought. Fire seldom did what people expected. As he neared the *T* intersection, the smoke thickened noticeably, further blurring the light from his helmet lamp. He bumped Jonah's shoulder before realizing the big cat was there. Jonah was moving quickly too. He stayed low, hunched with his unconscious rescue on one shoulder. It was lucky the cat was strong. Syd's body bumped and tilted as Jonah dragged him by the scruff of his turnout coat. Chris checked the tiger's aura. His light was lower than normal, but it was there.

"Syd's okay," he called back to Jonah before continuing.

He had to feel along the wall with his fireproof glove to find the final apartment. The door hadn't been kicked open, so Chris turned his back to it and forced entry. His adrenaline must have been pretty amped. He burst the hinges and the lock, toppling the door into the unit with a bang like a gunshot.

He ducked instinctively, just in time. A wall of heat blasted back toward him. The fire had got a good hold here. When he squinted through the rippling air, he spotted drapes blazing like torches against a wall. The windows were black from the smoke outside, the various furniture shapes burning or not with seeming capriciousness. If the kids who were supposed to be in here were mundanes, no way were they alive now.

If they were shifters or something else with juice, maybe he could save them.

"Fire Department!" Chris shouted. "Call out if you're inside!"

Hearing nothing, he crouched and looked lower. Most kids had the sense to keep to the floor if they were able to. He saw a wavering darker shape that might have been a body but couldn't tell from the threshold.

"Call out!" he repeated, using his tiger power to amplify the sound. "I need to know you're here!"

He forced his eyes to change a few ticks more. The unnatural partial shift triggered a sharp headache but allowed him to see the glimmer of a still-alive aura. He gasped in surprise at what he spotted next. There were *two* auras—two little guttering match flames inside the inferno.

"Chris." Evina's urgent voice crackled in his helmet. "Get out of there right now. The fire is spiking. Your floor is about to flashover."

She meant the temperature had increased enough for the bank of sooty smoke above him to reignite.

Chris wasn't crazy. His gear was good but not meant to withstand that kind of hell. Fear flooded through his veins, threatening to turn his powerful shifter muscles to water.

"Can't," he said, despite the reaction. "I've got two life signs."

"*Chris,*" she ordered in a full alpha snarl. "Back the fuck out of there."

Ignoring her, he edged inside the door, obliged to physically push against the thickness of the hot air. Alarms began beeping, the safety device on his suit going off. He didn't need it to tell him the heat had jumped dangerously. He could feel it through his thick coat. *Crap*, he thought, fighting panic. Was his faceplate melting?

Help, said the tiniest telepathic voice in his head. The voice wasn't Evina's. *Please,* said a second. *We're still in here.*

He couldn't get to them. There wasn't time, and the fire was too furious. His ribs tightened with distress. They were *kids*. He couldn't leave them behind.

Not after what had happened to his brothers.

"Chris," Evina growled through the radio.

His inner conflict was too great. Something snapped inside him, the sensation so visceral that at first he thought a bone had broken. He realized it wasn't that when his vision shifted completely to shades of gray.

His tiger nature had seized control of him.

He hadn't known it could do that without him changing form. Unlike his human self, his tiger wasn't afraid at all. It strode without hesitation toward where he'd seen the small life signs.

The kids lay together under a table. The girl might have been seven, and the boy was younger. No more than semi-conscious, they'd pooled their auras together, using their power as an envelope to shield them from the flames. Their skin was red but, as yet, they weren't burned badly.

Elves, Chris thought, noting their pointy ears. As he did, his tiger-controlled body crouched down and dragged them out. Time slowed strangely the moment he held their childish weight. Cinders and burning chunks were raining down on them. He sensed the fire gathering its strength for a new expansion—or maybe his tiger did. His tiger ripped off his fireproof coat, using it to wrap around the kids. Chris was a shifter. He *might* survive more exposure. These elf kids had exhausted their resources. They didn't stand a chance without protection.

The fire flashed over even as the scorching agony of the existing blaze registered on his skin. Balls of yellow and black flame boiled through the ceiling smoke. Chris's tiger ran for the door with the kids clutched to his bare chest. His shirt had ignited the instant his coat came off. He felt the blistering heat and didn't at the same time. His tiger was in charge of his limbs, bounding him at shifter speed down the hall, dodging falling timbers and open holes in the disintegrating floor.

His beast knew where they were going. Chris's eyes were too hot to see. Apparently, Station 12 had humped a hose up their ladder and opened up a stream. Steam boiled at him instead of fire, knocking him to a halt. Someone shouted and shut off the water. Given an opening, his tiger dove out the window, his precious cargo hugged tight to him.

Chris would have killed human firemen, catapulting at them that way. The tigers on the ladder caught and slowed him.

"Get a medic!" someone shouted as strong hands passed him to the ground. "He's still alive!"

His arms were paralyzed in position. Someone pried them apart.

"Jesus," they breathed. "He's got two kids in his coat."

Chris couldn't choke out the question he needed the answer to.

"They're alive," the fireman who'd called for the paramedics exclaimed. "I hear faint heartbeats."

Chris tried to thank him but passed out cold instead.

~

Chris bolted up gasping and sweaty, the dream momentarily more real than his surroundings. He was in an unfamiliar bed, in an open loft, with a sleeping man lying face down beside him. The sight of his companion's muscular back restored Chris's memory. He'd woken at Nate Rivera's, his alpha's new fiancé. He'd had mind-blowing awesome sex with the cute gay werewolf from the party.

Chris rubbed his face, appreciating that the skin was smooth and not burn-scarred. The apartment fire was over. Chris had come through it.

"What is it?" his bed companion slurred into his pillow.

"Nothing. Go back to sleep."

Omega or not, Tony didn't listen. Unabashedly naked, he sat up and looked at him. They'd fallen asleep with the lights on, and Chris got a good eyeful. The strapping wolf was sleepy-eyed and gorgeous. His skin was tanned all over, his nipples tempting darker circles on his broad chest. His lips, which were flushed and kissable, curled teasingly. "Bad dream?"

The kid was the stuff of good dreams, for sure. Chris didn't want to darken Tony's brightness by explaining. Mind-blowing sex aside, they were strangers.

"I'm fine," he said, pulling his knees up and holding them.

Tony laid his hand behind Chris's shoulder. He didn't rub the muscle, just let the warmth of his palm sink in. "You were dreaming about that fire, the one that put you in the hospital."

His guess turned Chris's gaze to him. "You heard about that?"

"Please." Tony's manner was humorous. "Saving those kids made you a hero to heroes. You know how people talk in our lines of work."

Chris wasn't sure how he felt about that. In his mind, his tiger had done the deed. He hugged his knees closer, then released them. When he inhaled, he could smell his own fear sweat. "I need a shower."

"You want company?" Tony asked as he got out of bed.

Chris was tempted, but, "Not this time," he said.

Seemingly not upset, Tony flopped back and closed his eyes. "Wake me when you get back. I should have my second wind by then."

He'd completely stretched out his body, toes pointed, long leg muscles delineated, cock and balls rolling loosely between strong thighs. Chris remembered how it felt to fuck him, how Tony had cried out and bucked up him. His prick lengthened, more interested in another go than Chris's head was ready to handle.

Before his cock convinced him to climb back into bed, he strode to the nearby shower. The pelting spray washed the last of the dream away. His inner darkness wasn't entirely gone, but he was himself again: reliable, closeted Chris Savoy.

He found his clothes and dressed, deciding it was safer to have them on. Tony was fast asleep when he finished, curled around Chris's pillow with the sheets kicked to his ankles. His body was a true masterwork, not as substantial as a tiger's but genuinely strong. His cock lay limp, partially obscured by the pillow he was hugging. With nothing to stop him from staring, Chris curled his tongue over his upper lip. Waking that sleeping length—and Tony with it —would have been easy and pleasurable, especially since Chris would probably be the first man to introduce him to that delight. If Tony had been a different guy, Chris knew he'd have done it.

Sadly, Tony wasn't a different guy. He was out and sweet and a teensy bit flamboyant. Chris could get away with being pleasant to him but not with being secret fuck buddies. He believed Tony when he said he'd keep his mouth shut. The problem was, one hopeful look from those soft green eyes would give the game away. All his years of playing normal would have been for nothing.

Chris's job was his life. Being a leader, saving people, gave him a sense of worth nothing else equaled. He loved knowing he did it well. Hell, he loved the excitement. He wasn't about to throw that away just to admit he was gay. Chris *needed* to be a fireman more than he needed that.

He, of all people, couldn't afford to indulge his longing for honesty.

His eyes burned as he watched Tony sleep. The wolf's cheeks were untouched by lines, his slumber as untroubled as a child's. Chris wondered if he'd hit thirty yet. Tony seemed young to him, though he was older than Chris's brothers had gotten a chance to be . . . older than all their years put together, he suspected.

Leave, he ordered and made himself do it.

One night and done was what this had to be.

~

Tony wanted to kick himself when he woke hours later. The sun was extremely up. Nate's front windows were blazing.

He knew at once Chris Savoy was gone. Tony hadn't meant to sleep that long. The sex had just been so damn good and relaxing. Plus, he'd thought for sure the fireman would want a second round.

Him preferring to shower alone should have rung a warning bell.

Chris's nightmare had *not* been nothing. Tony should have pushed him to talk about it and not let him run away.

"Right," he drawled to the industrial struts on the loft's ceiling. Being pushed to talk always worked fabulous. Just think how he'd reacted back when women tried it on him.

He got out of bed and hit the bathroom—which smelled of Chris's shower. That didn't stop him from using it. Barely less grumpy but squeaky clean, he stumped to Nate's kitchen. Chris hadn't left so much as a post-it to say goodbye.

Thanks for last night. Sorry I had to rush out early.

"Fuck," Tony cursed.

He'd definitely heard Chris mention a next time. Maybe the cat had thought better of it, or realized the sex wasn't spectacular after all. Tony planted his forearms on the island's black countertop. He could find Chris's number. He was a detective. No one had to know he had it either. Not Evina and not those macho ass-hat tigers. So what if Tony's nature wasn't dominant? He was more than his wolf. He could make the next move if he wanted to.

He made a fist, thumping the counter for emphasis. "The sex *was* spectacular, damn it."

Of course, it might only have been great for him. Maybe Chris's *next time* was like other guys' *I'll call you.*

Tony had uttered that phrase a time or two.

"Karma's a bitch," he said. The flare of humor lightened his mood a smidge. He'd try to call Chris. Once. Discreetly. To prove he wasn't a crazed ex-virgin stalker boy. Then he'd see what happened. If Chris could forget their night together, so could Tony.

"We are done," announced a melodious voice. "Would you like to unload us?"

Tony's heart lurched into his throat. *Shit.* The voice came from the dishwashers. Nate must have programmed them to remind him.

"I'd love to unload you," he assured, though they probably couldn't hear. The Brownies' soap was magic. The dishwashers were just pricey machinery.

He began to empty them, oddly soothed by the simple task. Whether he saw Chris again or not, he'd finally popped his gay cherry. The experience had been good, probably better than most people's. That, he decided, was reason enough to feel all right.

~

Eight days later, Tony was catching up on paperwork in the spell-warded basement of the downtown precinct. The wards protected the squad room from magical sneak attacks, a consideration in a town like theirs. He and Carmine had the space to themselves. No more than once every ten minutes,

Tony checked the untraceable burner phone he'd stashed in his desk's locked drawer. Despite his vigilance, the cell refused to give him new info.

No calls. No texts. No fricking two-word voicemails.

He'd called Chris four days ago. Just a: *How are you, man? I've got that thing you were looking for. Get in touch if you still want it.*

The message was the soul of discretion. He'd used no names and no lovey-dovey stuff. Chris could claim it was a wrong number if he wanted. Despite the consideration, Chris hadn't responded.

Could the fireman have forgotten what Tony sounded like?

No, no, no, Tony ordered when his restless hand reached for the drawer again. He'd sworn he'd call Chris *once*. Shifters didn't forget voices. If the tiger wasn't getting back in contact, he wasn't that into him.

Across the detective squad room, Carmine hung up his phone.

"Hey," he called in Tony's direction. "You free to ride with me to Elfyunk? I need to interview a shop owner."

Carmine was Tony's older cousin, a married wolf with two boys in high school. He outranked Tony but not by much. He had to ask the junior man to do things; straight out orders wouldn't work. Carmine's ride-withs tended to be boring. Important cases rarely fell to him. Carmine was as solid as a fireplug but not brilliant.

"I'll buy coffee," he said when Tony hesitated.

Tony relented. Carmine was a good guy, and Tony had lots of reasons to respect him. "Coffee's on me. As long as you tell a story from the old days."

"Oh I've got stories," Carmine promised. "Your IQ will go up ten points before I'm done with you." The older wolf rose and hitched up his pants. He didn't really have a belly. That wasn't a shifter thing. Sometimes, though, he used the mannerisms of a fat man.

Like it was nothing, Tony shut and locked the drawer with the burner phone.

"Ready," he said. He pushed up from his swiveling chair, grabbing his jacket along the way. A touch of his hand verified that his gun was secure in its side holster.

When he was close enough, Carmine slung his arm around Tony's shoulder. "You okay, kid? You've been quiet lately."

With a start, Tony realized Carmine didn't actually need him to come with. He was checking up on Tony. He was concerned.

"I'm good," he said, touched enough for his eyes to heat. "I've been practicing shutting up so you can dump all your experience on me."

"*Dump!*" Carmine exclaimed. "More like honor you more than you deserve."

Tony smiled as they took the stairwell to the precinct garage. It was at least five minutes before he thought about Chris again.

CHAPTER
THREE

TONY didn't think it was right that Nate was calmer than him. Nate was getting married this afternoon. Tony was only the best man.

Nate and Evina's engagement had been brief. Barely a month had passed since the big party on his roof. The couple was sure about their feelings, and Nate wanted them to be official before the cubs' next parents night at school. He was comically excited about attending—in contrast to his I'm-too-cool-for-the-room demeanor over walking down the aisle.

The ceremony, once everyone had their tails on straight, was taking place in Tiger Park. Tony was keeping Nate company in the Groom's Pavilion, a fancy Indian-style building.

Unlike Wolf Woods—which was a private preserve for werewolves—the public had unrestricted access to Tiger Park. Today, the twentyish acres blazed with October color. The city's runners loved Tiger Park. It stretched along the North River, on the same side as Resurrection's downtown core. The paths were flat and shady, and the park's stray cat population kept it blissfully free of gnomes. Visitors who relished a slower pace could meditate in a peaceful garden honoring fallen firefighters. Most beloved by the city's children was a slightly inappropriate petting zoo.

It housed the sort of game wild tigers enjoyed eating.

The section of the park roped off for Nate's wedding included two enclosed pavilions, a banquet hall, and a nice grassy stretch for tents. Nate wasn't a tiger, but Evina had decided rather than exhaust the family savings hiring some swank hotel, they'd hold a less expensive, more eclectic celebration here.

The future Mrs. Nate was in the Bride's Pavilion, along with kids, mom, girlfriends, and some of her firefighters—one of whom in particular Tony tried not to think about. Nate would have had more of an entourage except for an unforeseen disaster involving marigold decorations inside the wedding tent. Rick, Adam, and Carmine had left to help sort it out. On the female front, their alpha's wife Ari had whisked their baby daughter to the petting zoo, in the hope that the antelopes would cure her fussiness.

Nate didn't seem to mind the general abandonment. He was dressed and ready, as sharp as a fashion plate in his close-fitting tuxedo. His trademark ponytail had a glass-like sheen only magic could account for. He knew he looked good. The long stretch of mirror in the dressing room had received his brisk nod of approval. His own fineness seen to, Nate turned his attention to Tony's lack of imposingness. Thus far, he'd redone Tony's bowtie, straightened his lapels, and refolded his pocket square.

Resigned to more of the same for the duration, Tony braced his hips on the back of the room's beat-up couch.

"Stop hunching," Nate scolded mildly as he tucked the now-perfect handkerchief where it belonged. "Don't you know how tall Evina's best man is? Do you want me to lose face in front of her tigers?"

Tony knew exactly how tall Evina's beta was. He also knew how many days it had been since he'd overoptimistically called him. Rather than share either fact with Nate, he tugged at his snug collar. "This penguin suit isn't very comfortable. Are you sure that demon tailor did what you told him to?"

"Idiot." Nate smacked his hands away from the shirt. "It's impeccably fitted. And you look great in it. Why are you so squirmy?"

"Why are you so calm? You're about to get leg-shackled."

"Sheesh." Nate slapped his chest lightly. "Just wait till you fall in love."

"Don't want to," Tony grumped. Him shoving the never-called burner phone in the very back of his closet was proof of it.

Nate didn't listen to his claim. Nate smiled beatifically. "You'll fall in love," he predicted. "And I'll tease you mercilessly."

Tony didn't doubt that part. His scowl deepened until he realized he wasn't being a good friend. "I am happy for you," he said.

Nate broke into a laugh.

"I am. Evina is terrific."

Nate's expression turned sappy. "She is, isn't she?"

Oh Lord, Tony thought. *Look how the mighty skirt-chaser has fallen.*

Nate's face changed without warning. He looked like he wanted to ask something important.

"I have the rings," Tony said, hoping to head him off.

"I didn't doubt it for a minute—though that's good. I was going to say, I went through the Civil Code."

The Civil Code was ten volumes in tiny print—basically a bunch of legal crap devised by the ever-so-superior fae on the Founders Board to keep lesser supes in line. The fae had created Resurrection. Letting anyone forget that wasn't part of their master plan.

"You've lost me," Tony said.

Nate looked awkward. "There's nothing in it to prevent gay people from marrying."

Now Tony was amused. "You couldn't give me time to find a boyfriend before you have me exchanging vows?"

"Oh shut up," Nate huffed. "I thought you'd want to know."

Tony hadn't been concerned, but the fact that Nate had was kind of sweet. The fact that he'd searched the whole ten volumes was impressive. "If only you were gay," he joked. "Think how easy my life would be."

Nate frowned. "It'd never work. You're too big of a slob."

Evina and her cubs were kind of messy, but Tony didn't mention that. When the right person came along, people forgave all sorts of flaws.

"I'm taller than you," he said. "That's why I hunch when you're next to me."

Nate looked at him like he was crazy.

"You told me to stop hunching, but you're dominant to me. My wolf thinks we should be lower down."

"Jesus," Nate said. "Really?"

"Really. You're a sucky subordinate, so you don't think that way, but I'm pretty good at being submissive."

"Shit," Nate said. This of all things seemed to upset him. "I don't want you to think that way around me."

"You don't?"

"I absolutely don't. You're my friend. You be as tall as you damn well please."

His voice was gruff. Tony dropped his gaze to his shiny black shoes and smiled. "Now I really want to marry you," he teased.

~

Chris had never seen his old friend this rattled.

"I shouldn't have worn this," Evina moaned, frowning at herself in the triple mirror in the bride's dressing room.

This was a breathtaking orange and gold sari with a sky-blue fitted top beneath. A coordinating gold-bordered veil covered her long black curls. His alpha had the coloring and the curves to carry off the outfit. She saw something different, apparently. She plucked at the shimmery silk that flowed down her legs like water.

"I look like I'm costumed for Halloween. I've never been to India. Why did I think these clothes were a good idea?"

"Maybe because you're beautiful in them."

Evina twisted around to glower at her back view. "This skirt makes my butt look fat."

Chris snorted.

"Sorry," she said, instantly repentant. "I'm being a girl, aren't I? Please don't tell the others I lost it."

The others were in the outer room. Evina's hot-as-curry eighty-something mother had yanked them there so Chris and her daughter could have a pre-wedding talk. As best man, it was his job to confirm her mental state. His job as beta was pretty much the same. Whether male or female, on the rare occasions tiger alphas married, their seconds ensured they made it safely to the altar . . . and that they wanted to.

"You *are* a girl," he pointed out, amused by her uncharacteristic insecurity. "Your butt looks exactly how it's supposed to—not that Nate would mind if you prowled down the aisle naked."

"He'd probably like that," Evina admitted.

She was still making faces at her reflection. Chris put his hands on her shoulders. His head topped hers in the mirror. For just a second, he felt like her big brother. He suspected she sometimes thought of him that way.

That was going to change. Nate would be her closest male family now. Chris gave her a squeeze he hoped didn't betray his own regrets.

"What matters is remembering you're marrying the man you love. Nate is a standup male. He's lucky to have you, but you're lucky to have him too."

Despite his intent to conceal his private yearnings, his voice cracked the slightest bit. Evina registered the sound. She turned and gave him a bone-deep hug.

"You're my bestest friend," she declared, imitating her five-year-old daughter's favorite exclamation of affection. "Just don't tell Mom or Freda that I said so."

Chris smiled against her veil. "You're my bestest friend," he returned. "For real."

Evina tipped her head back. Her golden eyes glittered with emotion. "I won't neglect you," she promised more seriously.

"I know you won't, but you have to commit to your new life."

She touched his face, gaudy wedding bracelets clinking, shining gaze searching his. He sensed her debating whether she should say more. Why hadn't he ever been in love? Why did he hardly date? In the end, *don't ask, don't tell* ruled her decision.

"Would you check on Nate and his pack for me?" she asked. "The tiger priest is due here in ten minutes."

"I'll check," he agreed. "No matter what, he'll marry you. If I need to, I'll have Liam sit on him."

A horror he didn't expect filled the tigress's expression. "You think Nate might have cold paws?"

"I meant I'd have Liam sit on the priest. The end of the Pocket wouldn't keep your wolf from being hot to trot to you."

Leaving her laughing seemed like a good idea. He slipped out the door to the outside, the cool autumn air a pleasure against his skin. Three feral cats scampered across the grass to him. Though they weren't pets, they were used to people. Lots of park visitors brought them treats. Chris crouched to pet them for good luck.

"Hello, cousins," he said as they wound around him. "Promise to carry Evina's prayers to the Tiger Queen?"

A gray and white female mewed, tilting her head for more scratches. Chris obeyed her bidding, then rose again. He was putting off the moment he'd have to face Tony.

Maybe the hot gay wolf would be gone. Maybe he'd have stepped out to fetch something.

Maybe the Tiger Queen of the Universe would help Chris win the Lottery.

Annoyed with himself, he closed the short distance to the Groom's Pavilion. He knocked, but no one answered. When he stepped in, the outer room was empty. The door to the inner was open a crack.

"You don't?" he heard Tony say.

Chris knew it was his voice. He'd replayed the message Tony left him a stupid amount of times. *I've got that thing you were looking for. Get in touch if you still want it.* Chris hadn't let himself compose even a pretend text in answer. He'd have been too tempted to hit *send.*

Nate said something Chris's roaring blood drowned out.

"Now I really want to marry you," Tony said.

Chris could tell he was joking. Nonetheless, the most extraordinary wave of rage rolled through him. The sockets around his canines heated, the tearing teeth verging on lengthening. Chris clenched his jaw. Tony shouldn't joke about marrying. Tony belonged to him.

The thought shocked him. If he believed it, he'd lost his ever-loving mind.

"Hello, wolves," he called in his steadiest voice. "I'm checking on you for Evina."

Nate stepped into the outer room, bringing his odd alpha energy with him. The wolf seemed relaxed, a *GQ* model in his tuxedo. The swiftness with which he popped out told Chris appearances might be deceiving.

"Is Evina all right?" he asked.

Chris had braced for Tony to follow Nate. When that didn't happen, he wasn't certain he was grateful. "She's fine. The priest is due pretty soon. Are you and your pack ready?"

Nate twisted his head over his shoulder. "Tony, can you make sure Adam and the guys fixed that flower thing?"

"Sure," Tony said. "I'll get Ari and the baby while I'm at it."

Nate didn't thank him. Then again, Tony didn't seem to expect it. He trotted briskly out, throwing Chris a sideways ghost-glance along the way.

Fleeting though it was, the look sent heat coursing through him for new reasons.

"He's a grouch today," Nate said. His eyes were coffee black, their sharpness going straight through Chris. "He'd have greeted you politely otherwise."

Tony was a grouch today? Had something happened? Was he mad because Chris was here? Chris forced his gaze away from the exit through which his hottest one-night stand ever had disappeared.

"No problem," Chris said to Nate. "Weddings mean changes for everyone."

His words were a wee bit pompous, but Nate broke into a grin. Chris respected and owed Nate already. The wolf won him completely over by bouncing on his heels like a ten-year-old.

"I cannot wait," he confessed. "I don't care if every flower in the park explodes. This is the best day of my life."

~

The flowers in the bridal tent hadn't exploded. The event planner had decided to save time by purchasing a spell to keep the festoons in place, rather than stringing them by hand. He'd also decided to save money, and the bargain basement enchantment expired early. Nate's packmates had snarled at the human until he quaked, but in the end the best solution anyone came up with was to arrange the flowers on the ground. Now a river of orange blossoms flowed from the door of the tent to its altar.

Tony thought the tigress bride looked stunning wading down the aisle through them.

When the groom tucked two blooms into his new children's curly hair, every eye in the house—no matter how macho—welled up with sentiment.

The wedding vows were short and sweet. As best man, Tony stood a few steps behind the couple, doing his best to act like Chris wasn't right beside him radiating his sexy tiger vibe through his tuxedo. Tony glued his attention to the couple, who swore to love, honor and cherish as if the words were invented just for them. Nate added a promise to respect and look out for Evina's clan.

"Me too," Evina said, surprising Tony by sending him a wink.

Unable to resist, Tony twitted Nate by pretending he couldn't find the rings in their safe pocket.

Nate shot a cool glare under lowered brows. *Idiot*, he mouthed at him.

Tony pretended he didn't notice Evina's beta's lips quirking.

The priest bound the pair's wrists together with a length of silk that was half tiger-print and half wolf. He covered their hands with his for the blessing. "May your mating prosper," he pronounced.

"Kiss her!" Evina's daughter Abby crowed.

"Kiss her good!" Her twin Rafi seconded.

Nate complied by bending the tigress backwards over one arm.

Wolves and tigers whooped and whistled in approval. The Bollywood-style musicians began to play, signaling the crowd to get off their folding chairs and dance to the banquet hall. The feast that waited was delicious, the champagne and humorous speeches equally plentiful.

Tony couldn't help but be happy through most of it. He was surrounded by his pack, and all of them were well. The tigers were on their best behavior —and similarly enjoying the party.

Joy could be shared when you were a group creature.

"Sweeten your mouths," the bride's mother instructed, helping the caterer wheel out the wedding cake.

Nate and Evina fed each other and their children a piece of it. Their auras were bright as dawn, their faces glowing with love and tenderness. Tony sat smiling a few more minutes. Then, suspecting no one would notice, he slipped from the hall for a breath of solitude.

~

Do not go after him, Chris ordered his twitching feet. *You and Tony have nothing to say to each other.*

Nothing Chris could follow up on anyway.

He stood with his back to the wooden wall of the banquet hall, slowly killing a bottle of ice-cold elf porter. He'd left the bridal table some time ago, unable to calmly sit with Tony next to him. He'd forgotten how sexy the young wolf was, with his smooth tanned skin and his full dark mouth made for slow wet kisses.

Chris shifted uncomfortably, his dress trousers going tight at the direction his thoughts drifted.

"Dance?" invited Evina's slightly tipsy female friend Freda.

She'd appeared through the crowd without him noticing. She was a paramedic: hot, fun, smart . . . and totally wasted on Chris. She'd shared her favors with a few of their station's tigers—to no one's harm, that he could see. Though she'd flirted with Chris before, he'd always evaded her.

Having sex with someone Evina cared about, just to shore up his damned secret, didn't seem right to him.

"Two left feet," he said, softening his refusal with a smile.

"Like I care!" She laughed and pushed his chest playfully.

Still smiling, he shook his head. "Liam looks like he needs a partner."

She pouted but danced off, the sinuous motions of her tight tigress body letting him know what he'd turned down.

Sighing, Chris finished off his beer. The table for the empties sat near the rear exit, the same exit Tony Lupone had slipped out of.

Don't, Chris ordered himself.

This time he didn't listen. He was a little drunk and maybe more than a little sad. Under those conditions, the lure of the hot young wolf was simply too powerful.

~

A stone half-wall separated the running path from the riverbank. Tony leaned on it with bent forearms, watching the dark current flow. The sun had set, probably after the first meat course.

Times like this he wished he smoked. That's what people did when they left a crowd. *Went out for a cigarette*, they'd say, not: *Needed to escape the hot fireman I've got a hankering for.*

Footsteps approached along the walkway behind him. Dress shoes. Worn by a large tall male. The swoosh of expensive fabric suggested a tuxedo.

"Tony," said the very fireman who'd driven him out here.

Tony turned and leaned back against the wall. He told himself he could be as cool as Nate if he wanted to. "You owe me a clean set of sheets."

Chris stopped, too close and too far at the same time. His handsome brow furrowed. "What?"

"You promised you'd wash the sheets yourself if we messed up Nate's bed. I guess your promises don't mean much."

God, Tony sounded childish. He refused to drop his gaze regardless. Looking at Chris fed something inside him he couldn't bring himself to deny.

"I'm sorry," Chris said. "About everything."

He wasn't looking away either. Perversely, Tony longed for him to move closer.

"You knew it was me calling you from that blocked number."

"Yes."

"I made myself only call you once."

"I appreciate that." Chris's cheek muscles worked, his jaw so square he was like a fricking superhero on a kid's cereal box. His shoes made a scuffing noise on the path as his weight shifted. "You know my situation."

His voice wasn't pleading but his eyes were. Tony wasn't used to having the upper hand. Now that he did, he wasn't inclined to give it up.

"Why did you follow me out here?"

The big cat rubbed the back of his beefy neck. "I drank too much and I couldn't not." He sighed out a curse. "You're too fucking hot in that tuxedo."

His words thrilled and hardened Tony, which angered him quite a lot for about three seconds. "You're not too shabby yourself," he grudged.

Chris's lips curved faintly. "I'm sorry," he repeated. "More than you probably believe."

Tony grunted a sound the fireman could take as forgiveness if he wanted.

"Truce?" Chris asked.

"I'd agree if I knew what you meant by that." Suddenly, he couldn't look at the man anymore. He turned back toward the river, hoping—stupidly— that he didn't seem too rude. He guessed he didn't. Chris came to lean on the wall with him. His thickly muscled arm brushed Tony's.

"I want to make this up to you," he said.

Tony's blood already sang from the light contact. At this, his hard-on lurched vertical. "Given your 'situation,' I don't see how you can."

Chris was silent for a few heartbeats. "Maybe—"

Tony cut him off. "Don't start with me like that. I like you. You and I have good chemistry. If I'm going to screw around—which I don't rule out—I'll choose a Maybe I don't mind getting kicked to the curb by if he decides I'm too risky."

Chris wrapped his hand around Tony's and squeezed tightly. "Have you?" he asked in a low voice.

Tony was trying to get his head around the fact that Chris was holding his hand. "Have I what?"

"Screwed around."

"Jesus," he said. "It's barely been a month since you and I had sex."

"So you haven't." Chris's statement was smug.

"That's not your business," Tony retorted.

Chris's thumb rubbed the side of Tony's hand. It was a little gesture, but tingles immediately shot up his arm, through his body, and into his throbbing dick. The downward surge of blood was so dramatic Tony went lightheaded.

Wanting this man so badly was dangerous.

"Christ," he breathed. The fireman knew why. His chest started going in and out as fast as Tony's was.

"Come with me," he said, tugging him away from the river view.

Tony guessed where he was headed. A gingerbready gardener's shed sat slightly off the path not too far from them.

"It'll be locked," Tony warned even as Chris pulled him into a run.

Chris grinned, yanking the cheap padlock so that it snapped.

Tony did love a bad boy. His heart knocked his sternum as Chris pushed him inside and backed him into the dark shed's wall. He smelled mulch and damp concrete, the scents mingling weirdly well with Chris's grassy savannah aroma. Tony was a big guy, but Chris seemed huge in the confined space— hot and male and totally powerful. Being crowded by his taller body chased delighted shivers down Tony's spine. Probably Chris noticed. His hands gripped him at the waist.

"You are something," he murmured, taking Tony's mouth in a blistering kiss.

Tony could only moan. Well, he also grabbed Chris and kissed him back. The days it had been since he'd kissed this man multiplied. Knowing what he'd been missing made going without it worse. Now Tony needed kissing like he needed oxygen.

"Get this off," he urged, wrenching Chris's tuxedo jacket down his arms.

Chris removed it while energetically Frenching him.

God, that was good—his taste, his aggressive tongue, the hardness of his chest as they pushed against each other. Chris's long leg edged between

Tony's. Tony resisted for the heady pleasure of feeling Chris force his thighs apart. The tiger was really strong, his palms clamping Tony's buttocks. His cock was steely as he rolled it beside Tony's.

Tony sucked in air at the rush of hot sensation along his dick. Even with both their clothes on, he could have come.

Panting, Chris tore free of the kiss. One hand shifted forward to Tony's bulge, his cock continuing to rub next to it. "I want to make up for hurting you."

Tony gasped louder. Chris's powerful fingers had just squeezed him.

He didn't know what to say. *You don't have to? Hurry up if you're going to?*

Chris didn't need a response. He grabbed a folding chair from the jumble of equipment in the shed.

"What's that for?" Tony asked as he opened and placed it in front of him.

Chris sat, brushed his tousled bangs back, and looked up Tony's chest. His big hands settled on Tony's hips, thumbs stretched to stroke the arch of his erection. Tony ordered his wolf to shut up about who was above whom. Chris wanted to do this. A good submissive shouldn't refuse. Illumination from the running path's lampposts filtered through the small window. Chris wasn't smiling, but he was still gorgeous. A pair of red suspenders broke his white shirt into sections, making his chest seem even broader.

"Anyone ever suck you?" the fireman asked.

Tony's cock jolted. "Not a man."

He guessed this was the answer Chris expected—and maybe had hoped for. The tiger wet his lips, and Tony's penis pulsed harder. Chris unfastened Tony's trousers, his fingers careful but titillating as they lowered his strained zipper. Just as carefully, he freed Tony's throbbing length from his underwear and shirttails. Being touched by him felt amazing. Tony's breath sawed like a bellows; he was that excited.

When Chris looked at the massive boner he'd just drawn out, his tiger fangs shot down.

"I'm going to do us both," he announced harshly.

Tony didn't know what he meant until Chris's surprisingly dexterous fingers opened his own trousers.

"Oh God," he moaned without meaning to.

Chris grinned whitely in the dimness. "Like to watch?"

"Never got the chance to, but I expect I will."

Beads of pre-cum squeezed from his dick, generous enough to be embarrassing. Chris rubbed the fluid over him with his thumb.

"I'm leaking too," he confessed.

Tony's hands clenched into excited fists. If they hadn't, he'd have grabbed Chris for sure. He had to clear his throat before his voice came out. "Show me."

Chris dug his cock out, grabbed its root, and stroked upward. Since he was sitting, Tony saw the prodigy from above. Chris's shaft was thick in his hand, the head rounded and swollen. Seeming to like showing off, the cat let go and stroked again from the bottom. His grip was tight, compressing his flesh slightly. Tony shuddered with arousal.

"One hand for me," Chris said. "And the other plus my mouth for you."

"Shit," Tony breathed, watching moisture well from the tiger's slit, loving that he was uninhibited. He swallowed, wanting to suck that big cock so badly he ached.

Chris must have known. "This is my show. Everyone expects you to jump when they snap their fingers. You let me do for you."

Tony didn't know how to respond to that. He was what he was in the pack. It was natural to him.

"Can I hold your head?" he asked instead.

Chris grinned. "I'd be disappointed if you didn't."

Tony placed his hands on either side of the tiger's skull. He wasn't gripping hard, though he couldn't resist sinking his fingers through Chris's thick gold-streaked hair. Chris's eyes briefly closed, liking the gentle stroke.

When his lashes lifted, citrine glints lit his irises.

Tony held his breath as Chris bent forward on the seat. He was big for the folding chair, and the shift in his weight made the metal creak. His thumb and fingers angled Tony's cock toward his mouth. His breath fanned the tip, his tongue licked once, and then he swallowed him.

Tony's lungs emptied at the ferocious surge of pleasure. Chris's tongue and cheeks were sleek, the band of his lips firm and tight. Tony's head fell back as Chris drew slowly up his shaft.

He'd been blown before, but this one pull was a revelation. Chris's mouth was bolder, more encompassing than a woman's. Or maybe Tony's reaction had nothing to do with technique. Maybe this was a revelation because Chris really, truly attracted him.

Helpless to stop himself, he tightened his fingers on Chris's head.

"Mm," Chris said. "You are as smooth as silk."

He licked across Tony's glans, tongue flat and pushing hard. Tony's nerves did a happy dance. "You can guide me if you want," Chris offered.

Tony shook his head. Did he remember how to speak? "I just . . . want to feel you go up and down."

"You like it slow?" His partner demonstrated the speed he meant with his fist. Tony noticed his left hand, the one he'd wrapped around himself, moved identically. That was a charge, knowing Chris would jack himself in synchrony.

"I like it any way." His thighs tightened, pushing his pelvis forward without quite intending to. "Just don't leave me hanging."

Chris might have been smiling as his mouth took him in again. Tony's spine arched with renewed bliss—too much bliss maybe. As the tiger sucked slowly up and down, his free hand burrowed into Tony's trousers, fingers ringing the top of his ball sac. When he had him the way he wanted, he pulled down and held firmly. The protracted tug surprised him. Tony knew it was meant to help him last. What he didn't expect was Chris wanting to linger over this.

Chris seemed to know when the imminent threat of orgasm had backed off. He released Tony's balls and changed tactics. The pressure of his lips had been relatively light. Now he gave Tony more of everything: more tongue action, more pressure, more speed as he rose and fell. Tony's scalp tingled at the intensification of wet friction, his hands passive but very interested riders on Chris's head. The sound of the blowjob was a turn-on all by itself. If Chris had been crap at this, Tony probably would have enjoyed it. As it was, Chris's skill and interest drove Tony to the trembling edge.

Once he sensed he was there, Chris tugged his balls down again.

This time the yank inspired a brief flare of pain. Heat followed in its wake as soon as it registered, spreading out from his groin to suffuse his whole body.

"God," Tony gasped.

Chris rolled his eyes up to check that he was all right. Tony was so good it wasn't funny. He was on the balls of his feet, his whole being straining for more pleasure.

Maybe more pain too; he wasn't certain about that part.

"I'm okay," he assured Chris breathlessly. "That was just the right kind of snap."

Chris sucked upward, thumb and hand following his mouth up Tony's shaft. He kissed its tip, licked, then brushed his lips across more softly. The look on his face was like nothing Tony had ever seen—not directed toward him at least. *Worshipful* was the word that came close, though a guy like Chris was no one's acolyte.

The look made him wonder how Chris had resisted answering his message.

"No more teasing," Chris said like sandpaper. "This time I'm going to suck you until you come."

His pupils had changed. Within the orange glow of his irises, the slits were more catlike. This thrilled Tony more than he knew how to hide. His hands tightened helplessly on Chris's head.

"Yes," he said. "Please."

Chris's smile was feral. He stretched his tongue out between his fangs, making sure Tony got the best possible visual of its pinkness dragging up and over him.

"Shit," he gasped, feeling a strange difference. Chris's tongue was rougher, more textured against his skin. "What the hell did you do?"

Chris chuckled, low and dirty, leaving Tony to guess the answer.

Cats weren't like wolves. They didn't need the moon to change; they could shift any time they pleased. Lengthened teeth or shining eyes were common shifter reactions to excitement. Chris altering his tongue to have more feline traits wasn't something Tony had known a cat could do. Maybe most cats couldn't.

Maybe Chris was special.

He moaned as the tiger began sucking him full throttle. The chair scraped back as Chris scooted forward to perch on its edge. He was going fast, and his tongue was busy. Tony was going to fuck his mouth. His cock longed for that so much he didn't think he could stop himself. His hands tightened on Chris's head. His ears were between his palms. He was pulling him down his prick, forcing him to take more of him.

"Fuck," he gasped, trying to stop himself.

Chris wrapped one massive arm behind Tony's thighs, refusing to let him escape his own urges. His bobbing head bumped Tony's stomach through his tuxedo shirt. Despite the crazy groans Tony was letting out, he heard Chris jerk off faster. The sound of his grip clicking on sweat and flesh was incredibly arousing. Unable to resist, Tony shoved his hips at him harder. Chris grunted and took him, swallowing against the tip so that Tony's cock went even further down his throat.

It felt amazing—sexy and sweet and totally accepting.

Tony's come exploded.

As it did, Chris's fist sped up manically. With Tony taken care of, the tiger wanted his own climax. Tony wasn't about to miss watching. He'd spread his legs to brace himself for Chris's blowjob. Now he shook his head to clear his pleasure-blurred vision. Chris was pointing his stiff erection toward the space between Tony's feet, his hand streaking up and down. His mouth was clamped around Tony's cock, though Tony had stopped thrusting. Chris breathed through his nose, uneven huffs of a man lost to everything but his need for release. His fangs were hard, his big body tense. Suddenly, he moaned around Tony and cut loose.

Long bursts of seed spattered the floor of the gardener's shed.

The noise of them hitting sent pleasurable spasms through Tony, like Chris had the power to share his ecstasy. Each mini-thrill weakened already wobbly knees—though of course it was worth it. Finally, both of them finished quivering.

Wow, Tony thought, grateful for the support of the worn wood wall. Without it, he might not have stayed standing. He wondered why Chris wasn't pulling off. Then he realized he was clutching his head to him.

"Sorry," he said, immediately letting go.

Chris wiped his mouth and straightened in the chair.

"I've got a pocket square," Tony said.

Chris smiled like this was a silly thing to offer.

"No?"

"You tasted good," he said simply.

That was flattering, Tony guessed. He didn't know how to interpret Chris's current expression. His glimmering smile had faded, and he'd closed his features down like Fort Knox. Tony wasn't expecting hearts and flowers, but the change knocked him off balance. Aware that he'd been extremely well serviced, he tucked his cock away and zipped up. Chris rubbed his knees and half watched.

"Are you sorry we did that?" Tony asked, finding Chris's man-of-few-words habit frustrating.

Chris pushed the folding chair back and rose. He shook his head, somehow not making it a *no*. He looked down at himself and wagged it again. His cock was thick but as well sated as Tony's. Tony definitely watched him put himself away, no halfway about it. He wanted to store up the image of that yummy length of man flesh.

His trousers set to rights, Chris pulled on his tuxedo jacket. His breathing was almost normal. As a rule, shifters recovered from exertion quicker than normal folks. He'd swallowed Tony's ejaculate and had been careful not come on himself. Once he wiped the sweat off, it would be difficult to tell what he'd been up to.

Maybe he hadn't been as uninhibited as Tony thought.

"I should get back," Chris said, shrugging his big shoulders into position within the black garment. "Before someone notices I'm gone."

Tony hoped he wouldn't kick himself later for opening his mouth now.

"Okay," he said, dragging the other man's gaze to him. "I get it. If you're spotted alone with me, your men will get suspicious. I understand being outed would make your job harder."

"That's . . . understating it," Chris said.

"You can really pretend this never happened?"

"I'm going to try to."

"Hell."

"You're dangerous," Chris explained, a hint of a plea in it. "I don't think I can sneak around with you like I . . ." He trailed off.

"Like you do with other men," Tony finished for him grimly.

"We're likely to be thrown together, since your packmate married my alpha. If I'm remembering what we did or hoping what we'll do next, my reaction will be hard to hide."

Tony pressed his fist to his brow. His head wasn't aching, but it felt close. "So you only did this with me tonight because you're drunk?"

"Not only because of that." Chris touched Tony's arm. When he felt how stiff it was, he dropped his hand. "You've got to believe I wish things were different."

"We're a good fit." Tony tried to say this without sounding emotional.

"You can't tell me sex with other men is this amazing."

Chris's breath trailed out. "We're too good a fit." He lifted his palms before Tony could protest. "I can't, Tony. Please don't push me to do this again."

He hadn't pushed him tonight. Chris had followed him out here. Tony clamped his jaw shut on that little fact. Pointing it out wouldn't change anything.

Seeing he'd given up, Chris stepped to the shed's shut door.

The cautious cat had remembered to pull it closed.

"Go on," Tony said when he hesitated. "We can't return to the party together."

His tone was sarcastic, but Chris didn't take offense. "You're a good man," he said before slipping outside like a shadow.

A good man. Too bad there was no reward for that.

CHAPTER FOUR

CHRIS'S mood hadn't been sunny since walking out on Tony two nights ago. His catnaps were history. They'd been chancy enough before, but now that he'd been with Tony a second time, he dreamed of the hot young cop each time he closed his eyes.

His subconscious mind seemed determined to torture him with details. At random moments, Tony's scent teased his nose. His ears rang with Tony's gasps, the pleasure the wolf had experienced clearly new to him. Chris had loved being the first man to give him head. The prick of Tony's claws on his scalp was a sensation he wouldn't soon forget. More times in the last few days than he cared to count, he woke with pounding erections he was too annoyed to deal with. Jacking off would only summon more images. Remembering Tony in that shed—the way they'd come, the way they'd said goodbye—tempted Chris to put a fist through something. Tony wasn't kidding about them being a good fit. Chris didn't think he'd ever felt that *himself* with someone.

All of which proved he'd been right to walk away. If any man could inspire him to out himself, Tony "Hotstuff" Lupone was that person.

Given that this was so, the sight that came toward him now didn't make him happy.

Their homophobic omega Liam was straggling across the concrete apron outside the station like he had all the time in the world. The big tiger was relaxed, yawning behind his fist as he paused to check the street in both directions. The autumn blue sky above him drew his attention next.

The forecast for Liam was cloudy—as he'd have known if he'd had the self-preservation the Tiger Queen gave a gnat.

"You're late," Chris said loudly enough for his voice to carry.

He sat inside Company 5 with the rest of the men. The lounge's secondhand chairs and sofas offered a view through the truck bay into their

44

egress street. Chris had been halfheartedly paging through *The Pocket Observer*, looking for articles to occupy his thoughts. He'd finished all his administrative chores, sure sign of his desperation for distraction.

Having time to kill was nothing new. Resurrection wasn't a nonstop fire city. Firemen here waited around a lot, though portions of their shift were taken up with training and equipment maintenance. Aside from that, they ate, they napped, and they studied—if they were so inclined. Sometimes they raced out on calls that turned out to be someone's cat spelled into a tree by an ornery neighbor. Maybe twice a week they answered an alarm for a fire that required more than a ten-second burst from an extinguisher.

Despite facing only occasional life and death circumstances, one rule of their profession wasn't open for debate.

Firemen showed up where they were supposed to when they were expected.

Liam seemed to have forgotten this. He added a full-body stretch to his yawn, cracking the joints in his muscled back with a tiger-grunt of pleasure. When he finished, he grinned boyishly. "Sorry, boss. I do have a good excuse. Ever since the wedding, Freda and I have been knocking boots. That tigress knows how to wear out a man."

Chris's insides went very still. Their best cook Syd had been frying eggs and sausage in the open kitchen behind the lounge. Naturally, Liam's ill-chosen words reached him. The sizzle dissipated as the cat clicked off the stove's burners. Along with everyone else, he'd stopped what he was doing to see how Chris responded. Syd was laidback by nature, his family having originated in Jamaica. His reaction reminded Chris *laidback* wasn't the same as *indifferent*. Every member of the clan cared how it functioned.

Jonah was probably their hardest man to read. He lost his cat-cool enough to lean forward in his easy chair.

"What's the deal?" Liam asked, noting all eyes on him. Slowly though his long legs were moving, they'd brought him into the truck bay. "I'm only ten minutes late. The big boss isn't even here."

Evina and her new husband were on a whopping two-day, two-night honeymoon. Liam shouldn't have assumed their alpha's absence meant he could slack. No one else at the station was. Vasur, their shortest man at a mere six three in his turnout boots, had been working out when Liam made his gaffe. Vasur outranked Liam, a fact he didn't let the junior cat forget. He felt obliged to point out the error of his co-worker's ways.

"You really should not have said that," he murmured from the weight bench.

Recognizing he needed to make a few things clear, Chris set down his paper and got up from the couch. "You think you have no one to answer to when 'the big boss' is gone?"

He didn't put a growl in it, but Liam was just smart enough to perceive one.

"Um," he said, rubbing one flushing Irish cheek. "No?"

In his unsureness, he'd paused beside their lime green and black tiger-striped pumper. Chris prowled out, giving the other man a taste of his heightening beta energy. He stopped an arm's length away.

"Freda is your alpha's friend. You think it's appropriate to be bragging to your buddies about what she did with you in private?"

"Freda doesn't care," Liam said stupidly. "She sleeps with everyone."

Chris wasn't an ordinary person, and sometimes he couldn't afford to act like one. He didn't fight his tiger's instincts on how he should respond, though his beast was probably more ticked by Liam questioning its authority than by the slur to a member of tigress-kind.

Powered by sureness and dominance, his arm lashed out in a split second, moving too quickly for even Liam's shifter perceptions to see it coming. He cuffed the omega across the face the way a grown tiger would a cub, knocking Liam off one foot and causing his body to swing around. He didn't break Liam's cheekbone, but it was close.

"Shit," Liam gasped, hand to the place his superior had walloped.

"Freda is a tigress," Chris bit out. "Not some prostitute you met on a corner. She risks her life every day the same as you. You will not speak of her with disrespect."

Liam was the bottom man, but he wasn't short on pride. If Chris had punched him, it would have been man to man. To swat at him like he had was an insult. Embarrassment and anger fought for control of his expression. In the end, foolishly, he tried humorous wheedling. "Come on, boss. Just because you couldn't hold Freda's attention—"

He didn't finish. He lost his nerve when the men behind Chris sucked in matching breaths of shock. Chris's gift for astral projection expressed itself in different ways. Now his energy swelled with anger, expanding to such a height that for a second he could have been looking down at an ant. His eyes flared bright in the monstrous feline form, claws jutting from the spirit shape like talons. Liam quailed and fell to his knees, finally doing what Chris's tiger believed he ought.

When Liam covered his head to shield against a strike, all Chris felt was satisfied.

He pushed down the emotion, settling for long warning growl. Understanding it, Liam cowered lower.

"Boss," Jonah said. He had a hard time seeing his buddy scared, however much Liam deserved it.

Without moving his gaze from Liam, Chris pulled his energy almost completely in.

"Check the hoses," he ordered the cowering cat, his vocal chords still projecting an animal threat. "Every inch of every length." Liam drew breath, but whatever he meant to say Chris cut off. "Not another word. When you finish, scrub the bathroom. While you're at it, consider how lightly you're getting off. You were late *and* insubordinate. Tigers have been fired from this crew for less."

He turned away before he saw Liam's inevitable resentment. Chris didn't need more triggers to force the man to submit. He'd already come too close to seriously hurting him. Within tiger clans, betas were enforcers. Sometimes they had to use physical force. For better or worse, that was the language their beast halves understood. If, however, a beta used force to settle every damn argument, he'd lose a bigger battle than the one for obedience.

Maintaining his men's respect meant his human side had to rule his animal.

He strode from the truck bay into the kitchen. His hands tried to shake, but he controlled them. He wasn't like the man who'd killed his brothers. He understood Liam was just a temporarily stupid kid and not a threat to him. Both sides of Chris's nature wanted to keep the omega safe more than they wanted to put him in his place. Liam was shaping up to be a good fireman. Making sure he became one was Chris's priority.

He'd calmed a bit by the time Syd slid him a plate of food. The caramel-skinned, dreadlocked tiger was mellow to the *nth* degree. In addition to this, he was mid-rank on the power scale and not short on confidence. All the same, he offered Chris the steaming meat and eggs as if needing to placate him.

"I'm all right," Chris said. "Storm over."

Syd nodded soberly. The kitchen's concrete prep table was between them. Syd made no move to change that. He visibly squared his shoulders before he spoke. "You sure you don't need a day off? You came straight back to work after your accident."

He meant after Chris was burned so badly he'd been in too much pain to change and heal. This was the official explanation anyway. Chris knew his issues were more complex.

"I wanted to come back to work. I'd have been bored to death at home."

Chris had never met a fireman who didn't feel that way. Seeming to accept his claim, Syd leaned more sociably on the countertop. "*Are* you interested in Freda?" he inquired cautiously.

Chris rolled his eyes. "I'm not jealous of her and Liam."

"But if you were," Syd said, "I or one of the other tigers could warn him off."

Chris rubbed his forehead, unable to explain how many different ways this was wrong. "No," he said. "Freda is a free agent."

"Getting shagged is a good tension reliever."

"I am aware of that," Chris said.

The desert dryness of his response wasn't lost on Syd. "Okay," he surrendered with a small grin. "You can arrange your own love life."

Chris grimaced and said nothing. He wished he could arrange it. He dug into the food, aware he'd dodged more than one bullet in the last few minutes. It occurred to him he hadn't worried about dominance issues during his two encounters with Tony. He'd pushed the wolf to be *less* submissive . . . though he couldn't deny enjoying that side of him. Frankly, everything Tony did was enjoyable.

Thinking about the wolf wasn't a good idea. Chris's blood was up from facing off with Liam. One salacious mental image would dump him in libidinal hot water. The klaxon going off for a new alarm was undeniably good timing.

Because Liam probably needed bucking up, Chris squeezed his shoulders before they rolled out. He wished he could swear Tony hadn't been in some corner of his mind when he struck the gay-phobic cat.

What the otherwise likeable tiger might do to a wolf like Tony didn't bear thinking on.

~

Tony's disreputable running shoes felt like they were cemented to the unnaturally clean sidewalk. P.J. Brit's wasn't the sort of bar he was accustomed to. For one thing, it was uptown, with shiny plate glass windows and perfectly groomed green ferns hanging from a stamped tin ceiling. The predominantly male clientele looked just as snipped and trim. Most sat in laughing groups at too-small tables, wearing *GQ*-ish suits Tony wouldn't have dreamed of wasting his paycheck on. For variety, a smattering were tricked out in motorcycle leathers, reminding him of greaser movies from the Fifties.

Fetishwear, he guessed it was.

Tony doubted the men who wore it actually rode Harleys.

Fuck, he thought, cursing his unpreparedness for this.

Their precinct dispatcher Dana had recently come out as a lesbian. Because everything Tony had found on Elfnet seemed skeevy, he'd asked her if she knew where gay men hung out.

P.J. Brit's and the Central Park public johns were what she'd come up with.

Tony probably should have consulted Nate instead.

Stop dithering, he scolded his reluctant feet. His tiger fireman was a write off. He needed to get his gay self into circulation some other way.

A group of laughing pointy-eared yuppie elves bumped him on their way in. They didn't glance at him as they passed. They were oblivious to everything but their own circle.

God, Tony hated going out alone.

Too bad, he told himself, ordering his legs forward. If he wanted to be who he really was, he'd have to function without wingmen.

His sweaty palm gripped the door handle. Nervous strength caused him to nearly bash himself in the face. That embarrassment narrowly avoided, he stepped inside with his heart pounding. Going to hookup bars was so much easier when you didn't care about the outcome.

"Meeting someone?" inquired a sharp-nosed effeminate shifter behind a podium.

Okay, what the fuck sort of watering hole had a maître d'?

"No," Tony said. "Is it cool to hang at the bar?"

"You can't order food there, just snacks."

"That's okay," Tony said. "I doubt my stomach can handle food anyway."

The host looked to where Tony had pressed his hand over his belly. His lips slanted to one side, making him abruptly seem friendlier. "First time?"

"I guess that's obvious." Tony tried to breathe out his nervousness. "I'm dressed all wrong, aren't I?"

He'd pulled on a clean yellow polo shirt and new jeans, nicer than what he'd have worn to a cop bar. He'd also showered and shaved but—given that he was a dark-haired wolf with a persistent beard shadow—he wasn't ever going to look as polished as most of the men here. Given that he wasn't a wannabe anything, he wasn't going to carry off fetishy either.

The maître d' laid one finger beside his mouth to consider him. When he finished the slow once-over, he was grinning. "I expect you'll do. Variety is the spice of life."

This should have reassured him, but his butterflies flapped harder.

"Why don't I show you through to the bar?" the host suggested with a kindness Tony didn't expect. "I'll let the bartender know you're new."

"Thanks," Tony said, falling gratefully into his wake.

"Just take it slow." The host threw the advice over his shoulder. "Nurse your drink. Watch how people interact. Make your decisions with a clear head."

"You're alpha," Tony said, the realization surprising him.

"Werefox," the host replied. "We don't care so much about who's butchest."

They'd reached the packed but not rowdy bar. The flat screen that hung above it had the financial news on instead of sports. The werefox caught the bartender's attention and then pointed at Tony. The tall bald man was polishing a glass with a drying cloth. He nodded at whatever signal the werefox sent. He was part-demon, Tony saw, his all-black eyes giving him away.

Not gay, Tony decided, and not as kindly as the maître d'. "I'll have a faerie stout," he said. "On tap, if you've got it."

The bartender pulled one with quick motions. Tony paid, braced his shoulders, and looked around. One of the leather daddies was looking back. He raised his whiskey tumbler in salute.

No, no, no, Tony thought, not feeling that at all. Hoping it was enough for politeness, he nodded very slightly and looked away. *My, how fascinating the* foam in his beer glass was. He could stare at it all night.

The man on his other side bumped his elbow, almost triggering his fight response. "And then I told him if that's a genuine Rolex, I'm Brad Effing Goddamned Pitt."

Whoever the stranger spoke to laughed like a hyena.

Fuck, Tony thought. He couldn't do this. These so were not his people.

"The first visit is the hardest," the bartender said.

Tony hadn't heard him return. He looked up from his beer into black-as-a-black-hole eyes. Maybe he shouldn't have, but he blurted a confession. "I don't think I'll find someone I like in a place like this."

The part-demon's smile was a flicker of broad thin lips. "Don't assume. Corporate a-holes and leather posers are people too."

Tony laughed, because he was right. The bartender moved away, but the burst of shared humor had relaxed his taut spine a notch. He'd stay an hour, he decided, and take it slow like the werefox said.

Every journey, however excruciating, began with a single step.

~

Two and a half hours later, Tony fell into bed alone. More or less sober, he was thankfully tired enough to sleep. Though he'd stuck with it, his exchanges with the bartender and the host turned out to be the highlight of his bar adventure. A couple men had approached him, but he hadn't been tempted to encourage their overtures. That had troubled him a bit. What if he never found a partner he liked as much as Chris? What if the only gay bar he'd found kicked him out for being too picky? Worst of all, what if he settled and was sorry?

Miraculously, he didn't dream of his lost fireman, or not that he remembered.

Morning—or pre-morning, because their squad was on early shift—came way too soon. Tony's big brother lived one floor above him in the historic brownstone they owned together with their alpha. Rick called him at half past three to make sure he was up. He'd done that a lot since Tony's big announcement, as if being gay had erased a decade's worth of birthdays and a few IQ points. Tony was thirty-five, not stupid, and not a baby—even if shifters aged slowly.

"I'll drive you in," Rick said.

Of course you will, Tony thought grumpily.

To be fair, he didn't totally mind. Not driving that damn early was easier. Too, after the night he'd had, he looked forward to being with his brother. Ass or not, Rick was his comfort zone.

He reminded himself of that as he wolfed down breakfast and dressed for work. He *almost* let the brownstone's street door slam behind him, but stopped at the last minute. Ari was human and could sleep through a lot of noise. Her and Adam's daughter Kelsey had baby shifter ears. Not waking *her* made life easier on the entire pack.

Rick hadn't forgotten. Though they were three floors down and outside, he shut the driver's side door as gently as possible.

"God, I need more coffee," Tony grumbled as Rick rolled out and turned onto Saltpeter.

River Heights—their solidly blue-collar, largely cop neighborhood—was dead at this hour. The shifters and other folks who resided here were safely tucked in bed. Sadly, Rick and Tony had nowhere to make a caffeine stop. The local restaurants and corner groceries were shuttered.

Tony wondered how soundly Chris Savoy was sleeping.

That train of thought annoyed him. His trip to the stupid bar had been about forgetting the hot tiger. Frowning, he pulled his long legs up between the dash and him. Rick's stodgy gray Buick was used this treatment. Two shiny patches marked the ledge above the glove compartment. Maybe Tony should have been a cat. Sometimes he liked having walls on more than one side of him. Maybe he'd have enjoyed curling up in a cardboard box.

His left ear prickled, warning him his big brother was staring.

"Do I have Faerie O's in my hair?"

"What?" Rick asked, startled by the question.

"You're staring at me."

The prickling stopped, so Rick must have looked away. Good thing, considering he was driving. "I just wondered," he said. "You were out late last night."

Tony did not want to recap his experience. "I went to a bar."

"And?" Rick prompted, ignoring his please-let-this-drop signals. Tony lost his patience.

"And what?" he snapped. "I'm not hung over. It's four in the frick a.m. You want sprightly, you need a sprite for a brother."

Rick laughed and shot another glance at him. "I'm trying to ask if you met someone nice."

Was this what Tony was in for while his brother adjusted to his gayness? Being pestered about his romantic life like Rick was his mother?

"You haven't had a date since you came out," Rick explained.

"That you know of," Tony retorted. His cheeks were a few degrees hotter than he wanted them to be. To compensate, he glared at the dirty rain spots on the windshield.

"Have you been dating?" Rick persisted.

Jesus, Tony thought but didn't say. Did getting blown in a gardener's shed count as a social life?

"Tony—"

"You know," Tony cut him off. "If you were getting laid yourself, you wouldn't worry so much about my sex life."

This was true but a low blow. His brother's dating record was worse than his lately. Tony would have felt guiltier about the dig if it had actually shut Rick up. His brother's hands shifted on the steering wheel. "You could tell me if you met someone special."

Lord. Rick *was* turning into their mother.

"I wouldn't be rude to them," Rick swore.

Okay. Maybe Rick's attempt at being open-minded was sort of sweet. Tony tried to answer less snippily. "Just give me a chance to get my sea legs."

The radio between their seats crackled, causing Tony to snap upright. Please God, let whatever call was coming in put an end to this heart to heart.

"RTA requests assistance," said an unfamiliar dispatcher's voice, referring to the Resurrection Transit Authority. "10-34 M at the Elm and Fifth north station. Witness describes two perps going at it with long swords."

The subway stop the dispatcher named wasn't far from their location. As detectives, Tony and Rick weren't obliged to take the call. Breaking up fights was a job for uniforms. On the other hand, 10-34 M was code for an altercation involving magic. Plus, the long sword thing could be cool.

"Not unheard of," Rick said in response to his raised eyebrows. "But intriguing."

The advantage of being brothers was that they often thought alike. Certain they were on the same page, Tony grabbed the radio. "Car 65 responding. We're two minutes out, no more."

"10-4," the central dispatcher said. "Be advised suspects are fae."

Now that really was intriguing. Fae had created the half-magic Pocket that enabled Resurrection to straddle realities. More often than not, they remained aloof from its citizens. Most fae stilled lived in Faerie, only visiting the Pocket when they felt like slumming. If they had beefs with each other, they didn't settle them in front of inferiors. They certainly didn't have knockdown drag-outs at subway stops.

Tony saw Rick grin right before he floored the accelerator. The Buick shimmied and then took off, forcing Tony to brace himself. Though the streets were practically empty, roaring down them was fun. The public might not want to know, but most cops loved this stuff. Tony had a feeling his and Rick's inner tails were wagging.

Because there was more to think about than fun, he grabbed one of the padded vests that lay on the back seat. The straps that fastened it were Velcro, the black material spelled to block magical and mundane projectiles. Rick stuck his arm out for his even as Tony readied it.

They ran down their checklist of protections.

"You packing electrum loads?"

"Yup. You got your depowering charms?"

Familiar as it was, the ritual heightened their confidence. They were an experienced team, and they were ready to rock and roll.

The Elm and Fifth subway stop appeared. Its circular aboveground plaza hosted a mini-park. Rick spun the steering wheel one-handed and hopped the heavy Buick over the curb. The car was still rolling slightly when they leaped out. Slamming the doors in tandem, they ran across the grass side by side, toward the clearly marked subway stairs. Lamplight sparkled on concrete, the special city glitter they could only admire at night. Tony sent his wolf senses questing through their surroundings. He didn't hear a swordfight, but he scented a whiff of blood.

The scent came from underground. It had mingled with the stale tunnel air. Rick must have caught it too. He put his arm out to signal Tony to take a beat.

"Be careful," he said in a deeper than normal voice.

His words acted like a trigger to the city's mystical underpinnings. Tony could have sworn the night around them drew in and held a breath. His adrenaline went crazy, his pulse filling up his throat.

A man-shaped star burst up the RTA entrance steps.

The star was a faerie, a pureblood to go by the blinding dazzle his skin shot off. Tony's lungs stopped working as an inappropriate buzz of interest awakened between his legs. Tony had never seen a pureblood this close before. When faeries were in the Pocket, they usually dimmed their looks with glamour. This dude was letting all his gorgeousness hang out. The leather boys at P.J.'s would have drooled over his gladiator-style getup, the briefness of which showed off his tall body. His frame was slenderer than Tony favored, but so fabulously proportioned in its ratio of shoulder to hip to leg that he couldn't have said how to improve it. If that weren't theatrical enough, the faerie's waist-length hair was silver—like a zillion floaty strands had been spun from pure sterling.

Tony had an insane urge to bury his face in it.

The faerie stopped, as surprised to see them as they were to encounter him. His eyes were electric blue, like they'd been plugged into a battery. When his gaze locked onto Tony's, his feet would no longer move.

He cursed silently. Faeries were top dogs on the magic heap. They could out-charm gargoyles and demons and any flavor of shifter imaginable. This faerie's power felt like it was trying to crawl inside Tony. His hands, which were lovely and white as snow, wrapped the hilt of a medieval-looking sword. *Long* didn't cover how big it was. Pointing up at the moment, the blade was nearly as tall as the shining male. Thick streams of blood dripped down it, coating his exquisite pale fingers.

Tony wanted to lick those fingers for more than one reason.

The faerie's glowing blue eyes widened.

Tony had a strong impression the faerie knew what he was thinking.

He's going to kill us, he thought, realizing Rick wasn't any less faerie-struck than him. The faerie's literally stunning looks had paralyzed them both.

Feeling disloyal to Chris for letting that happen was ridiculous.

"Fuck," he choked aloud.

The faerie's face flickered, no expression in it that Tony recognized. Time had seemed to stop while they gawked at each other. Tony's curse kick-started it again.

Wolf, he heard very clearly inside his head. *Move out of my way or die.*

Tony wore an enchanted Saint Michael medal around his neck. Though the thing was designed to protect him against compulsions, it didn't help him then. Like a puppet, he stepped out of the faerie's path. The male zoomed by and then cut left across Elm Street. The air he displaced blew Tony's hair like storm wind.

As soon as he was out of reach, Tony's anger recovered. The faerie—who'd probably just murdered someone—had passed close enough to grab. Tony wasn't a puppy, he was a wolf. And an officer of the law. He didn't care how much juice this fae bastard could draw on. Tony's city wasn't his personal playground.

"I got this," he barked to Rick, sprinting after the fleeing male.

"Call for backup," Rick shouted.

"Will," Tony promised over his shoulder.

Tony wasn't stupid. He notified Dispatch through his shoulder comm before he'd finished bounding across the empty lanes.

After that, he needed all his breath for running. Sheesh, the faerie was fast. Tony had heard some fae could fly or levitate. Sword Guy didn't do either but was moving at better than average shifter speed—with no sign of slowing down. Buildings rushed by as Tony strove to keep up. The fae was still glowing, which made him hard to lose. Tony wondered if the male not hiding his light with glamour was a good sign. Had the fight in the subway sapped the fae's energy?

If this was Sword Guy tired, Tony didn't want to see him daisy fresh. He pushed himself to his limits, a stitch beginning to grab his ribs. It was too bad he couldn't change at will. Four wolf legs would have been an improvement on two flagging human ones.

"Fuck," he breathed. Sword Guy had just veered sideways between two office towers.

Did the alley dead-end? Was the faerie setting a trap? He knew Tony was behind him. Had he decided to make a stand?

Tony had a small spell-charged crossbow in his right bulletproof vest pocket. The tips of its bolts were solid electrum—unlike the ammo in his sidearm, which was only electrum plate. The bolts *might* disable the pureblood, if Tony hit him right.

Deciding this weapon was his best bet, Tony snapped the bow out and activated it. Too quickly to make himself a target, he ducked his head into the gap between buildings.

The alley went through to the next street. The faerie's star-bright glitter was disappearing from the far end.

Tony took off after him again.

Beyond the alley, the city's landscape opened up. The buildings were lower, with more space between them. Tony signaled Dispatch again, hoping they understood the update in spite of his hard breathing. A sparkle trail led across the empty lot of a gas station up ahead. If Sword Guy was shedding faerie dust, maybe he really was losing steam.

The stuff went up Tony's nose as he ran through it. Gritting his teeth against the mild high it caused, he armed the light crossbow.

Seconds later, he skidded to a halt.

He'd caught up to the fae. The male was cornered, or seemed to be, against the graffitied front of Demon Dan's Motorcycle Repair Shop. The street art was some of Tony's favorite, showing Demon Dan riding a black-winged Harley across a Van Gogh-esque starry night.

Since he didn't have the luxury of admiring it right then, he brought both arms up and aimed. An order to *Freeze* was literally in his throat when an invisible wall of force drove the air from his lungs.

"That's far enough," the faerie said.

Well, fine, Tony thought. He'd shoot him from where he was.

"RPD," he managed to wheeze.

Tony wasn't the pack's best marksman. That honor belonged to Nate. Nonetheless, what he pointed at, he generally hit.

"I don't think so," the faerie said.

The crossbow fell from Tony's suddenly nerveless hands.

Crap, he thought. His shoes were stuck to the cracked asphalt. He couldn't reach far enough to retrieve the weapon. For the second time tonight, the faerie had frozen him.

Tony noticed Sword Guy wasn't winded from the chase. He held his bloody long sword at horizontal, its great weight no trouble for him to lift. Seeming more curious than angry, he came a few strides closer.

"Why do you pursue me, wolf?" he asked.

"I'm pretty sure you just killed someone. Pursuing you is my job."

"You aren't powerful enough to subdue me. And what I do isn't your business."

"Everything that happens in this city is my business."

Okay, maybe that was a tad dramatic. The faerie seemed to realize he'd exaggerated. His perfect lips curved the slightest bit in his snow-white face. Tony immediately wished they hadn't. The smile sent extremely distracting waves of lust coursing through his bloodstream.

"Wolf . . ." the fae began but stopped.

The blood that coated his sword had just ignited like a Fourth of July sparkler. The faerie's smile broadened. "Ah," he said as the dazzling light swiftly consumed the gore. "It appears my mission was successful."

"You killed another faerie," Tony realized. That's what happened when fae died. Every cell of their bodies, including blood they'd shed, reverted to faerie dust.

The faerie regarded him with his flame blue eyes. "You are brave. I shall spare your life in honor of my victory."

Given the circumstances, Tony thought it best not to argue. The faerie took two steps back, murmured an unintelligible incantation, and cut a glowing slit in the air with the tip of his now spotless sword.

"Wait!" Tony cried. From the standpoint of apprehension, what the fae was doing couldn't be good.

The fae looked at him like he was nuts. Probably he was, but it didn't matter. Ignoring him, the faerie took hold of the slit's shimmery edges, stretching them wide enough to slip inside. Once all of him was in there, the magic door to wherever winked out of existence.

Tony's feet agreed to move again.

"Crap," he gasped, because his sudden loss of balance had dumped him onto his hands and knees. At the same time, he became aware that he had the mother of all hard-ons, the thing pounding like a jackhammer between his thighs. This wasn't just because Sword Guy was sexy. Among other things, faerie dust was an aphrodisiac. Tony had sucked up a lot of it.

The pain of the monster boner made him want to curl into a ball. Well, that or call his hot fireman and screw him for an hour or so.

The thought of Chris intensified his arousal. Tears squeezed from Tony's eyes. He couldn't even curse; the surge of need was so powerful. Naturally, this was when he heard sirens. His requested backup was finally approaching.

If he were caught like this, he'd never live it down. Gay wolf gets hard-on for homicidal faerie. That was years of jokes begging to be cracked.

There really was no question what he'd do. Desperation drove him onto his feet. He ran around the corner of the repair shop to a scrubby patch of weeds. It was all the cover he could find. He had his cock out in nanoseconds, zipper whining, right fist pumping his unnaturally engorged rod while he drove the left down to squeeze his balls. He couldn't separate pain from pleasure. The ache of need was the same as the bliss of racing to fulfill it. He had to rub one off *now*, before the cavalry arrived. Chris's mouth flashed into his mind: the sound of him sucking, the feel of his tongue working around the rim. Tony didn't fight the image. It was making his pleasure surge. Pressure built, swelled . . .

His nerves went supernova half a breath before his testicles contracted.

His seed hit the ground hard and copious. Tony bit back the moan that wanted to come out with it.

He couldn't quiet his exhalation. Luckily, the climax was quickly done. Tony cleaned up, zipped, and returned to the parking lot. He'd wiped most of the sweat from his brow when two squad cars squealed up. He shielded his eyes with one arm to keep the headlights from blinding him.

The first uniform to exit his vehicle swaggered over like a cowboy. "Lookie who we've been called to help," he drawled. "Where's your perp, Detective Lupone? Did he run away when he found out a wolf of your persuasion wanted to cuff him?"

"Funny," Tony said. "Did your mother help you make up that joke?"

It was a stupid comeback, but the other policemen laughed. Yet another awkward moment made better with humor.

"I was chasing a fae," he explained, his weariness complicated. "He magicked himself away when I cornered him. Maybe one of you could call the forensic psychic to see if he left trace behind."

"I'll do it," said a cop Tony thought was called Jessup. That they all knew him was no surprise. The RPD only had one openly gay werewolf.

"You need a lift somewhere?" asked the cowboy. He'd made his joke, so he was being respectful now.

"Yes," Tony said. "To the Elm and Fifth subway stop. My brother Rick is mopping up a fight there."

Tony guessed he looked pretty ragged. The cowboy's partner got out and held the blue-and-white's door for him.

CHAPTER

FIVE

THE faerie Tony chased to the repair shop had indeed killed someone. Tony and the uniforms arrived on the subway platform to find EMTs sucking up dissipating sparkles with a handheld vacuum. They weren't collecting evidence. The volatile magic dust had medical applications, and the vacuum canister preserved it. Rick seemed upset about them hoovering up the victim but was controlling his emotions. Tony guessed he'd arrived in time to see Sword Guy's opponent die.

Tony didn't like explaining he'd lost his man, but Rick absorbed the news absently. Per usual for a homicide, too many cops milled around the scene. On this occasion, their presence was especially pointless. A couple chunks had been knocked out of the station's concrete, as if something fast-moving had hit them. Aside from that, once the sparkles were vacuumed up, you couldn't tell a murder had occurred. Tony had no idea how they'd pursue the case. The combination of no body, no trace, and a killer who could poof himself away didn't seem promising.

"Where's the victim's sword?" he asked, remembering the report of the fight that had led them here.

Rick jerked as if coming out of a dream. "I don't know. I didn't see it when I came in."

The cowboy who'd given Tony a ride said he and his partner would search the tracks. No cop in his right mind wanted some commuter finding a potentially magical fae weapon. Tony could tell the uniforms were excited to be part of a homicide. If he were lucky, they'd end up feeling indebted to him for getting them involved.

No wind so ill it doesn't blow someone good, he thought cynically.

Rick took a statement from the RTA employee who, along with Rick, had tried to save the victim with first-aid. The human was more openly shaken than Tony's brother. The skewered faerie had been female. Big guys like the transit cop didn't like seeing delicate women die. It didn't matter that a pureblood, male or female, had the juice to tear any and all of them apart. Instinctive responses to seemingly vulnerable people were hard to get over.

Tony pondered that as Rick drove them to the precinct—along with whether he should have confiscated his car keys.

"You okay?" he asked when Rick took a good five seconds to notice a light was green.

"Huh?" he said. "Sure. I'm wondering what's on the surveillance footage the transit guy handed over."

More was on Rick's mind that that. Not sure he ought to push, Tony pinched his lower lip and said nothing.

~

The surveillance footage showed the sword fighting faeries going at it like supercharged ninjas. All five members of the squad had crowded into Adam's office to watch his monitor. At Rick's insistence, Adam had shut the blinds. Soundlessly—because audio hadn't been recorded—the faeries flipped and rebounded off the station walls while parrying each other's tremendous swings. Their blades clashed so hard sparks flew off. Even more impressive, they moved so fast Adam had to slow the playback to follow it. Despite getting the worst of the exchange, the female faerie had been valiant.

Witnessing her death made Tony extra sorry he hadn't caught her killer. It also made him feel bad for his brother. Even with no sound, he saw Rick beg the bleeding faerie to hang on.

Naturally, his brother kept his upset to himself.

"Doesn't her outfit look familiar?" he asked. "I swear I've seen it before."

The faerie's black silk pants and tunic looked like standard ninja princess clothes to Tony.

Nate's recent honeymoon hadn't blunted his faculties. He snapped his fingers and supplied the answer. "*Mini-Dragons to the Rescue!* Evina's kids are obsessed with that cartoon. That black costume is what the dragon keepers' protectors wear."

An odd cool prickle crawled over Tony's scalp. He'd seen the cartoon too, with his sister's five-year-old pup Ethan. It followed the adventures of small underwater dragons that saved people, usually with the help of a group of kids. The stories were fiction and pretty ridiculous, but they contained a grain of truth. In one of the Pockets that had been founded beneath the sea, there *were* actual mini-dragons called Meimeyo.

"So . . . what then?" their alpha asked, leaning straight-armed on his desk. This was his unconscious I-am-the-master-of-this-room pose. "Our vic is a mini-dragon fanatic?"

Rick rubbed the back of his neck like he was experiencing the same prickle as Tony. "Maybe she's a member of the actual Dragon Guild. As I understand it, full-sized dragons are supposed to be extinct, but their guild could still be active in Faerie. We don't know the half of what goes on there." Rick paused and looked embarrassed. "The faerie said something weird before she died."

Adam was Rick and Tony's blood cousin. The green eyes he shared with them sharpened. "What did the faerie say?"

Rick cleared his throat uncomfortably. "She, uh, was bleeding out, and she told me I was 'The One.' She said I had to warn some woman she was in danger."

Strictly speaking, Tony should have left questioning Rick to Adam, but this was just too weird.

"Who did she mean?" he asked.

"She said I already knew," Rick responded. "She said the universe chose me for a reason, and the destiny of the city depended on me succeeding. She said, 'Don't trust anyone. They're watching.'"

Nate and Tony shivered at the same time, which made Tony feel better about the fear response. He guessed the warning explained why Rick had asked Adam to shut the blinds. Probably they were safe. Their basement bunker had anti-eavesdropping wards galore. All the same, if the dying faerie meant her fellow fae were watching, no one could guarantee what they might spy through. Fae avoided revealing the full extent of their powers. They certainly didn't let on what their limits were.

"She might have been nuts," Tony said for the hell of it. His back was braced on a shelf of procedural manuals. Like the presence of his pack around him, the support made him feel more secure.

"She didn't seem crazy," Rick said slowly. He had one hand shoved in his jeans pocket. Tony assumed he'd stuck it there because he felt sheepish, but when he drew it out, he held something in his fist. "She gave me this before she died."

He opened his fingers with seeming reluctance. Along with the others, Tony leaned in to see. A set of brass knuckles lay on his brother's palm. Runes Tony couldn't decipher marched around the four finger holes, which were topped with wicked spikes. They'd deliver a nasty punch, maybe even kill if you weren't careful.

"I think that metal is electrum," Tony said. If it were, it would hold spells better than silver or gold alone.

The knuckles' soft buttery-white gleam was mesmerizing. Unable to resist, he stretched his index finger to touch them.

A spark the size of a walnut jumped out at the contact.

"Ouch," he said, unaccountably insulted as he stuck his zapped finger in his mouth. "You didn't warn me that thing bites."

Rick seemed as surprised as him. "I didn't know it would."

"The pureblood keyed the knuckles to you," Adam concluded.

Tony's twinge of annoyance intensified. Of course a badass faerie would choose Rick to save the world—or at least their city. Tony's brother was exactly what a hero ought to be: brave, true, and as hetero as they came. Even his modesty was perfect.

"Why would she do that?" Rick asked. "I'm an ordinary wolf."

"You're 'The One,'" Carmine teased. "You're supposed to warn some chickie she's in danger."

Rick swore he didn't know who the faerie meant. Maybe he thought he was telling the truth, but the more he denied it, the less Tony believed him. He'd known his brother all his life. He'd learned to tell when Dudley Do-Right wasn't being completely frank.

~

Tony didn't see much of Rick over the next two days. He knew his brother was working the fae-on-fae homicide but not the details. Adam knew what he was doing. Rick had called in and spoke to him. Nate had an assignment too, tracking down a professor at City U. No one seemed to remember Tony had been right beside Rick when the case began. No one seemed to think he deserved to be kept informed.

Sometimes, being the pack's omega sucked.

Part of why the exclusion ticked him off was that he'd have preferred to stay busy. He'd spent way too many free minutes checking the news for fire stories.

Today he was off, which he'd normally have enjoyed—especially since it was Sunday. His parents were great cooks, and they loved to spoil their youngest with a big breakfast at their house. Handily enough, they lived in the next brownstone over across the street. Admitting he was gay hadn't changed the habit, though he did have to put up with extra hand patting from his mom. She tried not to say it, but he knew she worried about his future. She wanted him to be happy. She'd been hoping for more grandkids.

This Sunday, his folks weren't in Resurrection. They'd won a trip for two to Oceana on a cruise submarine. They'd been over the moon excited, this being their first journey out of the Pocket they'd been born in. Tony was glad for them, just sorry for himself.

He contemplated inviting Ari and baby Kelsey to join him on a trip to the park. That idea appealed for about a minute. Hoping his alpha's wife would rescue him from his doldrums seemed selfish. He should offer her his company when he knew he could be pleasant.

He *could* spend the day cleaning his apartment, but that prospect was too dreary. He wouldn't be doing it for himself. He was fine with its current state.

Comfort was Tony's goal for his home, and to his mind, he'd achieved it. Found furniture was his favorite, the more dinged up the better. Making something broken useful was a hobby he found soothing. Maybe he didn't finish every project right away, but why should a source of pleasure become a chore? So what if the result was messy? A person could put their feet up anywhere without fear. Well, assuming they found room for their feet. His stray magazines did overrun everything a bit. This didn't mean Rick was right in claiming the place ought to be condemned. Tony had a good nose. He threw out old food before it stunk up the joint.

When he spotted his ElfBook sitting on a stack of newspapers on the coffee table, he knew exactly how to entertain himself.

Once he'd shoveled half the sofa clear, Tony sat on the leather cushion sideways. Ignoring the inner nudge that said this wasn't a good idea, he propped the laptop on a pillow his sister Maria had cross-stitched with a straggly wolf in high school. A couple of key pecks later, he'd typed "Chris Savoy" into Oogle's *FindThis!* window.

The popular search engine offered up three results. The first was a record of Chris's graduation from the Fire Academy. He'd trained in the same class as Nate's wife, and both had earned top honors. The accompanying grainy picture showed Chris with his brawny arm around his future boss's much more petite shoulder. He was leaning toward the camera to bring their heads level. Possibly they'd already decided to work together. Their smiles were broad and happy, their body language totally connected. Chris in particular looked younger.

Almost carefree, Tony thought.

He realized his fingertip was stroking Chris's expression through the screen.

Shaking that off, he clicked the second link. That sent him to a website listing Mayor's Medal honorees. Chris had been awarded his for saving a bunch of kids from a school bus that careened off a bridge and into a lake. He'd done this without the aid of his crew. He'd simply been driving by and saw the accident. With no regard for his own safety, he'd dived into twenty meters of black water. While underwater, he'd shifted into his tiger form, using his teeth and back legs to peel the bus's side off like a tin can. Most of the kids were shifters and mixbloods. They'd swum out on their own as soon as they weren't trapped. Chris had saved the three remaining riders with CPR, including the werebear driver.

Tony assumed he'd done that in his human shape.

"Wow," he marveled. Tigers were tough, but this story was amazing. No wonder Chris was committed to his job. Tony could hardly imagine the rescuer's high you got from a day like that.

He sat thinking about the story: how Chris could be so brave in one situation and so cautious in another. People weren't simple, that was for sure. Also, what did it mean that a virtual superhero was attracted to a low-ranking wolf like him? Was it flattering? Crazy? Or maybe it was proof that Chris was out of Tony's league. At least it suggested Tony's instinct for who was worth sleeping with was good.

Tony grinned to himself. Maybe that was *his* superpower.

The second link digested, Tony glanced at the final result Oogle had delivered. If he hadn't known the search engine was magically enhanced for relevance, he wouldn't have bothered to click on it. The date was nearly thirty years ago.

Maureen Savoyard Death Ruled a Suicide, it said.

~

The body of Maureen Savoyard, weretiger, 42, was found early Sunday morning in her home by her eighteen-year-old son Christophe. The M.E.'s office ruled the likely cause of death as a self-administered overdose of Benzodiazepines infused with faerie dust, colloquially known as Benzi-Wings.

Ms. Savoyard was believed to suffer from depression following the murder of two other children by her then live-in boyfriend, weretiger Mark Naegel.

Naegel's trial, at which Ms. Savoyard's surviving son testified, resulted in a guilty verdict. Due to evidence of diminished capacity, the death penalty was not invoked. Naegel is currently serving a life sentence at Rykers in Poughkip, a demon-run maximum-security penitentiary.

Determination as to whether Naegel's clan owes Mr. Savoyard restitution for his brothers' murders has yet to be decided.

~

"Shit," Tony muttered beneath his breath.

The article he'd read came from the *Courier*. It included a single photo—that of Maureen Savoyard. Her eyes were sadder and her features more delicate, but she strongly resembled the man he knew as Chris Savoy.

Chris must have shortened his name, presumably so the old tragedy wouldn't follow him everywhere. Tony wasn't certain why it came up in his search. The Elfnet worked on bits and bytes much like the Outsiders' world wide web. Occasionally the magic that powered it threw in its own two cents, as if the software *knew* who ought to get which info.

Tony suspected the software had glitched today. It didn't take a genius to realize Chris wouldn't want him discovering this. They weren't dating. Tony had no excuse for checking up on his background. Lack of excuse aside, he wasn't a stranger to this sort of event. Being a cop exposed him to the darker side of extra-human nature. What humans did to each other, supes sometimes did in spades. It saddened him to see it, though it also made him realize how important his job was.

Even if justice came too late to save a life, it told survivors their loss was important.

His cordless phone rang, causing him to jump guiltily. He hopped off the couch to dig it out from under a discarded pillow and an old magazine. This left him standing by his front window. On the sidewalk below, the corner grocer passed. He appeared to be having a one-sided conversation with his friendly but not-magical golden retriever.

"Hello," Tony answered, smiling in spite of the other things in his head.

"Tony!" Evina's voice exclaimed. "Thank goodness I caught you in."

"What's up?" Tony asked, a call from Nate's new wife not a common occurrence. Was it weird that he'd just been looking at her photo?

"I'm so sorry to ask you this. I know it's your day off, but could you look after the twins today? My mom's out of town, and I've been called in as backup on a three-alarm."

"Not a problem," Tony assured her. "You're at Nate's now?"

"Yes," she said, though *Nate's* was now the whole family's house. "You have the key? I've given the cubs strict orders to mind you."

Tony grinned. He knew kids . . . and how long those orders were liable to last. "Don't sweat it. I'll keep them out of trouble."

She gave him a few more breathless instructions: what Abby and Rafi liked to eat; which of the six-year-olds' toys he should probably grab and bring with them.

"Uh," Tony said, a smidgen of alarm rising. "You don't want me to babysit them there?"

"The painters are coming to do the kids' new bedrooms. I'm afraid they'll be underfoot."

The twins were cats, so *underfoot* could be literal. Tony looked around his epically cluttered apartment. He found it comfortable, and the cubs might not disagree. Their mother, however, would have a different perspective.

"Okay then. I'll, uh, probably watch them at Rick's place."

Evina was so relieved to have her kids taken care of she didn't question this. "Bless you," she said. "You're a lifesaver."

Tony hung up . . . and immediately wished he'd found a way to ask if Chris had been called out on the fire with her.

~

Being the baby of his generation meant Tony was half kid himself. He and the tiger twins plunged right into having fun. They made pancakes and bacon and built a fort by overturning a sofa and draping it in sheets. A slightly too-competitive game of Portals and Ladders seemed like it might end in tears, but Tony was able to distract his charges with a giant pad of paper and the kids' own mess-proof magic markers.

No matter how hard you pressed, they wouldn't write on walls.

Quiet for the time being, the cubs lay on the floor beneath Rick's sunny front window, drawing from either side of the large manila sheet. Rafi's tongue stuck out in concentration, and Abby colored so energetically her dark mop of curls jiggled.

Enjoying the opportunity to catch his breath, Tony watched them fondly from an armchair. Maybe his mom was right about more grandkids. These two had certainly turned his day around. He wondered if the rules of Resurrection allowed gay men to adopt. Did Chris like kids? Chances were he had issues on account of losing his littermates. If that hadn't put him off parenting, a cat like him would make a great father.

Tony sucked in a breath at the errant thought. Talk about romantically deluded.

He sprung up like a Jake In the Box when he heard his brother's tread coming up the brownstone's stairs. Rick was supposed to be at work. Tony guessed this wasn't his day for relaxing.

His brother was talking to someone—a female someone, he realized. Rick seemed to be trying to convince her she shouldn't be shy to meet Tony.

Hm, Tony thought. Maybe one of the Lupone brothers' romantic stars were aligning.

"I hear you out there," he warned Rick.

Too curious to wait for them to knock, Tony opened the door himself. To his surprise, he recognized the woman Rick was with.

"Whoa," he said. "Snow White."

It wasn't really Snow White, of course. It was Cass Maycee, a half fae, half human girl they'd gone to high school with. Her family had founded Maycee's, Resurrection's version of the similarly named Outsider store. Thanks to a happy combination of genetics, Cass was like the fairytale come to life: snow-white skin, ruby lips, hair as black as a raven's wing. Her rich girl pantsuit didn't fit the image, but other than that she was exactly as he recalled.

Also front and center in his memory was that Rick used to have a huge crush on her.

Tony guessed he wasn't over it. Rick glared at Tony like he'd committed a cardinal sin. "You want to step aside and let us in?"

"Uh, no?" Tony cut a look at Cass. Her cheeks were pink, but she didn't seem upset—not at him, anyway. "We, um, made a bit of mess."

"*We?*" Rick said, which meant Tony had to explain.

Rick wasn't happy about Tony using his apartment to babysit, or turning it into a disaster zone. Tony was lucky they weren't alone. The cubs were part of their pack now. Even if Abby and Rafi hadn't been likable, which they were, Rick shared Tony's instinctive drive to ensure they were safe.

"It *is* Snow White," Rafi breathed, looking up from his drawing.

Blushing, Cass explained she wasn't. She was just half faerie.

More down to earth than her brother, Abby had her own question. "Are you Uncle Rick's girlfriend?"

Tony noticed Cass couldn't help glancing at Rick. Despite his naturally tan skin tone, he'd gone redder than she had.

"She's my friend-friend," he answered in an admirably level voice.

He kept his temper even when Rafi suggested he ought to ask Snow White to be his girlfriend. "Clarence's dad says part faeries are hot stuff."

"O*kay*," Tony said, grabbing both cubs before they could further embarrass the supposed non-couple. "Why don't you two go color in Rick's kitchen?"

The kids grumped about it but went, freeing Tony to follow Rick into his bedroom for an obviously overdue word alone.

Rick walked straight to his dresser, rummaging in it for a clean shirt. As he peeled off the one he wore, Tony realized he'd recently had sex—with Cass, apparently, because her scent was mixed with his.

Slightly shocked and possibly envious, he dropped onto the side of Rick's bed. How had this happened? He'd thought Rick was busy working the faerie case.

Unless Cass had something to do with that.

"Holy smokes," he whispered, figuring Rick wouldn't want the cubs hearing. "Is Cass Maycee The One?"

"The one what?" Rick said, purposefully being dense.

"The person the dying faerie said you had to protect."

"Oh. Yes, it's looking that way."

"Wow," Tony said. "You and Snow White. Your high school fantasy."

"Her name is Cass," Rick said a tad prissily. "She's an actual person, not a storybook character."

Oh his brother still dug her. Tony gave up fighting his grin. This was too good not to tease him over. "You might want to shower, Prince Charming. I can tell you and 'Cass' got sweaty."

Rick cursed at him, which Tony found amusing. "Call Nate," Rick snapped. "I need to know everything he found out about dragon keepers."

Tony knew how to jump to conclusions. Rick must think Cass was a dragon keeper—or why would the dead faerie want him to protect her? Assuming she was one, didn't she need a dragon to take care of?

Wow, he thought, digging out his cell to call Nate. Maybe reports of the beasts' extinction were premature.

~

Once Nate hugged his excited kids and was introduced to Cass, he confirmed Tony's suspicion. The snazzy wolf sat in a fat armchair, leaning forward across his knees. Tony's pulse sped up.

Finally he was being clued in on what had been going on.

"So," Nate said, pausing to smooth his shiny ponytail. "I went to see Professor Pliny, the expert on faerie culture at City U. According to him, true dragons—the ones that are supposed to be extinct—could make and unmake worlds. They feature in fae origin tales, including the one explaining how our Pocket was formed. The story claims our reality was created from the death energy of T'Fain, the last true dragon to walk Faerie. Once she was gone, there weren't any more."

"Except there must be," Rick said. "Or why did the faerie who ran away from Tony attack Cass's father at home last night? The female who died in the subway was a protector. Cass's father is a pureblood whose origins we can't trace. All we really know is that he's been living in the Pocket, under the radar of his fellow fae. I think Sword Guy was trying to get intelligence about dragons from both of them."

Sword Guy had attacked Cass's father? Tony looked at her. Snow White was chewing her thumbnail unhappily.

"Is he okay?" Tony asked.

"We think so," Rick said. He was on the now righted sofa with Cass perched next to him on its arm. "His apartment was a shambles, from a battle involving magic is what we guess. A witness saw him running away alive."

Cass squirmed uncomfortably. "Dad never talked to me about dragons. I don't know any more about them than you."

Her tone struck Tony as peculiar. It reminded him of Rick claiming not to know who the dying faerie wanted him to protect. Cass might think she was being truthful, but Tony wasn't convinced. Nate shot her a look that said he also doubted her claim.

"Here's the thing," Nate went on without challenging her. "Professor Pliny said there were rumors that T'Fain wasn't actually the last dragon. He said three eggs might have survived from an earlier clutch, eggs the Dragon Guild hid away for their own reasons. Someone, maybe even Cass's father, could have smuggled them to Resurrection for safekeeping. Faeries don't age like other folks. What if Cass's dad was T'Fain's keeper? In the legend, he let her die at the king's command. Maybe he feels guilty. Maybe helping to hide those eggs is his way of making up for it."

"My father's not that sort of person," Cass burst out. "He's a simple toymaker."

Rick put his hand on her leg to calm her.

Tony thought that was cute, but decided to keep his amusement to himself. He leaned back on the couch on the other side of Rick. It seemed to help his brain when he wagged the foot he'd pulled onto his knee. "What are we thinking here? That some block of faeries wants to hatch new dragons and make their own Pocket? One they can lord it over without interference from rivals?"

Faeries loved lording it over folks—the faerie who'd poofed away from him being a prime example. Tony had no trouble imagining him wanting to rule a world.

"Professor Pliny suggested another possibility," Nate said. "That some people in Faerie want to *un*make us. Evidently, certain factions think Faerie should be Faerie, and Outside should stay Outside. They're very much opposed to our blended reality."

Okay, that was a grim idea. Tony's life wasn't perfect, but he certainly didn't want it to cease to be. The others didn't look any happier than him.

"Maybe we should try to dig up more facts," Rick said sensibly. "All we've got now is speculation."

"We could put out an APB on Cass's father," Tony suggested.

"Let's hold off on that. We wouldn't want to inadvertently lead his enemies to him. If he's got the eggs, or knows where they are, we can't afford to let them fall into the wrong hands."

"We shouldn't discuss this outside the squad," Tony said, sounding unnaturally serious even to himself. "If this is a faerie plot, they could have glamoured anyone to help them."

"Agreed," Nate said.

"Agreed," Rick seconded.

Their concurrence didn't gratify Tony the way it otherwise might have. He'd live without pack respect if it meant his world weren't in danger of ending.

CHAPTER SIX

CHRIS had braced himself for the challenges he'd face after his alpha married. Not on his list of scenarios was watching her husband walk around in front of him, fresh out of the shower, in nothing but a designer towel. Men that lean weren't Chris's ideal, but the anatomy manual look suited Nate. The brown and black towel he'd wrapped around his waist showed off his olive skin tone and also his tight rear end.

Evina seemed to be admiring both from her stool at the kitchen island across from Chris. This prevented her from noticing her beta's stoic expression. Should a supposedly straight man look or not? Neither tigers nor wolves were shy about their bodies, but Chris always had trouble deciding.

"Where's my blue shirt?" Nate asked, returning from a brief disappearance into his new bedroom.

The open-plan loft had changed since Chris had last been in it—a visit he definitely wasn't mentioning. Walls had been added, and a second bathroom, and a modern bookshelf-type storage unit for housing toys. One look at the items strewn around the living room indicated this wasn't being used as conscientiously as Nate must have hoped.

The kitchen, where Evina and Chris were going over their station budget, remained pretty much the same. Well, maybe its counter hadn't hosted a zoo's worth of little rubber animals before.

"Your blue shirt is at the dry cleaners," Evina said.

"Damn it."

Evina's eyebrows rose.

"Sorry," Nate said. "I'm not damn it-ing you. I'll pick up both our stuff tomorrow, if you want. I had another blue shirt at work, but Tony borrowed it. I don't know why he does that. My shirts are too snug for him."

Chris was grateful Nate had pulled trousers on. Hearing Tony's name was sufficient to send a helpless hot thrill through him.

"Tony likes you," Evina responded. "Remember when you couldn't find your dress shoes, and it turned out Rafi hid them in his tiger roost?"

"Tony's not a six-year-old."

"No," Evina said, the gentleness that was a big part of her in her voice. "Tony's a full grown man."

"Tony doesn't like me *that* way," Nate protested.

Evina smiled. "He likes you that way a little."

Nate's face twisted as if he wanted to argue. "He practice-flirts on me is all. He doesn't really have a crush."

Evina didn't answer, just continued to smile lovingly at him. Chris fought an urge to clear his throat. This conversation was making him uncomfortable. He knew he had no right to be bothered by the idea of Tony having a crush on another man.

"I'll wear the gray Armani," Nate decided, turning away again. "Witnesses respond to that nearly as well as the blue."

"Is he serious?" Chris asked once he'd shut the bedroom door.

Evina laughed softly. "He is, though he isn't usually this wound up." A sober expression replaced her amusement. "This is hush-hush, so please don't repeat what I'm going to say. One of his pack members has disappeared."

Chris's blood went cold. "Not Tony," he blurted before he could stop himself.

Evina blinked at him. "No. His brother Rick. He was guarding someone for a case—a witness, I guess—and they were attacked by goblins at her home. They escaped, but no one has heard from them since Sunday. Their alpha thinks they've gone off the grid on purpose."

"Goblins," Chris repeated. Goblins were one of Resurrection's more controversial ethnic groups. They were smart and worked cheaply, but the few who weren't law abiding could be vicious.

"That's what I hear," Evina said. "The pack's been in a tizzy. You know how tight-knit wolves are. One of them going missing is upsetting."

Chris gripped the island's black marble edge. Tony must be worried. Rick was his brother.

"I'm sure he'll be all right," Evina said. "Those wolves are resourceful."

Chris knew she meant Rick would be all right. He doubted anyone would remember Rick's jokey younger brother might need support. He realized too late that he was rubbing his right eyebrow, a nervous habit he tried not to indulge in.

"You're probably right," he said, forcing his hand to drop. "And speaking of resources, we'd better get this budget ready to submit . . ."

~

Tony stepped out of the interrogation room and closed the soundproofed door carefully. He wanted to slam it, but he'd probably break the thing.

The squad had pulled in a bunch of goblins for questioning. All were criminals with known or suspected faerie ties. The attack on Cass and Rick had left one goblin dead and quite a lot of goblin blood splatter. Happily, this suggested Rick and Cass weren't injured. Sadly, goblin DNA was complex. The lab took extra long to work up profiles. Complicating matters further, goblins didn't have fingerprints. As a result, they had no I.D. for the attackers, not even the one who'd died.

The goblin lawyer for the thief Tony tried to grill had accused him of police prejudice.

Possibly he was right. Tony found the lawyer as suspicious as his client. Frustrated, he thumped the back of his head against the cinderblock in the hall. Rick had been missing four days now. As far as Tony could tell, they weren't any closer to locating him. Sword Guy hadn't popped back onto the radar either, a fact Tony did not find comforting.

His gut told him the fae was still in Resurrection—and up to no damn good.

The door next to his opened. Adam looked at him as he exited and shut it. "Any luck?"

Tony shook his head. The alpha grimaced and rubbed the frown lines beside his mouth. "These goblins do not like talking to police."

"It doesn't help that we can't mention the you-know-whats."

They'd decided it was best not to let the rest of the city know a trio of dragon eggs might be floating around somewhere. If they existed and could be hatched after all this time, they'd attract too much potentially dangerous attention. Tony had no idea how you got a dragon to make or unmake a world, but any number of faeries might. In a town like Resurrection, an unexploded nuke would cause less trouble.

"How are you doing?" Adam asked in a more personal tone.

"Frustrated." Tony leaned harder against the wall. "Interrogations go better when Rick and I do them together."

"Sure," Adam said. He hesitated, his green eyes too compassionate for comfort. "You sense anything? About Rick, I mean. You two have a strong brother bond."

Tony guessed they did, but he was no psychic. He shrugged and looked down at his running shoes. His eyes were pricking with emotion. "I'm having a hell of a time not calling my folks back from vacation, but I think that's just me wishing they were here. If things get hairy, they'll be safer where they are."

"Why don't you have dinner with me and Ari? We'll grab a pizza. Kelsey's decided she likes gnawing on pepperoni. Ari thinks it isn't good for a five month old, but she *is* a five-month-old shifter."

"That's a nice offer," Tony said, "but I think I'm going to crash when I get home tonight."

"You sure? We'd love to have you. You might . . . settle easier with company."

Tony supposed he seemed like he needed settling. He just didn't think an evening playing fourth wheel to his alpha's cozy family would make him feel better. "I think I need sleep more than I need company."

"You do look tired," Adam acknowledged. "We're spinning our wheels here. Why don't you knock off now and start fresh in the morning?"

Tony's lieutenant didn't wait for him to respond. Instead, Adam slapped his shoulder like it was decided and strode past him down the hall toward the squad room.

Well, hell, Tony thought, watching him disappear around the corner. More free time to climb the walls wasn't what he'd been hoping for.

~

When Tony arrived at the brownstone a half hour later, he was shocked to discover Chris sitting on the front steps. The sun had set, and the light was on in the vestibule. Like most shifters Chris wasn't sensitive to cold. Though it was November, he wore cotton trousers and a light sport jacket. The simple button-down shirt that covered his big chest made it seem like he'd almost dressed up. He looked amazing—his 6'8" height, his gold-streaked hair, his running back's solid legs. Tony hardly knew what to stare at first; every part of Chris seemed designed to appeal to every part of him. In the end, he targeted Chris's eyes.

They squinted at Tony like he wasn't sure of his welcome.

"Hey," he said, rising a little awkwardly as Tony came around the front of Rick's car. Before he went off the grid, Rick had ditched the Buick at Cass's place. Tony had reclaimed it for him.

With a sense of unreality, he beeped the doors locked with Rick's key ring remote. He stopped an arm's length away from Chris. He wasn't going to react, not until he knew what the tiger was doing here.

"You know this is a nosy neighborhood, right?" he said. "Everyone around here knows who belongs where."

Chris smiled faintly. "I did notice a few inquiring looks." He shrugged one shoulder more than the other. "I wanted to make sure you were okay. Evina mentioned your brother, um, hasn't been reachable lately."

"She did."

"I don't think Nate told her much. And I haven't told anyone."

Tony didn't want his heart to race, but it was. He tried to remember the man who'd walked out on him in that gardener's shed, not the one who'd lost his mother and his brothers to a long-ago horror story. Sympathy for Chris wouldn't protect him. Neither would inhaling his spicy-sweet aftershave. "You didn't have to check on me."

"I wasn't sure . . ." Chris shoved his hands in his pants pockets. "Your pack is busy. I wanted to make sure someone was paying attention to how you are."

"And you honestly thought that someone should be you?"

"Tony."

"Fuck," Tony said, knowing he'd responded too harshly. He pressed the heels of his hands into tired eye sockets, abruptly as exhausted as if a twelve-story building had flattened him. His arms dropped like they had no muscles left.

"Couldn't we go inside?" Chris asked in a low voice. "You don't have to talk to me. I can just sit with you for a bit. If nothing else, the company will soothe your wolf."

The funny thing was that he was right. His wolf felt like it had been pacing back and forth inside him since Rick disappeared—despite his alpha's attempt to be supportive. His wolf wasn't pacing now. It was focused on Chris's presence—not happy but calmer.

As they spoke, Chris and Tony's gazes had locked onto each other. Chris's eyes weren't glowing, but little lemon lights flickered in their brown-orange depths. He was feeling strong emotions, whatever they might be. The pulse that beat in his neck matched the one in Tony's. Tony wanted to lick it so badly his mouth watered.

"If I let you in," he said. "It won't be just to sit."

Chris's breath caught softly. "That would be okay with me."

Would it be okay with Tony? He'd been trying to put Chris behind him. Did he really want another taste of the tiger's advance and retreat school of seduction? He knew what his body wanted. He was hard enough to go then and there. He had an urge to grab Chris's hand, but they were outside, in plain view of the neighborhood.

He squeezed the key ring he was holding. "All right. Follow me if you're going to."

Chris followed far enough behind him that their entry wouldn't look intimate. Tony's niggle of resentment over that didn't quash his arousal. His palm was sweating as he twisted his doorknob.

"Holy crap," Chris exclaimed as they entered the apartment. "Are you opening a junk shop? How do you walk in here?"

Tony's current work in progress was a set of harp-backed chairs that might one day grace his dining room. If it turned out they didn't suit, he'd sell them on eBuy. He wasn't the only person in Resurrection who liked fixed-up old things. Of course, since there were six chairs, and none were finished, they did fill up the living room.

Maybe a sensible person would have started off by repairing two?

Flushing, Tony shut the door sharply. "Fixing stuff is my hobby. Anyway, what are you worried about? You're a cat. You're supposed to be surefooted."

Chris turned back, his lips rolled together to control a smile. He gave up a moment later and broke into a laugh. "How the hell do you and that neat freak Nate get along?"

"We get along fine," Tony huffed, fists planted on his hips.

Chris's grin softened. The cat was inside Tony's house, his territory, and they both knew they weren't here to fight. Chris stepped to Tony, taking his shoulders in a partly reassuring, partly erotic hold. Tony's anger fell away, his hands moving a bit too naturally to Chris's waist. The man was literally hot, waves of warmth beating out from him. Tony's fingers dug into hard muscle. His dick was so stiff it hurt.

"I want you," he said, the only confession that seemed both honest and unlikely to get him in trouble.

Chris's eyes darkened. "I'm here to be of service."

His manner was humorous, and Tony felt a need to be clear. "I want to fuck you. You know: me in charge and you taking it."

Chris's mouth twitched at the corners. "Do you hear me objecting?"

Tony didn't. The desire inside him seemed to explode. He grabbed both sides of Chris's face, pulling his head close for a deep kiss. Chris's big arms surrounded him, the fingers of one hand forking into Tony's hair. Tony's wolf fangs slid down and a second later Chris's followed suit. The point of Chris's canine nicked Tony's lip. Blood welled up in the moment before it healed.

Chris drew back just far enough to apologize.

Tony growled, seized his head, and sucked his tongue again.

He guessed Chris found that exciting. He body-slammed Tony against the wall, hands sliding to his butt, erection grinding up and down over his. The cat was all the way hard—long, thick, and apparently indestructible. The pressure he used felt so good Tony nearly forgot his intentions. *Nearly* wasn't the same as really. Grunting at the strength it took to shift Chris's greater weight, he shoved the cat around until *he* was backed up to the wall instead.

"Jesus," Chris breathed. His eyes slid shut as Tony worked his crotch over his. Chris looked like he was in heaven, but not convinced he ought to be. Determined to decide him, Tony pulled Chris's hands from his butt.

Another grunt of effort slapped them up beside Chris's head.

Chris gasped and looked at him. Tony was treating him like he was dominant.

"You sure?" Chris's expression glazed as Tony continued to hump his thigh and crotch. "You don't want me to take care of you?"

Tony did—and that's why he couldn't. "I want to fuck you," he repeated.

He wasn't a hundred percent sure how to go about it, which angered him. He let go of Chris's wrists, but only to wrench off his light jacket. Chris started to undo his own shirt buttons. Not wanting that, Tony took over.

The feel of Chris breathing faster as his skin was uncovered was really arousing. Tony knelt to remove Chris's shoes and pants. When he rose, Chris's touch felt too good not to let him undress him. They kissed again wearing only their underwear. Tony decided soft cotton stretched by hard cock was a great combination, especially with two dicks to rub together. Their hands went everywhere they could—backs, arms, heaving chests, and rib cages. Tony loved the hairy muscles of Chris's legs jostling his.

With a groan of pleasure, he drove his fingers into the tiger's briefs and around his clenched butt cheeks.

Squeezing them caused Chris to tear his mouth from his. "You want a little guidance, or would you rather figure this out by trial and error?"

Trial and error sounded uncomfortable for Chris.

"You won't get bossy?"

Chris smiled at him. He was caressing Tony's arm muscles, fingers sliding from elbow to shoulder. Tony decided he liked the cat's expression. Chris wasn't laughing at him; he was just amused in general.

"You have good arms," Chris said, avoiding answering Tony's question. "Nice and brawny. I think you might be strong enough to control me."

Tony snorted. "Only if you let me."

Chris's grin broadened. "Want to take the shower we missed out on the first time?"

They'd missed out because Chris had declined Tony's offer to join him. Tony's brows lowered at the memory.

"Showers are handy," Chris pointed out. "Lots of slippery stuff. Plenty of hot water for cleaning up."

"Wait here," Tony said in his sternest voice. "I need five minutes to get ready."

The bathroom was what needed getting ready, not himself. He stalked to it, and—as soon as the door was shut—commenced to scrub it at shifter speed. When he'd moved into the brownstone with Rick and Adam, rather than gut this room, he'd painstakingly salvaged the bits he could. The toilet groaned when you flushed it, and the antique white-and-black patterned hextile wasn't a breeze to clean. Oddly enough, he had plenty of energy for it now. Chris guessed what he was doing. Tony heard him chuckling outside the door.

"I told you to stay put," he objected.

"I'm flattered you're fussing on my behalf," Chris said. "Also, I'm jerking myself off out here."

Okay, Tony didn't need an incentive to go faster, but that certainly worked as one. The tiger was a sex fiend, apparently. How he'd sneaked around successfully for so long Tony couldn't imagine. Or maybe he was a sex fiend because he didn't allow himself to sneak around very often. That idea sent a painful throb of excitement through Tony's cock. He could identify with never getting as much sex as you wanted.

"Done," he said, practically flinging the door open.

Chris hadn't been lying. He had his hand down his briefs, and he was tugging his erection. Not rubbing it, just gripping the shaft around the middle and pulling in and out from his groin. Seeing Chris do this was like having a window shade snap up to reveal something extremely personal.

"Jeez," he said, his attention glued to Chris's working hand. "Watching you do that is really hot."

"I can't not touch myself," Chris confessed. "But I don't want to go over."

His voice was husky. Tony shivered in reaction. Their gazes rose at the same time. Staring into each other's eyes was becoming a compulsion. Orange fire flared in Chris's irises. This made Tony's libido squirm.

"Come in," he said, moving back from the doorway.

Now that it was clean, the bathroom was kind of romantic. The tub was the centerpiece. Positioned in the floor's middle, it was one of Tony's left-by-the-curb rescues: a re-glazed cast iron clawfoot with a white shower curtain draped around it. Probably Tony's pack should have realized he was gay long before he told them. Instead, they'd assumed he was a packrat.

Chris stopped tugging his erection and came inside. "Nice," he said, taking in the space. He gripped the edge of the tub and gave it a testing pull. That the heavy basin didn't budge pleased him. "Sturdy."

Tony was too nervous and excited to come up with smart response. "I have lube in the medicine cabinet."

Chris's eyes were calm, only hinting at amusement. "You should probably get it out."

"I don't have to do this. You could—"

"No," Chris interrupted. "You want this, and I want you to have it. I want you to fuck me. I'm not all one thing or another. You get to me. Everything you do gets to me."

The way he said this was so raw Tony shuddered. He knew exactly what Chris meant. He wanted him any time, any way, more than any person he'd ever met. He bit his lip and opened the cabinet.

When he turned back with the lubricant, Chris had shucked his briefs, stepped into the tub, and was cranking the water cocks open.

He smiled at Tony over his big deltoid. "Do my back?"

It was the most gorgeous naked back Tony had ever seen—his dream back, probably. Spray bounced off Chris's mile wide shoulders to run teasingly down his tapered lats.

"Yes," Tony said, suddenly feeling very lucky. "I want to do your everything."

He swung in behind him and grabbed the soap. The tub was a good size, but the two of them filled it up. With the curtain pulled closed around it and the shower pelting them with sound, it was an intimate enclosure. Chris rolled his neck with pleasure as Tony ran lathered hands up and down his satiny back muscles.

Chris didn't resist when Tony urged his arms upward.

"Grab the piping," he said.

Obedient for the time being, Chris's fingers wrapped the structure the curtain rings hung on.

"Will it hold?" he asked doubtfully.

"Enough to swing your weight on. I tested it."

"Enough to swing *your* weight on, you mean," Chris laughed.

Tony shuffled closer to nuzzle his wet shoulder. "You can tug it hard, big man. I don't build things that break."

Chris stopped laughing and shivered. Liking that, Tony mouthed and growled into his warm neck muscle. Necks *meant* things to their animal halves —vulnerability, for one thing. Admiring how strong Chris's was, Tony circled his chest with his arms, soaping his broad pectorals and ribs. The tiger's nipples had drawn into hard points. When he moved restlessly in response to Tony pulling them, the cleft of his soapy ass brushed Tony's erection.

"Mm," Chris sighed. "You feel good against me."

Tony gave in and grabbed the object of his desires, pulling his slippery hands slowly up Chris's erection. The thick shape of it felt wonderful: the rim, the veins, the curve of the head and the strut beneath. His balls practically invited a gentle going over. Seeming to agree that this was a good idea, Chris widened his stance and made a purring sound. Tony ran three slick finger pads behind the swaying sac, over Chris's perineum.

Chris grunted, his head falling back onto Tony's shoulder.

"More," he urged, his wet hair clinging to Tony. "I love you rubbing me there."

Because it was easier to reach from the other side, Tony shifted his right hand back to massage the firm stretch of flesh between his balls and hole. There were nerves underneath that skin that connected to his penis. Chris arched unselfconsciously to give him more access. Tony took the invitation to press harder. Chris's spine writhed with luxuriant enjoyment.

He made Tony feel like he was good at this.

"Do you want my fingers in you first?"

Tony didn't expect his voice to break. When it did, Chris glanced back at him and smiled. The curve of his lips was both sensual and devilish. "I'd like it," he assured him. "And you can get a feel for the territory."

The *territory* certainly intrigued him. Fortunately, Chris was relaxed. Tony slid two fingers slowly in with no trouble. The tiger's passage was smooth and tight. Tony remembered how Chris had scissored his fingers apart to stretch him.

"Shit," Chris gasped, his back arching.

"Is that good?" Tony asked, thinking he recognized the reaction. His cock thought Chris was enjoying it. It was throbbing, nearly touching his belly.

Chris groaned and pushed closer. "Just don't . . . give me too much of that. I want to come with you in me."

Smiling, Tony stroked his fingers out and in again. "I thought you weren't going to be bossy."

"Just—" Chris squirmed and groaned some more "—expressing a preference."

Tony withdrew his fingers. Chris made a sound that, if you stretched it, could have been a whimper.

"You lube me up," Tony said.

Chris turned at his peremptory tone. His eyes were burning, their lids hooded. Looking authoritative was a challenge when you weren't the tallest, but Tony tried his best.

Giving in, Chris held out his hand for the tube of lubricant.

He oiled Tony more than he had to, pulling his fists up him hand over hand, slowly, tightly, until his cock felt stretched. From base to tip, his shaft hummed with readiness.

Chris let go to put one hand on Tony's shoulder. As if he were Tony's coach, he gave the muscle a little squeeze. "You don't need to be hesitant. Take me hard if that's what you're in the mood for. You know how strong shifters are. Trust me, I'll enjoy it."

Tony searched his face. He meant what he said. Tony could pound at him if he wanted. Tony could put everything into this. He didn't speak. He turned Chris around with his hands, guiding his arms up to grab the curtain pipe again. He wedged one bare foot between Chris's two, nudging his ankles wider for his soon-to-be entry. More than arousal or nerves had his pulse jumping in his throat. This was a different kind of first than the obvious.

Chris said *trust me*, but what he meant was: *I'm trusting myself to you.*

After the last four days, this was what Tony needed—more than being coddled or comforted. Chris had handed power to him at a time when he felt powerless.

He rubbed his face across Chris's shoulders, knowing the shower washed away the emotion that stung his eyes. One hand slid to Chris's hip. The joint was strong like the rest of him. He tipped his lubed cock to Chris's anus. Chris took a firmer grip on curtain pipe.

Tony's heart went crazy.

Chris pushed back as Tony pushed forward. Tony caught his breath at the sensation of going in—sort of what he expected and sort of not. The feeling was amazing. For a second he thought he'd come before he was all the way. Fortunately, the feeling eased. Chris gave a final wriggle, and Tony was surrounded.

"Good?" Chris asked in a harsh whisper.

"Really good." Tony drew back and thrust again cautiously. He moaned at the lush pleasure.

"Put . . . a little more pressure toward the front," Chris advised.

This was where his prostate was located. Tony smiled to himself. Chris couldn't help bossing him a bit. He pushed as the cat requested.

Apparently, he did it right.

"Unh," Chris said, his neck arching.

That was a thrill. Tony gave his cock to him harder, earning a louder groan.

"Fuck," Chris breathed.

A long noticeable tremor rolled up his back. Tony's excitement swelled at his success. Setting his feet more firmly in the tub, he gripped Chris's narrow hips, and went at him with real strength. Chris must have been longing for him to do this. A dozen deep thrusts later, his spine stiffened.

His seed spurted noisily against the shower curtain.

"Don't stop," he urged Tony, continuing to shove at him. "God, I need another."

Tony moved his hand to Chris's cock. His erection had flagged a little, but when he gripped it, it hardened up. Tony held it like Chris had earlier, tight around its middle, rubbing the skin over the firm center. Chris released the curtain pipe so he could wrap his palm around his own crown.

Oh that revved Tony's motor: to be pleasuring Chris's dick *with* him. He grunted and went faster, his stomach slapping Chris's hindquarters.

"Yes," Chris said, his hand screwing the crest wildly. "*Yes.*"

Tony's beast seemed to take over. He hammered Chris, not holding back anything. He went so hard he nearly hurt himself. Incredible sensations blazed through his penis, down his thighs, and finally up his vertebrae. He hadn't known he could feel so much and not go over. His whole body was on fire.

Chris cried out, his ass squeezing Tony's cock.

Knowing Chris was coming, Tony gulped for air and shot out his pleasure.

One climax wasn't enough for him, any more than it had been for Chris. As soon as the contractions petered, he sped up and went again.

"God," Chris choked.

His cock twitched in Tony's grip. He'd had one last orgasm with Tony.

For half a minute all either could do was pant.

"Relax," Chris said, stroking Tony's knuckles. Tony's grip on his penis hadn't loosened at all.

"Shit," he exclaimed. "Sorry."

The tiger laughed breathlessly. "That's all right. I knew you weren't really going to wrench it off."

Tony cursed again, easing off him completely. Chris turned to face him. He was smiling in that I-know-a-joke way he had. "That was good, wolf. Nothing like an edge of danger to make for a great blastoff."

Tony blushed but managed not to repeat his apology. Chris had straightened. He'd bent forward to be taken, but now he reclaimed the inches of advantage he had over his partner. Seeming like he wanted to savor the aftermath, he stroked Tony's cheeks with his fingertips. His exotic eyes were wistful.

"I'd stay if I could," he said.

Tony believed him, but this didn't stop a cloudbank of heaviness from dropping over him. He forced himself to respond. "It was nice of you to stop by."

Chris let out a wry amused sound. "*Nice* is one way to put it. Look, I could make you something to eat if you're hungry. Or call for takeout."

"I'm not a kid."

"I'm aware of that." Chris cocked his head to one side at Tony's anger.

Too drained to argue, Tony exhaled a sigh. "I'm going to finish showering. Maybe you could let yourself out of the apartment."

Hurt tightened Chris's features, satisfying the child Tony had denied being. He clenched his jaw and didn't apologize for that either.

"Okay," Chris said. He touched Tony's arm, his fingers gentle on his bicep. "Call me if you need anything. I . . . Tony, I know this situation isn't perfect, but I want to be here for you."

Tony nodded. He couldn't slap at Chris for the offer; it was too decent. He drew the shower curtain aside for him. Chris stepped out, looking back at Tony from outside the tub. Though the tiger's expression didn't plead, it was very serious.

Tony thought Chris might say something. He turned instead, grabbed a towel on his way out, and left the bathroom to Tony.

~

Chris scrubbed the towel over his wet hair as he strode back to the entryway. The terrycloth didn't push any happier feelings into his brain. Chris knew Tony wasn't a kid. Okay, maybe he seemed like one compared to Chris. In this instance, however, Tony was being more mature.

The wolf was smart to keep an emotional distance. Getting attached to Chris would be a bad gamble. The problem was Chris had gotten attached to him. Though he tried to breathe more air into it, his chest was tight as he dried himself and dressed. His briefs were still in the bathroom. He'd have to go commando. Somehow, his shirt had ended up in the living room, hanging off the sofa arm. As he tugged it free, something else fell along with it.

It was another shirt, a dark blue Hugo Boss. The tiny stitches at the shoulder seams were stretched out enough to be visible.

This was the shirt Nate had been looking for, the shirt Tony had nabbed from Nate's work supply and worn. It must have been laundered before he borrowed it. Nate's scent barely clung to the fine cotton.

Chris balled the garment against his breastbone. This was how Tony had been comforting himself: not merely with the scent of pack but with the scent of a man he maybe wished were available. Was it a coincidence that Chris and Tony had their first sexual encounter in Nate's loft? Had the setting been an extra charge for the wolf? Maybe subconsciously?

He shook his head and set the shirt back where he'd found it. This wasn't his business.

He glanced back toward the bathroom. Though the sound of the shower had stopped, the door remained stubbornly closed. Chris wanted badly to open it. He wanted to kiss Tony, to lead him to his probable hurricane aftermath of a bedroom. He wanted to hold him safe in his arms while he slept soundly. Tony deserved real support from someone.

Tony deserved a man who'd be there in the morning.

Grimacing, Chris buttoned up his plain white shirt. He'd made his choices, and he'd long ago learned to live with them. Chris couldn't blame Tony if, right that moment, he ached with regret.

CHAPTER SEVEN

TONY was at his desk in the pack's squad room. His feet were stacked on top of a pile of files, and he'd leaned his weight steeply back in his swiveling chair. In response to a dull headache, he was squeezing his temples.

He'd been on hold for half an hour.

His own brainstorm was to blame for this. He'd had the brilliant idea of contacting the city's gargoyles. Not only was their species magically sensitive but, due to their roosting habits, they were in a position to observe unusual fae activity, including the sort Sword Guy was engaged in. Unlike normal psychics, gargoyles wouldn't gossip about what they'd seen—or about being asked. Gargoyles were protective of Resurrection, but they also were telepaths. Aside from Pidgin English, most avoided communicating verbally. The idea of letting the general public know they were highly intelligent didn't appeal to them.

Stupidly, Tony had called the Gargoyle Liaison Office, whose nighttime staff consisted of a single nervous human girl. She was attempting to contact her employers with mind power, because of course they didn't use cellphones. Every time Tony tried to tell her she could give up, she insisted she just needed one more minute.

"My bosses love helping the police," she declared.

Tony should have driven home instead. Their friend Grant the gargoyle lived on the brownstone roof. He flew out a lot after dark, but eventually he'd have landed. He spoke better English than Tony, at least when they were alone. Tony was totally spinning his wheels hanging on this line.

He wished he had a better use for his time. Rick and Cass had been gone ten days. The tracking chip in Rick's phone and the LoJack in their getaway car had been disabled. Tony told himself the pair had likely shut them off to avoid being followed by dragon-hunting fae. If his assumption was correct, their strategy worked equally well on friends. Cass's rich girl clique had no idea where she was, and they were worried too. As discreetly as he could, Adam had requested a high-res sat-search of the city and its environs. Nothing abnormal had turned up—or nothing abnormal for Resurrection. The squad was forced to return their focus to other cases. Working past regular hours was how they made up for it.

All of them were at the office now.

A sudden extra buzziness in the air caused Tony to jerk straight. "Sorry," he told the well-meaning gargoyle liaison. "Gotta go."

He hung up and dropped his beat-up running shoes to the floor. Without stopping to wonder why, he swiveled toward Adam's office, where the blinds were open but not raised. Nate and Carmine had just done the same as him.

Adam was on the phone, standing with his back to them. The abrupt flaring of his aura was what had alerted them.

"Jesus," Adam said. "Where the hell are you? Are you all right?"

He had to be talking to Tony's brother. Tony jumped up and bounded to Adam's door, his hearing automatically sharpening to listen for Rick's response. Adam didn't turn, just lifted his hand to prevent Tony from speaking.

"I'm fine," Rick's voice said tinnily. "But I don't have much time. Is this line secure?"

"Of course it is. What the hell is going on?"

"We have the dragons. We need you and the pack to protect them. Don't involve anyone you don't trust a hundred and ten percent. There's a second faerie involved in this. She's unaccounted for."

"And the first?" Adam sounded a helluva lot calmer than Tony could have done.

"Sword Guy is torturing Cass's father for information. We're hoping to rescue him."

Tony didn't like the sound of that. Faeries were dangerous. Getting between two of them in a fight wasn't an objective for sane people. Adam knew this as well as him.

"Rick," their lieutenant said. "Wait for us. Wherever you are, don't do anything crazy by yourself."

Tony was aware of Nate and Carmine scrambling to trace the incoming call. Tony couldn't move. His white-knuckled fingers were glued to Adam's doorframe.

"We can't wait," he heard Rick say. "Track my cellphone. If you lose the signal, we're in a spot only Nate and Evina know about."

"Only Nate and Evina . . . Rick—"Adam spat out a curse. Rick had hung up on him.

"Why does he want you to track his cell? Why can't he just tell us where he is?" Tony's voice was high, his energy ragged and uncontrolled. He swallowed and reined it in as Adam spun around.

The alpha's expression wasn't reassuring. "He's probably hoping to delay us. I suspect he doesn't want our help rescuing Cass's father. He must be afraid he'll get us killed."

"That's fucked," Tony said angrily. "Packs are stronger together."

Adam met his gaze without comment. That he agreed with his omega was obvious.

Carmine came up behind Tony. "Boss," he said. "We couldn't pinpoint the signal. Outside the city and to the south is the best the software is giving us."

The older wolf put his hand on Tony's shoulder, squeezing the muscle there. Tony realized he was shaking.

With anger, he told himself.

"Nate," Adam said, pitching his voice to carry. "What spot do only you and Evina know about?"

Nate was on his feet, leaning over Carmine's desk as he tried to narrow down Rick's location on the computer screen. He looked back at Adam. "I don't—"

His face changed as a possibility occurred to him.

"Shit," he said, so Tony guessed the memory wasn't pleasant. "He's in Wolf Woods. He's at the hidden lake where I almost ate Evina."

Okay, that was a story Tony hadn't heard. Adam either, to go by his raised eyebrows.

"Uh, hey," Carmine interjected. "Anyone but me notice Rick said they had *dragons?*"

They goggled at each other.

"Dragons," Tony repeated, the word sinking in. "Not eggs."

"And not 'dragon' singular," Carmine said.

"He said he needed us to protect them," Adam finished.

In spite of being furious at and frightened for his brother, Tony's heart thumped with excitement. His brother had hatched some dragons. He couldn't deny that was cool.

Their allotted period for amazement ended when Adam shook himself back to the task at hand.

"Call Johnny," he said to Carmine, meaning the husband of Tony's sister Maria. "We need a chopper and a pilot, and he just got his license. Tell him to keep it quiet. Better he steal a bird than officially request one."

"Done," Carmine said, pulling his phone from his back pocket.

Normally he'd have made a crack about the instructions. Going black ops wasn't Adam's style. Their alpha went by the book, generally. Not tonight, Tony guessed.

"Nate," the alpha said next.

"Boss," Nate responded, as straight and respectful as a soldier—sure sign of how dire the circumstances were.

"Do you trust Evina's tigers?"

"With my life," Nate said.

His lack of hesitation surprised Tony—pleased him too. Chris was one of the tigers Nate had no doubts about.

Adam rubbed the side of his face, less sure than his third was. "Could you ask Evina to call them together as a guard? Ari and the baby—" His green eyes flared at the thought of his wife and child. "Ari has power but not enough to defend against pureblood fae. I want the pack's family members to have protection. Maria, Ethan, everyone. There's another dragon hunter on the loose. I don't want any hostages to fortune."

"I'll take care of it," Nate said.

"And me?" Tony asked.

Adam leveled a very sober alpha gaze on him. "You won't like this, but I need you to do it anyway."

"Do what?" Tony asked, the back of his neck tensing.

"I want you with the cats. They're brave, but they're not cops. I want someone with your instincts watching over the women and children."

"But Rick's my brother! I should be on the team that goes after him!"

Adam's hand squeezed the side of Tony's neck. His top-dog authority radiated through the contact of palm to muscle, something Tony resented the hell out of right then. "It's not an insult. You're the pack's heart, Tony—and probably its sense of humor."

"You're calling me a joke!"

"No." Adam put his other hand on him too. "I'm placing what I love most under your protection. The last thing that could be is a joke."

Tony dropped his head, unable to continue challenging Adam's gaze. This was his wolf's reaction to Adam's dominance. The man in him knew they couldn't afford to waste time arguing. Rick was probably tearing off already to rescue Cass's father from Sword Guy's torture.

"Okay," he said. "You can count on me."

Adam startled him by leaning forward to kiss his brow, the way a father would a son.

"You're stronger than you know," he said. "That's what I'm counting on."

~

Chris was with Evina at the station when she got the news that Rick had contacted Tony's pack. She didn't object to Nate's request that her tigers defend his wolves.

"Of course we'll do it," she said. "Station 12 can cover our calls. I'll tell them our truck was cursed or something."

Nate and she didn't speak for long. Chris assumed the squad was leaving ASAP to go to Rick's aid. Despite a twinge of concern, he was glad for Tony. Doing something was better than waiting.

"Wow," Evina said, setting the phone back down. "Where am I going to put everyone? Our place is big but . . ." She trailed off, fingers pressed together before her mouth as she mulled over the conundrum.

Chris was perched on one side of her cluttered desk, watching her rock slightly in the chair. Nate hadn't French braided her hair for work like he usually did. As a result, her curls were as unruly as her kids'. Chris wanted to smile but didn't. How pleased he was by her readiness to help surprised him. Actually, he was pleased by the prospect of helping people Tony cared about. That seemed . . . right. He and Tony should always be on the same side.

He pushed the pleasure aside so he could think clearly. As he did, he realized he had a solution. It meant risking a long-held secret, but that hardly mattered when weighed against these stakes.

"If these fae are watching Rick's pack, they must know where they live," he said. "I have a place. It's big enough, and it's not common knowledge that I own it."

Evina looked at him with her eyebrows up. "You have a place besides your townhouse?"

"Yes," he said, ignoring the discomfort of admitting it. "We can organize a couple cars. Pick up everyone Nate wants protected."

"All right," said his alpha. "I guess we're going to the mattresses."

~

Chris collected Tony's sister Maria and her son. She was girlier than he expected, greeting him in a flowered dress and a light sweater. She seemed like a normal mom: slightly frazzled but organized. Though it was the crack of dawn, she quickly packed the storage space in his Explorer with ready-to-eat food.

"You never know how long we'll be," she said. "Shifters with full stomachs are more pleasant to be around."

Ethan was a cute kid but sleepy. The five-year-old curled up in the back and dozed as Chris drove. He clutched a Met's jacket of his dad's like it was a teddy bear.

"You were at the wedding," Maria said, glancing at him from the front passenger seat. "You were the other best man."

"That's right. I'm Evina's beta."

"You tigers certainly grow up big."

Chris wasn't sure how to respond to that, especially since the comment sounded vaguely suspicious. Probably it was just a kneejerk cats-and-dogs reaction. "You warm enough in that sweater? I can turn on the heat."

Maria folded her arms. "I'm a shifter too," she said.

"Right. Radio?"

She shook her head tightly. "Where are we going?"

"Elfyunk. I have a place there that should be safe."

Elfyunk was neither the worst nor the best part of town. The 1930s had been its heyday. Today it was worn down and gritty. Some of Resurrections' less law-abiding citizens based operations here, but they were mostly old school and not violent. The saying went that there were as many strip joints in Elfyunk as there were Star's Brews downtown.

Tony's older sister didn't comment on the choice. When Chris checked on her from the corner of his eye, she was biting her lower lip. Her eyes were a different color than Tony's—golden brown rather than soft green. Even so, the gesture made her resemble him.

"Sorry," she said, shooting a glance his way. "I shouldn't be snippy. I'm worried about my husband. Adam called him in on this."

"Sure," Chris said. "I understand."

"You really are nice to be helping us."

"Nate is clan now. It feels right to pitch in."

"Nate always was a charmer." Maria's tone was dry. "Your alpha broke a lot of hearts when she snagged him."

Chris didn't want to dwell on Nate's charms. "He and Tony seem to get along," he said perversely.

"Tony *used* to be as big of a flirt as him."

This was said wistfully. Chris deduced she meant as big of a flirt with women. He hesitated, then decided to speak again. "The pack seems to have adjusted to him being gay."

Maria sighed gustily. "Yes."

Chris merged into the light early morning traffic on the freeway. "Do you wish they hadn't adjusted?"

"No." Maria squirmed. "Everybody deserves their pack's support. We just . . . . The family had hopes for him. I always dreamed of Ethan having more cousins. And . . ."

"And?"

"It makes me feel funny, knowing he lied to us for so long. I adore Tony. He should have trusted me."

"Maybe he wanted to trust you. Maybe he just was more afraid you'd stop adoring him."

"I didn't!" Maria lowered her voice so as not to wake her son. "I couldn't. I cried like a baby after he broke the news."

Chris smiled at the confession. He could tell Maria was a good sister. She turned to face him more on the seat.

"You're easy to talk to," she observed. "For a cat."

Chris laughed. She said this like he'd tricked her into it. "Cats are sly. You never know what we'll lure you into."

Soon enough they pulled into the weedy lot behind the boarded up social club. Lou's Place was a two-story bar and pool hall—or it had been until Chris took possession. The Shifter Courts had awarded him the property as restitution for Mark Naegel killing his brothers. Rejecting the settlement would have been an insult to Naegel's clan, but Chris had never had the heart to run the place. Every now and then he checked to make sure it hadn't fallen down. Aside from that, he left it alone.

As he jogged around the car to help Maria and Ethan out, he sincerely hoped the water and electric were on.

The back door creaked open before Chris and Maria got to it. Syd stuck his dreadlocked head out and grinned.

"Everybody's here," he said in his quiet Jamaican accented voice. "They want to know why you've been holding out."

Chris hoped he could avoid getting into that. "Help me unload the car," he said. "Maria packed it with food."

No different from any hungry shifter, Syd rubbed his hands together. "Nice to meet you," he said to Maria. "I'm Syd."

She returned his greeting and went inside with Ethan drooped over her shoulder.

"Seriously, Chris," Syd said, accepting a load of boxes into big arms. "We could have had awesome parties here. You've got four vintage pool tables gathering, like, thirty years of dust."

It was twenty-eight years, but Chris didn't feel like explaining that either.

"I take it you removed the covers."

"Vasur did. And was coughing for ten minutes. We got the lights hooked up and the water running. There's a stock of salted nuts and pretzels in the storeroom. Liam ate some and didn't die, so we're thinking they're all right."

Chris balanced his load one-handed and closed up the SUV. The thought of Liam playing food canary made him smile.

"Really, Chris," Syd went on more seriously. "Why did you keep this place a secret?"

"I sort of . . . inherited it. I have bad memories wrapped up in it."

Syd looked like he wanted to push. That was no surprise. Cats had issues about closed doors. In the end, Syd didn't ask more questions, mainly because he had a trickier issue to bring up. He paused with his hand on the heavy back door's lever, obliging Chris to stop with him. Tiny flakes of rust fell down from the bad weather overhang.

"I should warn you," Syd said, "Adam Santini sent one of his wolves over. Apparently, he thinks we can't protect his people without a cop in charge."

"O-kay," Chris said slowly, not understanding Syd's sneering tone. It seemed to do with more than answering to a wolf. "Is there some reason the men can't put up with that for a while?"

"It's the gay guy," Syd said.

Chris required all his supe self-control to prevent heat from flooding into his face. Syd was generally laidback. Was Liam's prejudice spreading to the crew? "Being gay doesn't mean he can't oversee security."

"He's their *omega*," Syd emphasized. "It's insulting. Liam is fuming, and I'm not sure you can count on the others to stop the explosion."

"I doubt Santini meant to insult us. He probably trusts the guy."

"He's no higher ranked than Liam. And he's *little*."

Calling Tony *little* was stretching it. He was an inch taller than Vasur—not as heavy, Chris guessed, but no feather. Not sure whether to laugh or sigh, he rubbed his itching cheek on his shoulder. "I'll talk to Liam. I get why he's resentful. He probably feels he answers to enough people already. You others are going to have to be more mature. I mean it," he added when Syd drew breath to speak. "Wolf or not, omega or not, we're all working for the same things. Let's go inside now, before my arms fall off."

As soon as they entered the dark back hall, a mix of smells hit his nose. He identified Santini's wolves and his and Evina's cats. Tony's individual scent markers cut through them all. Chris realized he knew Tony's personal fragrance as well as any of his crew—and reacted to it more strongly. Feeling like he was back in high school, he ordered his dick not to get excited. All he needed to send this situation into a tailspin was to throw a big boner.

Jaw clenched, he followed Syd to the storeroom. As they finished stowing the food, Liam's voice rose above the rest. "I'm not giving a fucking dog my cellphone."

"*Liam*," Evina warned with a noticeable growl. This should have silenced the rebellious cat.

"I won't call anyone!" he protested. "I know no one's supposed to know we're here. This idiot needs to give me some credit."

Chris strode into the room with the now uncovered pool tables. Because the front windows were boarded up, most of the light came from the green-shaded cobwebbed bulbs overhead. The whole party, kids included, was spread out around the big space. Chris counted eight people on the wolf side and their own four tigers. The youngsters especially were round-eyed at the tension.

"Not 'upposed to say the 'F' word," Ethan pointed out from his mom's shoulder.

Chris's eyes flicked to Tony, a response he couldn't have suppressed to save his life. The wolf seemed all right. Though his cheeks were ruddy, he looked calmer than Chris felt. He didn't glance at Chris, though Chris didn't doubt he knew he'd come in. Whatever Chris might wish, they were linked enough for that.

"I'm not questioning your word," Tony said to Liam. "My alpha's wife—" he inclined his head in the direction of a petite woman with spiky red and platinum hair "—is a human Talent. Ari can shield the locator chips in your phones from being traced magically."

Liam's expression struggled. He knew this was reasonable but didn't want to back down.

"Give him your phone," Chris said in his deepest voice.

Liam turned partway to him but wouldn't meet his eyes. Maybe he suspected Chris's authority would override his will. "I'll give my ePhone to *her*," he countered childishly.

The alpha's neo-punkster wife rolled her eyes. Her small stature notwithstanding, she didn't seem intimidated by the rising testosterone. Then again, considering she was a human with naturally occurring magical abilities, she might have nothing to be afraid of. Depending on their particular gifts, human Talents could be more dangerous than supes.

"You okay with holding Kelsey?" Ari asked Tony. She made it a question and not an order, giving the baby she held a soothing bounce.

"Of course," Tony said. Smiling fondly at them both, he traded the plastic Holy Foods bag he'd been holding out for the wriggling child. Kelsey went to him like she'd done it before and knew that he was safe. Chris saw phones already in the sack. He prayed at least a couple belonged to his tigers, but that turned out not to be the case. Thankfully, Ari collected the rest without getting any lip.

"Thank you," he made a point of saying to the alpha's wife as he dropped in his own offering.

"Thank *you*," she responded with a mischievous little smile, obviously aware of the diplomatic nuances. "Our entire pack is grateful for your help."

"It's our pleasure," Evina said. She leveled her gaze on their recalcitrant underlings. "Maybe you guys could pull up your fangs and pretend you're civilized while Chris and I consult Tony on setting up watches."

Her words startled Chris. He was glad she was showing the young wolf respect. What made him less happy was that *all* his men's teeth had lengthened, rather than just Liam's.

That development didn't bode well for the near future.

~

Chris didn't think he or Tony had maneuvered the situation, but they ended up assigned together as part of the first watch team. Neither could protest when Evina suggested they pair up. Pushing Tony on someone else would cause problems.

Of course, Tony and Chris spending time together could be problematic too.

"There's a room on the second floor," Tony said. "It has good sightlines for monitoring rear approaches."

There was a joke to be made but Chris refrained. He was thankful no one else was near enough to pipe up.

"That's the poker room," he said, trying to match Tony's seriousness. "I'll grab some food and water so we can settle in."

The layer of dust on the floor of the upstairs room was pre-marked by Tony's sneaker prints. The wolf had explored the building apparently, doing the job he'd been sent to perform no matter what anyone thought of him. A different sort of admiration rose inside Chris for that. Tony might not like being treated the way he was, but he was no whiner.

The wolf preceded Chris into the room, fingers trailing across a large round table where old playing cards lay scattered. His hand dirty then, he smacked it on the side of his faded jeans. God, his butt was cute—not little exactly but tight and muscular. Chris watched it helplessly from his stance a few feet inside the door.

The straps of Tony's shoulder holster drew attention to his back's nice wedge shape. Probably it was immature of Chris to find his armed status arousing.

Unaware he was being ogled, Tony examined the plywood that covered the one window. He must have pried the side loose on his previous visit, because the nails didn't resist his pull. "If you turn out the light," he said, "it shouldn't matter if I remove this."

Chris smacked the switch and the overhead light went dark, leaving them with the overcast morning's dull sunshine. Tony yanked the board off and leaned it on the adjoining wall. He scanned the area outside like a professional.

He sniffed suddenly. What scent had caught his attention Chris didn't know.

"Magic," Tony threw over his shoulder the same as if Chris had asked. "The bars on this window have an old spell on them."

"Probably an anti-cop warning. I doubt the poker that was played here was legal."

"Mm." Tony pulled two chairs from the card table, knocking the dust off their wooden seats. He set them to either side of his chosen watching post.

As gingerly as if the chair might bite, Chris lowered himself to one. "You're wondering why I didn't tell my crew I owned this place."

Tony smiled, the curve of his lips transforming his features to true beauty. "I'm wondering how you kept it secret. They seem like a nosy bunch."

"I guess I'm good at keeping secrets."

"I guess you are." Tony's smile still crinkled his eyes, but their expression had gone sad. "You crew really is a bit macho."

"Sorry about that."

Tony shrugged. "It is what it is."

Chris had leaned closer without thinking. When his and Tony's gazes flicked together, the skin of Chris's face grew hot. Other things too. Things that had a hard time relaxing around this wolf. Before he got into trouble, Chris leaned back and looked away.

"I have a confession," Tony said.

That brought Chris's attention back to him. Tony wet his lips. Chris didn't think he was being deliberately seductive, though his cock couldn't help stirring in response. The wooden chair creaked as Tony's weight shifted. "I think I know how you got this pool hall."

Chris's brows went up. "You do?"

"I—" Tony grimaced. "I looked you up on Oogle. Elfyunk used to be Naegel clan territory. I'm guessing this was the settlement for what Mark Naegel did to your family."

A cold wave washed through him at the name . . . and at Tony uttering it. "You know about that."

"I'm sorry. I shouldn't have snooped. I'm not even sure why the search engine spit it out. I know your last name was different then."

Chris looked down at his hands. They were dangling between his knees: not clenched, not angry, almost relaxed in fact. He lifted his eyes to Tony's. The wolf was watching him intently. "It doesn't matter. You of all people seem to see me as I am. Going through a tragedy like that changes you forever, but it's never everything you are."

Tony reached over to squeeze his knee. Despite the topic, the nerves in Chris's leg tingled deliciously. "Do you want to talk about it?"

"What, now?"

Tony smiled crookedly. "I am a wolf. My big ears can multi-task. Naegel had Tomcat Syndrome, didn't he?"

"Yes," Chris said, weirdly relieved to be nudged into the tale. He rubbed his right eyebrow and decided. "Mark really liked my mom. She was pretty and sassy and a bit of a party girl. She tried to encourage us to like him and vice versa, but it never took. Since it's not *that* weird for a single mother's boyfriend to be more interested in her than her children, we didn't see it as a sign. We were the offspring of other men. He wasn't invested.

"One night, Eddie—my youngest brother—was in a play at school, and she wouldn't skip it to go out with him. Mark snapped. It's a genetic thing, doctors say. Mostly anyway. My mom tried to stop him from attacking. Tigresses are strong, but he was a big guy. He grabbed Eddie and Justin by their legs and swung them like they were toys. He bashed their heads into the walls and floor until they couldn't heal the injuries anymore. He swung them and swung them until they were dead."

Chris pressed one fist to his chest where his lungs had gone tight. The nightmare felt very close, the knowledge of how determined a person had to be to kill supe kids.

"You saw it happen?" Tony breathed.

Chris shook his head, his vision blurred by tears he couldn't force back. "I was out with a bunch of friends. We were . . . robbing a convenience store. I was seventeen and big for my age. If I'd been there, I could have stopped him."

"You don't know that," Tony said softly.

"I do." He dragged his forearm across his eyes. "I'd clashed with cats his

92

size before. God knows I had practice fighting. I knew my nature was dominant. I could have beaten him. My brothers were six and nine. They'd have taken a while to die. They'd have had time to be terrified. I could have saved them. My mom as well, chances are. She never got over her guilt at letting Mark into our lives. She committed suicide."

This information didn't surprise Tony. "So now you save strangers. That's why you became a fireman."

Chris pulled his hands down the wetness on his cheeks, stubble rasping on his palms. He let out a shaky breath. "That's why. I'd probably have been a hooligan otherwise."

Tony sagged back in his chair, long legs stretching out until his tatty running shoes knocked Chris's. "That's a hell of a turning point."

"Yeah," Chris said. He didn't move his feet away. He liked the contact with Tony's.

"You're a tough mother-effer," Tony observed. "Most people would have curled up in a ball after that."

Chris didn't feel tough. He'd done what his conscience demanded, what he'd had to so he could live with himself. Unexpectedly, a little grin broke through his dark feelings. "Fortunately, I like being a fireman."

Tony snorted. "If you'd stayed a hoodlum, I could have arrested you."

That idea had a certain entertainment value—possibly too much of one. Chris shook it out of his head.

"So . . ." he said, feeling a need to let the subject go. "When your brother turned up again, did you see the dragons?"

"I wish. Adam sent me straight to guard duty. I'm not sure what's going on with Rick. Hey!" He sat straighter. "You're not supposed to know about the you-know-whats."

"The last time I was at Nate's place, I noticed he'd been watching the cubs' collection of mini-dragon DVDs. Evina said we're on the lookout for pureblood fae. They'd have to be here for something big. I put two and two together."

"And I just confirmed your guess," Tony said ruefully.

"Sneaky is my middle name."

Tony nodded absently as his mood shifted. He drew in a long breath like he needed bolstering.

"What?" Chris asked.

Slowly, as if he thought he might be stopped, Tony reached across the space between them to Chris's face. His touch was like oxygen, allowing the grief that had risen in him to ease.

"I miss you," Tony said. "I respect your right to make your own choices, but I want you to know that."

Chris's throat thickened. Tony was everything he'd never dreamed of finding in a partner: sweet, brave, fun to be around. Even Evina wasn't this easy to talk to. Time and again, the wolf's simple decency blew him away.

Chris could be real around Tony.

"The other day," Chris said, not letting himself second-guess what he was about to share, "I struck Liam. It seemed unavoidable: a disciplinary thing."

"I've paddled Ethan a time or two," Tony said. "You wouldn't believe what that kid gets into."

Chris knew a swat on the bottom wasn't the same. "I'm the clan's enforcer. I try to keep physical stuff to a minimum, but sometimes I don't know how else to keep order."

"Are you saying you're afraid you're like Mark Naegel? Chris, I don't think you have that in you. Naegel wasn't even related to you by blood."

"I'm a shifter. Half animal. Don't all of us wonder what we'll do now and then? Add being dominant . . ." He trailed off, unable to continue.

Tony clasped him over the ears, forcing Chris to look at him. "Not you. You're not one of those dominants who always has to be on top. If you recall, I've had firsthand proof of that."

Tony's slanting smile invited Chris to smile back. He managed a choked laugh. "You're a good person, Tony Lupone. Even if I were out, I wouldn't deserve you."

"Feel free to call me Saint Anthony," Tony joked.

"*Anthony*," Chris repeated, loving saying his full name. He loved Tony, he realized. He'd be an idiot not to. Tony's expression turned inquiring at the kindling of Chris's eyes. So full of emotion he couldn't speak, Chris rubbed the wrists with which Tony had clasped his head. He wished he had the right to say what he was thinking.

He bent forward to claim Tony's mouth instead.

Tony welcomed his kiss with a hungry moan. His lips were smooth, his answering licks and sucks passionate. As bad as Chris had felt before, now he felt twice as good. He hardened in one long surge, his cock so tight against his zipper it seemed ready to rip through. Tony's hands shifted to his back, roaming up and down Chris's muscles like he intended to push compassion into each one.

Compassion was hardly all Chris experienced. He ached with a desire so strong it seemed impossible to sate. Tony's touch, Tony's heat healed the heavy sadness inside of him. He wrapped his hands around Tony's thighs and pushed the grip up his thick quadriceps. His thumbs found Tony's erection first. He folded their joints around it, teasing Tony and himself with how hard the long ridge was.

What he really wanted was to grab the whole thing.

"We can't do this," Tony whispered against his lips, fangs brushing him sexily as he did. "I want to, but not here. Not with all the sharp ears and noses in this building."

Chris groaned deep inside his chest. He longed to tear off Tony's clothes and take him, to enjoy the comfort of being intimate with a person he truly cared about. Unfortunately, the wolf was right. Not only was that idea crazy, it was irresponsible.

When Tony rested his brow against his, Chris closed his eyes. Unable to let go completely, he traced the shape of Tony's hard-on with all his fingertips.

"Chris," Tony whispered. "You're killing me."

Chris pulled his hands back, followed by the rest of him. Tony's green eyes were glowing, his mouth red from their kisses. His gaze searched Chris's for a long moment.

Tony broke the eye lock first. Clearly struggling for composure, the wolf turned to stare out the grime-hazed window. The cloud cover outside was thicker, the commercial area still quiet at that hour. A shopping bag blew across the rear parking lot, the plastic rattling over cracks in the old asphalt. The cast iron security bars were black silhouettes against the gray light.

Without warning, a tiny spark jumped off one.

Someone was approaching. Chris saw no one, heard no one, but he knew it was true. The watcher spell Tony had noticed earlier wasn't quite out of juice.

"Shit," Tony murmured, tensing up and leaning closer to the window to see out. His palm shifted to the butt of his firearm.

If fae were on the way, Chris knew they needed more protection than a gun. Gritting his teeth against his inevitable twinge of doubt, he let his cat's instincts take over. His heart center swelled, the energy of his tiger bursting free of its human cage. Clothing ripped as light swallowed his senses.

A moment was all it took. Chris's paws hit the floor, heavy but silent. He lifted his tiger's head, pulling back his lips to test any new scents across his tongue. He located the intruder with no trouble. He'd been moving faster than a human, blurring through the shadows where their sight couldn't follow him. He was at the back door now, jiggering the lock. That was too close for comfort. Chris had to head him off.

"Wait," Tony said.

The wolf couldn't change on demand. He needed the moon for it. In his current shape, Chris's tiger thought him too small to be of use. Chris butted him once for reassurance, then streaked off down the steps.

~

Watching Chris change stole what breath Tony had after their cut-off kiss. The way the other man looked at him, as if Tony were the center of his longings . . .

That marvel was shoved to the back burner by the effortless wonder of Chris's shift. In a literal twinkling, he became his tiger. His face went still, bright white sparks shot out from his center, and there his beast self was.

He was huge, his ears as high as Tony's shoulders, his black-striped flanks rippling with muscle. His cat's eyes glowed, their orangey color finally making sense. When his head lifted to sniff the air, Tony fought not to jump. Chris's fangs were longer than when he was in human form, maybe as long as five inches. If a person were caught within those toothy jaws, they weren't getting out.

Tony wanting to pet him in spite of this was admittedly crazy.

Once he'd overcome his distraction, he had a second to identify the scent that had sent Chris into protective mode.

"Wait," he said.

Chris's tiger butted Tony's side with sufficient force to make him stagger. Tony was still catching his balance when Chris's fur-covered muscles coiled. He streaked away before Tony could grab him.

"Fuck," he cursed, tearing after him down the stairs. "That's my brother-in-law! Don't attack!"

Johnny had just succeeded in picking the back door lock, after which he sped at shifter velocity up the hall. Why he hadn't knocked, Tony didn't know, but being leaped on by a thousand pounds of snarling tiger was unlikely to have been his goal.

Chris smashed Johnny to the poolroom floor, his immense weight stunning him.

"Shit," Johnny gasped as Chris bared his forest of teeth and growled.

"No!" Tony cried, jumping on Chris's back like a circus daredevil. He clenched both hands around the looser skin of the tiger's hackles, hauling backward with all his might. Chris grunted but didn't budge much that he could tell.

"*Friend*," Tony barked. "This wolf is Ethan's dad."

"Please," Johnny seconded. "If you don't stop growling, I'm gonna pee myself."

Chris's attack posture began to ease. Tony swung off him and retreated. Thankfully, Chris followed.

Freed from his weight, Johnny rolled—relatively slickly—onto his feet.

"What is your problem?" Maria cried, rushing forward from the others. Amazingly, Chris wasn't the object of her ire. They knew this because it was her husband's chest she punched.

"*My* problem," Johnny complained, rubbing it.

"You couldn't warn us you were coming? You had to pick the lock?"

"I was trying to be stealth. I figured you'd recognize my smell. Also, I have this cat I need to get rid of."

"*I'd* recognize you," she said, hugging him. "Some of the shifters here don't know you."

Johnny shifted his gaze to Chris. Still in tiger form and definitely still alert, he stood next to Tony with the dropcloth-shrouded bar behind them.

"Johnny Surrey," he said to Chris's inscrutable cat face. "And my wife,

Maria Lupone."

Maria shoved him again. "He's met me, you idiot."

"Stop scolding," Johnny said, a smile softening it. His arms wrapped snugly around his wife, who didn't resist the embrace. "I thought you and Tony might like to know your brother is all right."

"Really?" Maria pressed her hands to her mouth. She looked at Tony, and both their eyes welled up. For a moment, it was like being kids again, before life and its complications made them more separate. Rick was their big brother: their unasked-for boss, their playmate and friend, their rock-solid dependable protector. The idea that he might be harmed was intolerable.

"Really," Johnny assured her. "I dropped him and the others at a top-secret location. I'm afraid you guys can't stand down yet. Rick killed the first bad faerie, and his new girl and her dad are safe, but there's one more you-know-what hunting fae unaccounted for. On the bright side, Adam seems to think we'll have the second pureblood in our trap soon."

Chris's furry head butted him again. Giving in to temptation, Tony scratched him behind the ears. His fur was incredibly thick and soft.

"Okay," he said, voice hoarse with relief at hearing his brother was alive. "What's this you were saying about a cat?"

"Hold on," Johnny said. "I left her inside the back entrance."

He returned carrying the sort of plastic bucket professional plasterers used. As he reached Tony and Chris, a desperate scrabbling noise issued from inside. Tony peeked into the lid's air holes, which appeared to have been punched by Johnny's claws. Green eyes stared accusingly up at him. They had vertical pupil slits.

"It's a housecat," he said.

"Apparently," Johnny said. "We found her in the cave where Rick and his new girl were hiding the you-know-whats. We assume she's Cass's. I don't know why they took a pet on the run, but she doesn't seem to like me."

"You stuck her in a bucket," Tony said.

"Believe me, kid, her mood was worse before I put her in there."

The cat yowled as if agreeing.

"We'll take her!" Evina's cubs chimed in unison. "We're cats too. She'll like us!"

Tony considered the unhappy cat. Her gray ears were flattened against her bony head, her fur puffed up in threat or fear. Abby and Rafi might be fellow felines, but they were also six-year-olds.

"Uh," he said. "I don't think this cat is up for being played with. Chris and I will look after her. Maybe coax her to take a nap."

Braced for more angry noises, Tony took the bucket handle from Johnny. The cat stayed mum. In fact, she sat down in the container.

"Well," Tony said, surprised and pleased. Domestic cats didn't always get along with werewolves.

"Okay then," Johnny said. "I guess I'll go back to Adam."

"You're not staying?" Maria objected.

"I can't, sweetie. I'm the weapons expert, and they brought an arsenal."

Johnny *was* Special Tactics, but Maria knew her husband's penchant for being where the action was. She frowned at him skeptically. "An arsenal for one faerie."

"Faeries are the Big Bad, honey—at least some of them. We want to squash this one good while we have the chance." He kissed her forehead to mollify her. "You don't need me here. You've got Tony."

Tony was relatively certain that fact impressed no one.

Maria didn't seem happy, but she let her husband hug her goodbye. Ethan got a squeeze as well, plus a giggle-inducing growl. Then Johnny slipped out the back way again.

His exit left a brief lull.

Syd, the dreadlocked weretiger, ended it.

"Pants," he said, holding up a pair in one hand. Tony gaped at him blankly. "For Chris. He'll have ripped his when he shifted."

"Right," Tony said. "I'll, um, give them to him if you want."

Syd tossed the garment, which Tony caught. Abruptly awkward but not sure what else to do, he carried it and the cat bucket up the stairs. There was a pause, and then he heard Chris's tiger padding up behind him. His fur brushed the peeling wall, his substantial weight causing the steps to creak. Tony didn't think it was his imagination that Chris's strides sounded self-conscious. Everyone knew Tony was attracted to naked men. The idea that he might watch Chris pulling on the sweats was unavoidable.

When Liam muttered a snarky comment beneath his breath, Tony deliberately blocked it from his hearing.

~

Under other circumstances, Tony turning his back while Chris pulled on a pair of sweatpants would have been humorous. Deciding not to attempt a joke, he tied the drawstring without comment.

"Sorry I attacked your brother-in-law," he said.

To prevent the cat from fleeing, Tony shut the door to the poker room before prying up the bucket lid. "You didn't know Johnny was a friendly."

"I should have listened when you told me to wait."

The cat wasn't hopping out of her enclosure. Tony reached in and pulled her out. She hung in his hands and stared at him. She was a skinny thing, her gray fur crooked from having been puffed up.

"She doesn't seem to hate me," Tony said.

"You might have my scent on you. Try holding her on your shoulder."

Tony shifted her onto it and petted her cautiously. The cat closed her eyes and relaxed, as if her bones had magically melted.

"She's purring," Tony said, surprised by it.

Chris smiled. He could hear that from where he stood.

Tony turned to him. "Adam is probably right about this being over soon. Our alpha has good instincts."

Was he sorry about that? Chris couldn't read his guarded expression. "You must have good instincts too. You knew it was safe to drag my tiger off your brother-in-law."

"Why would you hurt me?" Tony asked reasonably.

That was the million-dollar question, wasn't it?

"We should go back on lookout," Chris said. "Just in case."

Tony carried the cat to the chair, petting her ruffled fur smooth with long slow strokes. Chris sat too, soothed by him soothing her. The neighborhood outside slowly came awake with businesspeople and vehicles. Nothing alarming happened. Chris and Tony didn't repeat their kiss. In truth, they barely spoke.

Despite the uneventfulness of their watch, Chris knew he'd always remember being here with the man he loved.

CHAPTER EIGHT

ADAM called Ari, keeper of all the cell phones, with the news that the danger was over. She sprinted upstairs to tell Tony as soon as she hung up. The bad faeries were dead, the dragons were safe, and Adam wanted the squad and its family members to gather at the estate of Cass Maycee's close girlfriends. Apparently, this was the top-secret hideout Johnny had mentioned.

It was afternoon. Johnny hadn't left them more than a few hours ago.

"That's great news," Chris said, squeezing Tony's shoulder.

It was great. Tony swallowed back his urge to ask if Chris could come to the house with them.

"I'll bring Cass's cat," he said.

Ari flashed a grin. "Adam says your brother was really brave. And his new half-faerie girlfriend is badass. I can't wait to hear the whole story!"

Ari had hung her weight on the doorframe as excitedly as a kid. "Me either," Tony said as she bounced one last time and then trotted down the stairs.

"So . . ." Chris said.

He didn't get a chance to say more. The tiger called Jonah, the one next in rank after Chris, stuck his head in the door. His glance flicked scornfully toward Tony before shifting back to Chris. "You hear, boss?"

"I heard," he confirmed.

"We're gonna head to the station, if that's okay with you. Cook a big feed for everyone."

That he meant everyone who was a tiger was obvious.

"Okay," Chris said. "Anyone need a ride?"

"We're good, boss. See you there in a bit."

"You need help closing up things here?" Tony asked.

"I'll be fine," Chris assured him. "You go be with your brother. It's been a long time since you've seen him."

It had, but Rick wasn't the only person Tony cared about. This place wasn't somewhere Chris ought to be alone.

"Shake a leg, boss!" someone called from downstairs. "Vasur's going to barbecue spareribs."

Because it seemed the circumspect thing to do, Tony extended his hand for Chris to shake. The other man looked at it like Tony was crazy.

"Please thank your crew for their help," Tony said.

Chris gripped his palm cautiously. "Tony . . ."

The door was wide open. Tony didn't allow him to continue.

"I'll see you around," he said. He pumped his hand once, briskly, before releasing it.

~

Evidently, the battle to save the dragons had been epic, involving fireballs, magical doppelgangers, and faerie zombies whose life force had to be sucked out to the last drop before they died. Tony heard everything Ari knew by the time he drove her and the baby to the mansion in Westchester.

Tony had gone to high school with Jin and Bridie Levine, but the half elf cousins hadn't lived here then. This was quite a spread, set in the sort of gardens people paid good money to tour.

"Holy crap," Ari said as they pulled up in front of the sprawling ivy-covered edifice.

Few things cowed their alpha's wife, but this seemed to do the trick. Ari's origins in the human world were humble. For a while, she hadn't had a home at all.

"It's just a house," Tony said, reaching over to squeeze her arm.

"They're on TV, aren't they?" Ari asked, meaning Jin and Bridie. "I think I've seen them throwing parties here on the gossip shows."

"They host *As Luck Would Have It*, the program where the guests have had a big stroke of good fortune."

"Uh-huh." Ari bit the side of her thumb.

"Jin used to fart in math class," he informed her. "It was after lunch, and she had . . . issues with Mystery Meat."

Ari narrowed her cornflower blue eyes at him. "You're trying to make me feel better."

Tony grinned. "Is it working?"

She swatted him but got out of the car in a better mood. She only cursed once while reversing the enchantment that helped secure Kelsey's super-safe car seat. Kelsey was used to her mother's occasionally salty language and didn't bat an eye.

An actual human butler in an actual uniform opened the door to them. Since the guy looked like he could handle anything, Tony handed him the cat bucket, explaining that the pet could probably use a meal.

101

"Very good," said the white-haired man. "If you follow me, I'll take care of this."

With measured steps even Ari had to slow down for, the human showed them to a large sunroom where the others were waiting.

Rick didn't see him immediately. He sat on a flowered couch next to Cass, holding the beautiful half fae's hand. Their sides were pressed together, and their auras were intertwined. They weren't radiating like Nate and Evina had at their wedding, but Snow White was definitely more than Rick's "new girl."

Unless Tony's wolf had lost its knack for sniffing out these things, Rick and Cass were soulmates.

The discovery rocked him. His big brother had found someone.

"Tony," Adam greeted, spotting him from the other side of the room.

Rick looked over and saw him then.

He patted Cass's hand before releasing it to stand up. A big happy smile spread across his face. Tony felt his legs move—one stride, two—and then he and Rick slapped their arms around each other.

"Bro," Rick said, hugging him.

Tony was nearly as big as he was, but he still hid his face in his brother's shoulder. Holding Rick was like coming home himself. He was pretty sure they hadn't done it this unabashedly since he'd fessed up to being gay.

"Bastard," he said into Rick's neck. "You ran off without telling me."

Rick laughed and pounded his back some more. Tony pushed back and dried his cheeks. "Had to keep the hero stuff for yourself, didn't you?"

"I needed the advantage," his brother joked. "You are the good-looking one."

"Tony," Cass said a bit shyly from the couch. Possibly she'd been badass about killing evil faeries, but she wasn't looking it now.

"Cass," he replied. "I'm glad you're all right."

"Me too," she said.

Her rose red lips curved with amusement. Faeries were Resurrection's power elite. Even a little smile from Snow White dazzled. The buzz that vibrated through Tony's brain made him glad he was sure of his preference.

"Uncle Tony," said a more peremptory female voice. A curly-haired cub poked her head above the back of, well, he supposed rich people would call it a settee.

"Yes, Abby?" he answered extra respectfully.

She narrowed her eyes, seeming to know he was teasing a tiny bit. "Uncle Tony, don't you want to meet the dragons?"

He certainly did. His heart rate accelerated as he stepped around the fancy piece of furniture. Abby and her twin sat on the floor behind it with Evina. Between them were three exotic creatures Tony's mind didn't immediately make sense of. The dragons had wings and tales and snouts—just like in fairytales. The difference was they weren't any bigger than Cass's cat.

The trio turned their heads to him as he appeared. Their toothy mouths gaped like curious children's, their bright wings lifting like birds testing out a breeze. Tony didn't think he'd ever seen colors as vivid as those of their perfectly formed smooth scales.

The power they emanated was palpable.

"Gosh," he said, jolting to a halt. Resurrection held a lot of wonders, but these beings surely took the cake.

"This is Verdi," Rafi informed him, carefully stroking an emerald green dragon beneath its wing. "The gold one is Auric, and the red one—she's a girl —is Scarlet."

Tony dropped to his knees to get closer, barely aware of Evina rubbing him on the back in greeting. The girl, Scarlet, hopped in front of her siblings and trilled a sound at him. She was the smallest of the three but apparently not the shyest. Her curved red claws stuck a bit in the sunroom's looped wool carpet.

"They're really smart," Abby said. "They helped your brother and my dad kill the mean faeries."

"That *was* smart," Tony agreed breathlessly.

"You can pet them," Rafi reassured. "They don't bite nice people."

Tony extended one hand for Scarlet to sniff. Her lizard tongue flicked out from her muzzle, tickling one finger. "Is it okay to say they're adorable?"

He guessed it was. Scarlet rubbed her head against his knuckles. Her acceptance enchanted him. He reached to stroke her back with his other hand.

"Watch out for her dorsal spikes," Evina warned. "Those little things are sharp."

He didn't have a chance to worry. Scarlet suddenly flapped onto his thighs, stretching her body up his chest in what seemed like a dragonish hug. Her belly scales were smooth as satin, her catlike weight negligible. Tony was startled but cupped one hand behind her as a precaution, in case she fell backwards. Her tail seemed to help her balance on her rear feet, though her claws did dig a little into his jeans.

"Nice dragon," he said laughingly. "You're pretty, aren't you?"

Scarlet cheeped as if she agreed. She rubbed her skull against his chest muscles.

"She likes you," Abby said.

"I probably smell like Rick."

"She's a flirt," Evina said. "Look at her batting her dragon eyes."

All the dragons' eyes were silver and protected by double lids. Tony scritched one finger gently under Scarlet's chin. "You flirt with me all you want. You can be my one and only girl."

"Finally a promise the man can keep."

The familiar voice came from above and behind him. Jin Levine was as pretty as the dragons—and as colorful in her way. Dressed in a pink kimono-style dressing gown, she wore her twenty-four carat hair cropped short. Her tone was teasing, but he had a feeling she wasn't delighted by his presence. Back in high school, she'd been one of the girls he occasionally dated as a cover.

"Jin," he said, unable to get up with Scarlet perched on his legs. "Nice to see you again."

"Uh-huh," she said skeptically.

"Did you need something?" Evina asked sweetly. Her hand was on Tony's arm, her manner silently saying don't mess with my husband's friend.

Meow, Tony thought, resisting an urge to grin.

Too smart to miss the message, Jin flicked her golden hair from her made-for-TV face. "Rick and Cass have had enough excitement for today. They'd like to take the dragons and go home."

Tony glanced over at the pair. They looked like they longed to slip away quietly, their body language saying "couple" and then some. No matter if Rick and he lived in same brownstone, he wouldn't welcome Tony accompanying them.

"Do they have a car?" he asked, remembering he'd driven Rick's.

"They're borrowing Bridie's," Jin said.

That was all right then. Ignoring the funny feeling in his chest, he looked at the girl dragon. "Scarlet," he said. "Much as I hate to say it, you and I have to part for now."

He handed her up to Jin, who took her gingerly.

The cubs thought the way Scarlet's wings drooped was hysterical.

"She's sad!" Abby exclaimed. "She doesn't want to leave you."

Tony wasn't sure that was true. Still, the idea that *someone* would miss him was agreeable.

~

Tony checked in with Adam, but his boss didn't need him for anything. The alpha and Nate had their heads together. From the sound of their discussion, they were strategizing how and what to report to their higher ups. Two members of the race who'd founded Resurrection had been killed at the hands of the RPD. Their deaths were justified, maybe even unavoidable. All the same, explaining how they'd come about was delicate.

Left at loose ends but not ready to go home, he wandered out onto the estate's back grounds. The weather had cleared since morning. A velvety autumn sky stretched over the groomed gardens. The beauty of his surroundings should have improved his mood. Instead, it saddened him. The person he'd been before he came out was haunting him—always hiding, often angry, rarely considering the feelings of the women he'd used to shore up his lie. Evina defending him was sweet, but to be honest, Jin was entitled to her grudge.

Maybe him being alone while everyone was finding soulmates was simply his just desserts.

Oh your life is so sad, he mocked himself. Friends that loved him. Family that cared. Family that was alive and breathing, for that matter. Plenty of people were worse off than him. He'd suck this up like he did everything.

He'd reached a grape arbor where bunches of purple fruit dangled between the leaves. The arbor overhung a bench, and on that bench a man who sparkled sat. Tony had no idea how he'd failed to notice the figure as he'd approached.

Pureblood faeries who'd dropped their glamours were hard to miss.

The male was slender and black-haired. He'd been leaning forward, his attention on some object he was turning between his hands. When Tony jerked to a halt and gasped, his head came up.

His soft blue eyes gave Tony the automatic soul slap faeries were so good at, as if their power could reach anywhere they chose.

"It's all right," the fae said through the sudden cotton in Tony's ears. "I'm Cass's father, Roald le Beau."

Of course he was. If Snow White had been a man, she'd have looked like him. Roald pulled his glamour back around him, and his skin stopped twinkling. He was still incredibly gorgeous—incredibly sexy too. Tony clenched his teeth against responding.

"Tony Lupone," he said. He started to offer his hand, then wondered if he should.

"Best not," the faerie said. "I'm still recovering from my wounds, and my control isn't what it ought to be. I wouldn't want you accidentally faerie struck."

Tony didn't see any wounds, but fae were hardly all body.

Roald le Beau lounged back on the wooden bench, considering Tony without speaking. The grace of his pose seemed as unconscious as his beauty. Tony wouldn't have been surprised if the grapes on the trellis had burst into being for him. He seemed so astoundingly vital it could have been catching.

"Would you like to join me?" Roald asked after a longer pause than most people would have found comfortable.

Tony jerked, realizing he'd been dazzled. "Sorry," he said. "I'm standing here like a dolt, aren't I?"

"You aren't a dolt," Roald said. "And my invitation wasn't mere politeness."

He patted the bench beside him. Tony didn't think the fae was using his juice on him. Nevertheless, he felt helpless to do anything but sit.

Roald let another silence pass. Tony tried not to squirm.

"Do you know what these are?" Roald asked at last. He opened his right hand, revealing the object he'd been contemplating when Tony walked up on him.

"They look like the electrum knuckles the dying faerie gave my brother in the subway." Tony squinted at the rings. "They're not exactly the same. These seem newer."

"They are newer." Roald sounded approving. "They belonged to the faerie my daughter killed."

"Ah," Tony said.

This was hardly a brilliant comment, but Roald didn't seem to mind. Maybe he liked being in teacher mode. Neatly avoiding getting nicked by the weapon's spikes, he flipped the thing around one-handed. "These are called protector gauntlets. People who defend dragon keepers wear them, and they can assume different shapes: swords, gloves, these knuckles that you see. They're difficult to fashion, almost a lost art. Whoever made this one knew what he was doing."

"I see," Tony said, though he really didn't. Faeries' ages were hard to gauge, but it seemed Cass's father was old enough to be eccentric.

"Would you like to try it on?" He held out the gleaming thing. "It's a beautiful instrument."

Tony shrank back without thinking. "When I touched my brother's, it zapped me."

Roald smiled, and Tony's brain cells went slightly numb. "I don't think this one will."

Tony didn't want to risk it. He needed no more reminders that his brother was the special one.

"Maybe some other time," he said politely. He stood, drawing Roald's attention up with him.

"As you wish, young wolf," Roald said.

His formality reminded Tony of the fae he'd pursued to the motorcycle shop.

"What was his name?" he blurted. "The fae I chased, the one your daughter killed."

"Ceallach," Cass's father said. "He had to die, but his loss saddens."

"He tortured you." Tony couldn't hide his surprise.

Roald inclined his head. "No man has only evil in his heart."

Tony couldn't argue that. "I should go," he said, fighting an odd urge to bow. "It was nice meeting you."

"And you, wolf," Roald returned gravely.

Tony tried not to look like he was in a rush to escape. Beautiful though they were, fae weren't the most comfortable people to be around. If Roald turned out to be Rick's future dad-in-law, that was one blessing Tony didn't envy him.

He shut the door to Rick's car before remembering he hadn't gotten his alpha's formal okay to leave. *Fuck*, he thought, reluctant to go back in. Not that he wanted to go home either, not with the lovebirds right upstairs doing whatever. He pressed his brow to the steering wheel.

Why did everything have to close in on him at once?

His stomach growled, reminding him of Chris and his tiger-only sparerib feast. God, he wished he were with the cat. How awesome would it be to be his truest self right then? His best self. His happiest.

He pulled out his phone before he could stop himself. He knew the number for Evina's station. Surely he could invent a reason for needing to speak to Chris. He could pretend Adam wanted a statement for his report. Nothing relevant to the case had happened at the pool hall, but firemen wouldn't know what cops put in paperwork.

~

Despite Vasur's spareribs smelling amazing, Chris couldn't work up an appetite. He kept remembering Tony shaking his hand like they were strangers.

When the phone rang in Evina's office, he hopped up from the station's meal table. Evina wasn't at its head today. She was hanging with Nate's wolves. Maybe the call came from one of them.

"I'll get that," he volunteered. Aware the others were watching, he bounded up the open steps to Evina's loft at a swift but not overeager pace. The space was glassed to provide a view of the truck bay below. Though their alpha's desk was cluttered, he found the phone with no trouble.

"Company 5," he answered.

"Chris." Tony was on the other end. The sound of his voice put Chris's hormones into hyperdrive.

He glanced at the office door, which he'd left open. "Why are you calling? Is something wrong?"

"No." Tony was quiet for a moment. His exhalation was too close to a sigh.

Chris turned his back to the windows and held the phone tighter. "Something *is* wrong. Tell me what I can do."

"It's nothing. Or nothing important." He paused and Chris waited. "When we were together at my place, you said you wanted to be there for me. Does that include if I'm in a funk and just really want to see you?"

Chris hesitated and then hated himself for it. "Yes," he said, attempting to inject the answer with firmness. He didn't do it quickly enough to fool Tony.

"Crap," the werewolf said. "I shouldn't be asking this."

"You should. I want you to. I—" He thought quickly. "I know a place that should be okay. I'll text you the address."

"You're sure?" Tony asked, relief evident in his voice.

"I'm sure. I'll leave in a few minutes."

He hung up, using Evina's computer to send the directions. Deleting the message from the *sent* folder felt more two-faced than usual.

You'd think he wanted to be caught.

"Got to go," Chris said as he jogged down the stairs again. "Personal business."

"Must be a booty call," Vasur teased. "My spareribs are too tasty to walk away from for less than that."

Chris didn't answer. The cat's guess was close enough.

"You're in charge," Chris said to Jonah. "Station 12 is still covering our calls. If anything big comes in, notify Evina."

"Sure, boss." Jonah leaned back in his plastic chair, his big body confident and relaxed. Something in his gaze gave Chris pause. The cat didn't precisely seem suspicious, but there was an extra distance behind his stare, like Jonah was measuring him. Jonah was Liam's bestie. Had Chris's recent run-ins with the omega triggered something in the higher ranked tiger?

"Everything okay with you?" Chris asked.

"Sure," Jonah repeated. He lifted his water bottle for a swig. "Go take care of your business."

His tone was respectful—at least on the surface. Chris shrugged inside his head. He'd have to deal with this later. Right then Tony needed him.

~

Chris had a wait ahead of him. He'd sent Tony the address for the Downtown Grande's attached coffee shop. Meeting there was less conspicuous than the hotel's Versailles-like marble and gilt lobby. Because Tony had farther to drive, Chris arrived first. He'd finished a cappuccino by the time the wolf strolled in.

He stood up without thinking.

"Hey," Tony said, glancing around the gleaming place. "This is a coffee shop."

He sounded like he was disappointed but trying to hide it.

"We're going to the hotel," Chris said. "I thought we'd meet here first."

"Oh." Tony looked at him and then down, his cheeks becoming a little flushed. He shoved his hands in his jeans pockets. "Good."

Chris smiled. Tony was so easy to read it was flattering. "Don't get too excited. I haven't booked the penthouse suite."

Tony cracked a grin. "A closet would do for me."

They'd spoken in low voices, the sort shifters used to be private. Chris had an overwhelming urge to take Tony's elbow—or even to hold his hand. Knowing that was reckless, he thrust his hands in his pockets too.

"Elevator's this way," he said.

They walked side by side down a back hall that led out of the coffee shop.

"You make a reservation?" Tony asked.

"Phoned it in." The elevator that arrived was empty, the music playing inside some peculiar Outsider pop. "The manager is a sort of friend. I resuscitated her significant other after an accident. She gives me half off room rates."

"And doesn't ask who you stay in them with," Tony guessed.

"Right." Chris jabbed the button for the tenth floor.

"You're blushing," Tony observed.

Chris rubbed his forehead. "If it makes you feel better, I wish I were taking you somewhere I'd never been with anyone else."

"Ever use this room before?"

"No," Chris said, though in truth he didn't remember.

Tony's silent laugh shook his shoulders.

"I'm glad you find this amusing."

"I find it *endearing*," he corrected. "It's nice that you're embarrassed. Heck, it's nice that you're meeting me."

The door chimed and opened, sparing Chris the need to answer. They walked down the corridor with a foot of carpet between them. The separation didn't matter. Chris's body tingled all along the side nearest to Tony. He was halfway hard and totally hot-faced.

He flubbed his first attempt to get the key card to work.

"Need help?" Tony asked archly.

"Shut up." Thankfully, on the second try the little lock light turned green. Chris swung the door open. The room was nice but small: a bed, a bath, a window—now nearly dark—overlooking Fifth Avenue and the park. Tony strode straight to it.

"Nice view," he said, peering out. "I can see the tiger carousel."

Chris shut the door and flipped the bolt. The sound turned Tony around. Sensation poured through Chris at knowing they were alone. Tony was so flipping gorgeous, standing there tall and serious. His face was sad, but that didn't lessen Chris's attraction. He loved how Tony's fingers curled into his palms with tension.

"I'm gonna sound like a girl," the hot wolf said, "but could you just hold me?"

Chris crossed the room quick as thought and wrapped his arms around him.

"God, that's good," Tony said, rubbing his cheek over Chris's shoulder.

His arms had circled Chris's back, his warmth and hardness better than a campfire. Chris stood there like that for a while. He was powerfully aroused—enough to be impatient. In spite of that, simply holding Tony was enjoyable.

"What happened?" he finally asked. "Even if it seems like nothing, I want to hear."

"My brother found his soulmate," Tony said.

Chris pulled back a few inches. "The girl he went on the run with? The half faerie?"

"That's her. We all went to high school together. She's a good person, and he used to have a crush on her. It's nice for him. Really nice. It's just . . ."

"A big change."

"Yeah." Tony smiled sheepishly. "Then there's the hero stuff."

"The hero stuff?"

"He and Cass kind of saved the world."

"Not really."

"Pretty much," Tony said. "The faeries they were on the run from, the ones they ended up killing, wanted to use the dragons' power to destroy the Pocket and everything in it. They viewed our mixed magic-mundane reality as sacrilege."

Tony let his arms drop and took a step away. Chris sat on the edge of the bed to absorb what he'd said. "There really are dragons?"

"There are. Rick and Cass hatched them, and they're adorable."

"Adorable."

"Well, they're only yea big at the moment." Tony held his hands a short span apart. "That information isn't for sharing, by the way. Adam and the others are debating if they should go public with the dragons' non-extinction. You could say the brood is in the closet for the time being."

Tony's mouth twisted sardonically. Chris reached to him and took his hands. He'd sat down with his legs apart. A gentle tug brought Tony between his knees. The other man looked at Chris, but he seemed distracted. Chris tried to figure out what was bothering him the most.

"You're a hero to me," he said.

Tony pulled a face.

"You are," he insisted. "You're out to the world. You don't get the respect or the credit you deserve, but you go right on living and protecting the city like you've sworn to. I think you underestimate what a big deal that is."

Tony smiled faintly. "Sometimes I think it's a big deal. Sometimes I feel damn sorry for myself."

"Fine. You're not a saint. I still admire you, Tony. Literal dragon slaying not required."

"Strictly speaking, Rick slayed a faerie."

"Whatever." Chris saw Tony was teasing him, his green eyes twinkling with mischief. Chris rubbed his hands with his thumbs.

Tony's amusement changed subtly. "I love you, Chris."

Chris's heart faltered, then started galloping. *Oh boy,* he thought. "I love you too," he blurted.

Tony's mouth stretched with pleasure, making him look about twelve years old. "All right then. I guess we're even."

"Tony—"

The wolf cut him off by squeezing his hands. "No. No warnings and no take-backs."

"I was going to say I stopped in the gift shop before you arrived."

Tony's expression turned puzzled. "You got me a present?"

Chris laughed. "Only if you count a toothbrush."

"Ah. Should I promise to treasure it?"

Chris got up to retrieve the bag he'd brought up here earlier. He dumped the contents out on the king size bed. Lube tumbled to the covers, a pair of razors, and the aforementioned toothbrushes.

"You *were* planning a sleepover," Tony said.

He sounded smug. Chris was suddenly illogically giddy. In that moment, he didn't care how impossible them being together was. "Say it again," he demanded.

Tony put his hands on his hips. "I think you ought to earn it."

Chris moved too quickly to be stopped, undoing Tony's faded jeans and whipping them down his legs.

"Shit," Tony gasped, trying not to fall over with denim bunched around his ankles. "You won't make me say *I love you* by pantsing me!"

Chris moved again, this time peeling Tony's long-sleeve T-shirt over his head.

"Chris!" Tony had managed to kick free of his jeans and sneakers.

"You're not really upset," Chris said. "Or why are your briefs bulging?"

They weren't bulging just a little. Tony had a super-size salami stuck in his black Calvins. Laughing and cursing at the same time, Tony shoved Chris onto the bed. Chris could have resisted but let himself topple. He felt breathless and excited even before Tony pounced and landed on both knees on top of him.

Tony noticed the reaction. "I see you're one of those gays who thinks wrestling is a turn-on."

Being called gay gave Chris a start, but it was also weirdly arousing. Tony pushed the hem of Chris's shirt to his underarms.

"Hm." He slid both palms up the skin he'd bared, then pinched Chris's beaded nipples tightly enough to thrill. "Why are you breathing so hard, *mon chat?*"

"I like you," Chris panted, giving in to his need to squirm.

Tony sat on Chris's crotch, exactly where his bulge pushed out his tan trousers. Because Tony was down to briefs, the muscles of his cheeks were easy to distinguish. He rolled like a dirty dancer up and down Chris's erection.

Chris had trouble speaking, but he tried. "That's an . . . interesting wrestling technique."

Repeating it, Tony grabbed his wrists and pinned them to the pillow.

Chris groaned at how sexy the restraint felt. "Undress me. I want to feel your cock on mine."

"Say please."

Chris arched up and nipped his shoulder. "Please."

Tony flushed at the love bite. Breathing harder himself, he swung off

Chris's body and stripped him. His hands were hot and sure—gentle too, which Chris appreciated but also found frustrating. Tony pulled off his own briefs in quick motions, his erection hard and high. Chris rolled onto his side to watch, stretching out one arm to grip the bouncing length. Tony's cock was a good handhold. Chris tugged him back onto the bed with it.

Tony straddled him with his eyes glowing. "Where's the lube?"

Chris fumbled on the bed until he found it. "Do you want it?"

"Yes," Tony said roughly.

Chris gave it to him. The wolf opened it, squeezed some into one hand, then rubbed his palms together. Chris's cock throbbed longer, anticipating what was to come. The payoff didn't disappoint.

Tony wrapped his slippery hands around both their stiff penises.

"Fuck," Chris breathed as he pulled a snug grip up them. Tony's hold squeezed their shafts and heads together. Tony's veins throbbed next to his, his fingers rubbing and admiring. The fact that Tony was jacking himself as well made the whole thing that much more intimate.

"Mm," Tony hummed, his pelvis doing the booty roll again. "I want to kiss you, but this feels really good."

"I'll hold your weight. You keep your hands where they are."

He braced his palm on Tony's sternum as Tony descended. When he was close to kissing distance, he stopped. "I'm not too heavy?"

"No," Chris said simply. He needed only one hand to hold him up. He drew the other down Tony's spine, across the small of his back, and onto the slope of his taut butt cheeks. Tony shivered as Chris feathered his fingertips around their curves.

"I want you on top," the wolf confessed.

This wasn't a preference Chris would ever object to. Too eager to pretend, he flipped Tony under him. Tony's hands worked even better from that position, his double grip massaging both their cocks. Chris felt like a zillion fingers were stroking him. Without half trying, he imitated the other man's stripper-style hip roll.

"Oh yeah," Tony growled. "Your big hard dick is so fucking hot on mine."

The dirty talk got to him. Chris dropped his head to Tony's and French-kissed him. Tony welcomed the tongue battle. His body tightened, and he drove one thigh up between Chris's legs, compressing Chris's balls on the firm muscle. The pressure could have hurt, but instead it felt incredible. They were naked on a bed, and they had all night to play.

Chris drew out the kiss until the sense of imminence in his groin built too high to ignore. Tony's double hand-job was becoming a little too effective.

"Let go of our cocks," he whispered in Tony's ear.

Tony stopped stroking but kept his grip where it was. "I want to come."

"Me too."

"I'm close."

"Me too," Chris said and grinned.

Tony unpeeled his fingers. Without their activity between them, Chris could drop his hips onto his. "Put your hands on my butt."

Tony was feeling sassy. He slapped them around Chris's cheeks. Though he appreciated the sting, Chris wasn't relinquishing control. He came down on one elbow. "Lick my finger. Nice and wet, if you know what's good for you."

Tony lifted his brows but gave Chris's middle finger the desired treatment. Chris wedged that hand under Tony, shooting the slickened finger up Tony's hole.

"Sh-sheesh," Tony stuttered but not with pain. He wriggled, driving the intrusion deeper. Chris couldn't doubt he liked anal play. Trapped between their bellies, Tony's shaft pulsed harder beside his.

That was enough prep, Chris thought. He lowered his upper body, dug his knees into the bed, and rubbed himself in quick short motions up and down Tony's groin.

Tony sucked in air, his cock going rigid, his hips pressing up to get more. His hands were iron clamping Chris's buttocks, but Chris still had strength to move. The friction on their erections drew repeated gasps from him. Tony's muscular body was heaven chafing his. Suddenly Tony shifted angles, apparently desperate to work the base of his cock against the base of Chris's. A new spot of heat had sprung to life down there.

Despite his own pleasure, Chris's hindbrain recognized what it was.

He grunted, pushing his finger far enough to manipulate Tony's prostate gland. Tony groaned with enjoyment. Knowing the wolf was too overwhelmed by good sensations to move effectively, Chris took charge of sliding their cocks even more vigorously together.

"Ah!" Tony cried half a second before Chris's climax broke.

They shot seed up each other's bellies, their strong bodies striving to get as close as possible. Undulating through the increase in slipperiness was messily pleasurable. Chris's cock shot one last salvo, after which the most luxurious warmth spread out from his center.

"Mm," he hummed. "That is so much better."

He didn't object when Tony rolled over him. Now above him, Tony's face was flushed and relaxed, his green eyes alight, his lips full and soft. He was truly lovely to Chris. A small gold medal dangled around his neck: Saint Michael, Chris presumed, the patron of policemen. Admiring Tony's post-coital glow didn't cause him to forget the extra heat that had kindled at the base of the wolf's penis.

"Your bulbus gland activated," he observed.

"Uh-huh," Tony said. He yawned and wriggled out a kink in his vertebrae. "You've made it do that before. It makes coming feel extra good."

"I thought it only swelled when male wolves had sex with women who were good genetic matches. I thought it was a fertility aid."

"What can I tell you?" Tony said. "I guess my glands are gay."

Chris laughed. He lifted a hand to stroke Tony's bangs from his sweaty brow. The locks fell again of course, but touching him was nice. "I wish we could do this every night."

"Mm." Tony shifted lower, laying his head on Chris's thumping heart. Coming that hard was good exercise. Tony's left hand covered Chris's pec, lightly petting the muscle. Chris sensed him making his mind up about something.

"If you trust me," Tony said cautiously, "we could do this now and then."

Chris gnawed his lip. He did trust Tony. "That's really tempting, but I'm not sure I trust myself."

Tony rubbed his chest with his cheek. "We love each other."

"Yes," Chris agreed. "You're out though. Doesn't sneaking around with me feel like a step backwards?"

When Tony lifted his head, his green eyes were serious. "I like you better than any man I've met. I feel more for you, in my heart, than I ever have before. I understand what your job means to you. The chance to be together sometimes instead of never seems like a compromise worth making."

"Wow," Chris said, moved to speechlessness.

Tony smiled at his inarticulate response. Chris knew he couldn't bear not to have that humorous, handsome face in his life.

"Okay," he said. "We'll give it a try. And . . . thank you, Tony. You— I feel more for you in my heart than I have for anyone."

He meant this to a degree that shocked. How much he loved Tony actually seemed disloyal. No one except Evina had come close to equaling his brothers' importance in his life.

They're gone, he thought, trying to assure himself this was natural. Tony was right here. Of course he would loom larger.

"I won't let you down," Tony promised. "I haven't forgotten how to be careful."

"I hope you don't end up minding."

"Never," Tony said and laid his head back down.

Doubt nudged unease through Chris. Never was a long time. Tony's fingers drew circles on his ribs.

"What about Nate?" Chris asked impulsively.

"What about him?"

Chris was sorry he'd brought it up, but he explained. "You said you'd never, you know, felt as much as this before."

"Oh my God," Tony said. "That is awesome. You're jealous!"

Chris squirmed on the bedcovers. "I'm not jealous. Exactly. You'd be abnormal if you'd never had a crush on someone."

Tony snickered into his chest.

"You're not denying you had a crush on him," Chris noticed.

"Am I supposed to?"

Chris frowned at the ceiling. Maybe Tony guessed he was miffed. Chris felt his grin broaden.

"I love you," he said, patting Chris's side gently. "Nate's a great guy, but you . . . call to me more than him. Even if he were gay, I expect that would be the case."

He *expected* that would be the case. "He's too fussy for you," Chris said.

Tony kissed his breastbone. "Go to sleep, *mon chat*."

Despite his lingering annoyance, Chris did precisely that.

~

They woke up starving a few hours later. Tony thought it was sweet that neither had been in the mood to eat without the other. Chris ordered burgers from room service. They ate, then showered, then made love nice and slow. Tony liked that more than he suspected he should let on.

Afterwards, they slept through the night. Tony forced himself to get up before the alarm, so he could sit and watch Chris sleeping. True to his animal's nature, the big cat was good at it. He slumbered through Tony's trip to the bathroom and him dressing.

His eyes only cracked open when Tony combed his wonderful gold-streaked hair behind his ear.

"What time is it?" Chris mumbled.

"Still early. I need to go home for fresh clothes."

Chris rolled onto his back and stretched, his massive chest a sight to see. "Last night was good."

"Yes, it was, *mon*—"

"If you keep up that *mon chat* crap, I'm gonna call you pup."

Chris was assuming Tony wouldn't like having a nickname. "You can do better than that," he said aloud. "When we were kids and I annoyed my brother, he used to call me Ant."

"'Ant' as in a bug?"

"That too, but short for Anthony."

"Ah." On his side again, Chris tucked his hands underneath his cheek. "I'll remember that."

His smile was Cheshire-like. Tony's heart welled up, but he kept the words he was thinking inside of him. A guy like Chris wouldn't want to hear *I love you* every five damn minutes.

"I better go," Tony said, pushing from the mattress onto his feet.

"Bye, Ant," Chris said teasingly.

Amused, Tony shook his head. His hand was on the door when Chris spoke again.

"Tony," he called softly. "I love you."

The grin that stretched Tony's mouth warmed his face all day.

CHAPTER
NINE

SHORTLY after rescuing the dragons, Rick moved into Cass's place. She lived atop the downtown Maycees department store, in a lavish penthouse with a pool and a roof terrace. Not only did it have room for Cass's menagerie, but the building's security made it easier to keep the press and other curious folks out of their business.

Operating on the logic that creatures everyone knew about would be harder to move against, Cass and Rick had introduced the brood to the city on Jin and Bridie's *As Luck Would Have It* show. Two months after the program aired, the resulting dragon mania hadn't yet died down. Every other kid Tony saw was either skipping in dragon sneakers or carrying a dragon lunchbox or—most goofily—warming their little heads under crocheted dragon hats. The latest trend in reptilian wear was charming it to smoke. The day before, Tony had spotted an otherwise conservative businessman with a fire-breathing dragon-shaped tiepin.

Tony was seriously considering buying Rick one for his next birthday.

Given that Rick had all but abandoned the brownstone, Tony didn't expect to return from a run and find him on his couch.

"What's up?" he asked, toeing off his shoes and leaving them at the door. Using his shirt hem, he wiped the worst of the sweat from his face. "Cass come to her senses and toss you out?"

Rick was picking at the label of one of Tony's beers. The living room was marginally less cluttered than usual, and there was room to sit. Though Tony was glad to see him, Rick's at-homeness made him grateful he hadn't left anything to do with Chris lying out.

To Tony's surprise, Rick didn't roll his eyes at the joke. Instead, he looked very serious.

"Cass agreed to marry me," he said.

Tony's face split into a grin. "That's awesome! When is the wedding?"

"I don't know. March maybe? She and her girlfriends say there's stuff to plan." Clearly, the thought of that *stuff* inspired anxiety. "We're throwing an engagement party on Cass's roof this weekend."

"Great. You want my help with anything?"

"I don't think so." Rick hesitated. "You're really okay with this?"

"Why wouldn't I be? You know I think Cass is super."

Rick rubbed his knees awkwardly. "We haven't . . . talked about you in a while."

"Why do we need to talk about me? I'm good."

Tony was better than good. Despite needing sneak around, seeing Chris on a relatively frequent basis made him the happiest he'd ever been.

"You're cool with being my best man?"

"I'm honored," Tony said sincerely. He laughed. "I totally know what I'm getting you for a groom gift."

Rick cocked his head like he had trouble believing him.

"Seriously," Tony said. "I'm happy for you. Cass loves you, and I can't help loving her just for that."

Rick set down his beer and rose. "I want the same for you, Tony."

Tony smiled and gave him a quick hug. "You're a good brother. Maybe Cass is a little bit lucky too."

"*A little bit*," Rick repeated humorously.

"Maybe," Tony confirmed.

He was conscious of a tiny shadow on his spirit but refused to dwell on it. He was loved, and he loved in return. He had reason to know that was no small blessing.

~

Chris was shopping at Holy Foods. He didn't always buy his food here. Their specially blessed groceries were expensive, though you couldn't beat the quality. He'd come here on impulse. With the exception of Evina, who'd moved to Nate's, Chris and his crew lived near each other in the same suburban townhome complex. He'd been thinking he'd look for a cabin to rent some weekend, where he could cook for Tony without tripping over tigers every time he walked out the door. Chris was no chef like Vasur or Syd, but he could certainly grill steak and bake potatoes.

He wanted him and Tony to have a night like that.

Lost in his daydream and not paying enough attention to where he turned his cart, he nearly clipped a guy standing in the line at the bakery.

"Sorry, man," he said, jerking back the wheels just in time.

The man looked up. Chris blinked. Tony's brother Rick was right in front of him.

"Hey," Rick said with a good-natured laugh. "It's Chris, isn't it? Evina's second."

"Yes." Chris felt pleased and awkward to be recognized. He was very aware that Rick was his lover's sibling. In a different world, a whole host of hopes and worries would be tied up in them liking each other. Chris tried to respond like none of them were going through his head. "I don't usually shop here. I had a craving for good red meat."

"Cake," Rick said, nodding toward the bakery counter. "I'm trying to get a rush job for this weekend. You're coming, right?"

Chris knew his face was blank.

"I invited you," Rick said. "Or I think I did. I told Evina her crew was welcome."

"I haven't spoken to her yet today," Chris said.

"Oh. Well, come. We're, uh—" Rick colored like his brother did sometimes, red suffusing his naturally tanned skin. "Cass and I are celebrating our engagement."

"Cool," Chris said, privately thinking his blush was adorable. "Congratulations."

"Thanks. There'll be plenty of food. And the dragons. Your crew really ought to meet them, considering you helped the pack when we were hiding them."

"I'd like that," Chris said. "I've only seen them on TV."

He'd found them fascinating: beautiful, exotic, and something more. They were, literally, creatures out of a tale—a living, breathing embodiment of the fae's Old Country. Even on television, looking into their silver eyes was like meeting the gazes of wild tigers. One of the dragons' forebears had given her life to form Resurrection. Her essence suffused every atom around them, making the magical reptiles a kind of cousin to every soul who resided here.

Recognizing them as kindred was instinctive.

Maybe it was obsessive, but he'd watched their appearance on *As Luck Would Have It* a dozen times.

"So we'll see you," Rick said, his attention splitting as the man behind the baked goods counter gestured him forward. "Bring your swimsuit. There's a pool, and we'll have a warming spell."

A swimsuit. Chris wasn't sure that was a good idea. Not if Tony was wearing one. Not unless his own were constructed of cast iron.

The wolf was sexy enough with all of his clothes on.

~

Liam's moods had been up and down since their volunteer assignment at the pool hall. One glimpse of his sullen face told Chris the big Irish cat wouldn't be a ray of sunshine this evening.

"I don't see why we have to waste our Friday night with wolves," he grumbled loudly enough for the rest of the crew to hear. "We don't get the weekend off that often."

Hoping to make the omega feel less overlooked, Chris had been helping him stack fire hose on racks in the engine bay. It was grunt work but necessary. Watching Liam sulk made wonder why he'd bothered.

"It's a party," he pointed out. "And it was nice of them to invite us. But feel free to miss out. No need to eat great food or listen to good music or meet the creatures everyone has been talking about for months. We'll muddle on without you if wasting time with wolves bothers you that much."

Liam stopped folding hose to gape at him. "I don't want to stay away by myself."

No, he wanted the crew to take his side against the pack who'd accepted Tony's sexuality. Chris shook his head silently. God save him from insecure twenty-five-year-olds.

"Grow up, Liam," Syd put in from his position hosing down their dirty hook and ladder. Evidently, Syd had decided which side of this squabble he supported. Chris would have been more grateful if Syd's support hadn't spurred Jonah to defend his buddy.

"Lay off the kid," he said. "Liam is entitled to his opinion."

"He's being a fucking tool. Nate's a wolf, and he's all right."

Jonah wouldn't have made a face if he'd known Evina had just entered the garage.

"Yes, he is," their alpha said, giving Syd's dreads a friendly tug. "All his pack are stand-up people. We're lucky to have this chance to broaden our horizons. Having closer ties to the city's cops can only help us in what we do."

"Sorry," Jonah said, realizing he'd put his foot in it. "I didn't mean to insult your mate."

"We're a team," Evina reminded, drawing on her alpha charisma as well as her motherly patience. "Every one of us needs the others. We can't let this kind of conflict drive a wedge between us."

"It wouldn't be so bad if Chris weren't always on Liam's case," Jonah said.

Evina's brows went up. "It's not my perception that he is."

"You don't see everything," their third muttered.

Evina glanced at Chris, who didn't know what to say. No alpha saw everything. That wasn't how clans worked. "Do the three of us need to talk?"

Chris was willing to if she wanted. He wasn't perfect, but he did the best he could. He *knew* he was the best cat to serve as beta. No one else had anywhere near his experience. No one else cared as much about all of them—even when they were being twits.

"Maybe we should," he said, trying not to sound like he was sucking up.

Jonah's resentful grimace said the cat thought he was. Chris suppressed a sigh. That reaction was exactly why Jonah couldn't step into his turnout boots.

"You're putting them first," the tiger said darkly. "You both like the wolves better."

Jonah certainly wasn't short on nerve. Chris gave him credit for speaking his mind straight out. What he couldn't do was let the statement stand.

"Whatever you think of me, you're being unfair to Evina—and maybe to Nate as well. Haven't you noticed how much happier she is since she married him? How much more affection she has to give? As for Nate, he cares about us. He's new to our lives, and he's been giving us a chance to get used to him, but you have to admit he treats Evina's cubs as lovingly as if they were his own blood. His whole pack has welcomed Abby and Rafiq. Those wolves are putting us cats to shame!"

Chris's voice had roughened, the topic one that affected him. He told himself he wouldn't be embarrassed about getting emotional.

"Well," Evina said, sounding choked up herself. She pressed her fingertips to the wetness beneath her eyes. Though she was their alpha, the sight of her tears brought out the protective male in her crewmembers.

Syd smacked her lightly on the bicep. "We'll work it out, chief. You know cats are stubborn. We take longer for some things. I, for one, am completely stoked about meeting those dragons. I've got a nephew who'll think I'm a god if I get a picture of me with one."

The tension eased as the others ribbed Syd over this.

Evina watched them a minute longer, weighing if the crisis really was over. It appeared to be. Jonah had returned to soaping the lime green tiger-striped hook and ladder. Chris wouldn't say he looked satisfied, but his manner was no longer challenging.

"You okay?" Chris asked Liam. "You should come to tonight's party. You'll be grumpy if everyone else goes and you miss out."

Liam's head was down. He glanced at his boss sideways. "I'll think about it," he said.

Chris rubbed the omega's back before stepping to Evina.

"Kids," Evina said, rolling her eyes at him. She'd moved to the station's weightlifting corner so they could speak privately.

"Jonah and Liam are close," Chris said. "I don't want to discourage them from sticking up for each other, but—"

"—they're being a pain in the ass right now?"

"I hope that's all it is, and that they'll get over it." If Jonah was gearing up for a challenge . . .

"We haven't done anything wrong," she said, a hint of exasperation in her tone. "Nate is an asset to this clan." Chris smiled, and Evina rubbed the wing of one dark eyebrow. "Okay, maybe I'm partial."

Chris thought she was right to be, which might have been part of the problem. "Did you have a favor you wanted to ask me?"

"You know me too well," she said with a little laugh. "I hope this isn't awkward, considering the timing, but could you give Tony a ride tonight? He's been borrowing Rick's car, and it's in the shop."

"Oh," Chris said, caught flatfooted.

"We can take him if it's inconvenient," Evina assured him. "Nate's Goblinati is just so small the cubs end up climbing all over him. Plus, my car's such a piece of crap Nate hates driving it."

"Not a problem," Chris said.

Evina searched his eyes for doubt. "You get along with everyone. I thought you and Tony might be a good bridge to build, but maybe not if the cats are feeling all *Mom and Dad don't love me.*"

"We shouldn't necessarily coddle their fears."

"No," she agreed, rubbing her brow again. "God, I wish they weren't so uptight about Tony being gay. He's a good man."

Chris squeezed the deceptively delicate ball of her shoulder. "Maybe Syd's right, and they're simply taking longer to wrap their heads around the change in our conditions."

Evina surprised him by going up on tiptoe to kiss his cheek. "You're a rock. I'm so glad I have you to help me."

Chris didn't know how much help he was in this particular situation—or how objective. He wondered if Evina would have been as quick to thank him if she'd known where he was truly coming from.

~

Chris's dusty white Ford Explorer was nothing fancy, but for a conversion it ran okay. As he pulled up to the brownstone's front, Tony jogged down the steps. He was grinning from ear to ear, so unabashedly excited Chris couldn't help but be infected by his good mood.

The wolf looked totally do-able in worn jeans, a black T-shirt, and a brown sport coat.

"Thank God," Chris said, leaning sideways to open the door for him.

The greeting surprised Tony. "Were you expecting me to be late?"

"No," Chris said as the wolf slipped smoothly into the passenger seat. "I meant thank God you're wearing clothes and not a bathing suit.

Tony grinned devilishly. "It's January. My swimsuit is underneath. It's a bright red Speedo, in case you're interested."

"Jesus," Chris breathed, putting the car in gear.

"Sorry, dude." Tony tossed his head airily. "I don't do grandpa trunks."

Chris refused to picture him in either. They always left separately for their secret meetings. This was the first time he'd driven Tony anywhere. Simply being in the front seat together added weight and warmth to his groin.

Some hint of his foreboding must have shown in his face.

"I didn't put Evina up to recruiting you as my ride," Tony said.

"I didn't think you had." Chris touched his leg briefly. "Half the time you're more careful than I am."

"FYI, I'd like to be kissing you right now."

Chris laughed, his cock twitching dangerously. "Me too," he admitted.

Tony surveyed the car, which for some reason seemed to please him. Probably the vehicle being Chris's was enough to cause the reaction. They both liked being around each other's stuff.

"What happened to your brother's car?" Chris asked.

"A vampire ran into it," Tony said gleefully.

"A vampire?"

"Uh-huh. We finally closed this re-homicide Carmine caught lead on. He and I chased the murderer six miles along River Drive and into an alley. Rick blocked the end with his Buick, exactly as we'd arranged. The timing was perfect until the vampire decided he'd try to blur through the vehicle. Those bloodsuckers are dense . . . in more ways than one. I guess he didn't realize Rick's car was solid Detroit steel, not some lightweight goblin composite."

"Why didn't he leap over the car?"

"Because we'd exhausted him. He couldn't do that semi-flying thing vampires like. Fortunately, the collision stunned Pointy Tooth. Carmine and I were able to cuff him before he recovered."

Chris tried not to show how much this story alarmed him. "Was your brother okay?"

"Oh yeah." Tony beat a drum riff on the sloping dash, still charged up by the incident. "Pissed off about his car, though. The whole front was crumpled. It looked like a tin can ran into a deer. And he temporarily broke his nose when the air bags went off."

"Does this kind of thing happen often?

His voice wasn't as casual as he meant it to be. Tony stretched his arm along the top of the bucket seats. "Don't go protective on me, Savoy. I'm a big tough werecop, remember?"

"I'm not allowed to worry?"

"I'm assuming you'd rather I didn't worry about you. Because *you* don't do anything all day except pull kittens out of trees."

Chris didn't want to smile, but he did.

Tender then, Tony stroked a lock of hair behind Chris's ear, stirring a pleasant small shiver. "I'm not the only adrenaline junkie in this car."

Chris glanced at him, suddenly wanting him so intensely he couldn't imagine how he'd survive the party. "We really fit," he observed, the wonder of it hitting him.

"I'll say," Tony agreed with a naughty leer.

The leer was all it took. Chris's cock overrode his control and jolted out full length.

Tony knew. Tony always knew things like that. "Pit stop?" he suggested with a throaty laugh.

"Where?" Chris asked through gritted teeth.

"As it happens, I know the perfect spot."

He directed Chris downtown to an automated carwash housed in the base of a tall building. The sign above the square steel door said "Pointy Tooth Carwash Emporium." The sign to its right said "Closed."

"I thought you were kidding," Chris said as he turned down the concrete ramp. "The vampire's name really was Pointy Tooth?"

"It was, and since he's currently in a cell, I don't think he'll be disturbing us."

Tony hopped out of the Explorer. Despite the place seeming shut, the access door wasn't locked. Tony needed a single thrust to shove the corrugated metal high enough to clear the SUV. He waved Chris forward like a traffic cop, though Chris couldn't recall seeing one with the wolf's lascivious expression.

Chris drove in and Tony rolled the door down again. For a moment, until Tony found the switch, the business was completely dark. Once the lights were on, their buzzing illumination revealed a washing tunnel and conveyor, both so grimy Chris had to wonder how cars got clean. The giant soaping brushes were black and red—vampire appropriate colors, he supposed.

The booth where drivers paid the attendant was empty. Tony poked his head in, then got back in the car, grinning.

Distracted by their surroundings, Chris craned to look at the flickering lights. "Why do those bulbs look strange?"

"They're EBUs," Tony said. "Everything But Ultraviolent. They don't singe vampires when they're indoors. According to the info we dug up, this place was mainly a cover for money laundering. I'm not sure the equipment works."

"I'm sure the equipment works," Chris quipped.

Tony glanced at his suspiciously bulging crotch. "This is okay then? I know it isn't romantic."

Chris's smile broadened. "You're all the romance I need, Lupone."

"Bullshitter," Tony said.

Chris kissed him like they'd both been wanting.

Tony let out a moan as their tongues slid together and their cheeks applied suction. Possibly too eager to get this going, Chris opened Tony's jeans and slid one hand inside. He was indeed wearing Speedos. His cock stretched them to capacity—no surprise, considering how hard and thick he was. Chris ran his fingers down the underside of his shaft, savoring its melting smoothness and its high-pressure veins. He bent his thumb over Tony's slit and discovered pre-cum beading. That was an invitation he wouldn't dream of declining. The silky wetness simply had to be rubbed around.

Still kissing him, Tony squirmed as his glans was circled, then closed his hand over Chris's trouser bulge. He gripped Chris's package tight, the firm massage sending intense sensations zooming through Chris's nerves.

"Fuck," he breathed, suddenly wanting more than a mutual hand-job.

"Maybe we could put the seats down and move this into the back."

Tony had switched to sucking Chris's neck. His canine teeth were down, giving the love bite an extra charge. He pulled back reluctantly, his green eyes glowing like Christmas lights. "How fast can you convert the seats?"

"Very fast," Chris promised.

Tony let go of him.

They were shifters. They could strip off full riot gear in under ten seconds. Chris had the back seats flat in three. Because the carwash's floor was covered in who-knew-what, Tony tossed his clothes into the makeshift bed ahead of him. Gloriously naked and arousingly erect, he made a hurry-up gesture.

"Time's a-wasting," he said to Chris, flashing sharp teeth at him.

"I need to stare a sec," he explained, "out of respect for your hotness."

Despite the words, he undressed nearly as swiftly.

"Not on the floor," Tony reminded, extending his hands to take Chris's clothes.

Stripped to his skin and too wound up to be self-conscious, Chris swung into the SUV. The car was no compact, but even seated on his heels, the roof was close to his head. Tony was hardly smaller. Going at it the way Chris craved would be interesting.

"Yummy," Tony said, running his hands over Chris's chest and shoulders. He squeezed Chris's biceps as if testing how strong they were. "I'm glad you wanted to be naked too."

"I always want to be naked when you're around."

Tony laughed. "You say the nicest things."

"I don't want to be nice," he warned, a growl sneaking into it.

"Really?" Tony said archly. "I guess you'll be needing this."

Not a bit afraid, he grabbed his discarded jeans, digging out a single-size applicator of what Chris assumed was lubricant.

"Okay, sometimes you're so prepared it's scary."

"I always want to be prepared for you." Tony's breathlessness sent a different message than his sassy tone. "I should warn you there's only one. You'll have to make it count."

Chris narrowed his eyes, fully intending to. "What if I want to fuck you hard? What if I want to push you around a bit?"

Tony's pupils expanded. "I'd say bring it on, tiger."

Tony had a way of being hot and funny at the same time.

"You'll want to be on your front," Chris said.

"Will I?" Tony asked without moving.

Grappling in a small space with a not-small guy like Tony was no cakewalk. Add to that the wolf resisting Chris's attempt to flip him over, and there was some cursing and bonked elbows before he accomplished it. By the time he planted his knee conqueror-style in the small of Tony's back, Chris's blood was extremely up.

This, of course, was what Tony intended.

"You're so mean," the wolf said in falsetto. "I don't want that big cock of yours ravishing me!"

God, it was weird that Chris found this arousing. His cock was hard enough to pound nails, so hot it should have been glowing. Tony squirmed, his ass going up and down. Chris pushed his shin between its cheeks.

"Be still," he commanded.

The growl the order came out on was genuine. Tony shivered, then filled his lungs with air. Chris just knew he was planning to make another joke. Rather than let him, he dropped a stinging smack onto Tony's right buttock. Tony sucked in a breath of shock, but Chris had no pity. Tony had once smacked him playfully. Ever since Chris had fantasized about returning the favor with interest. He rubbed the hot spot—caressed it, really—and brought his palm down again.

Tony stopped trying to speak. His breathing was deep and ragged. Unable to deny he liked the sound, Chris straddled his hips and sat. Muscle by muscle, he drew his touch down Tony's satiny back. Every one of his fingertips registered Tony's heart pounding. When he reached Tony's ass, its muscles were quivering.

The red mark he'd left was fading. Shifters rarely retained bruises. Chris's fingers curled. He wanted to hit the place again and wasn't sure he should. He'd been aggressive with partners, but he'd never seriously spanked one.

Some fantasies were safer not lived out.

"Go ahead," Tony whispered. "You know you won't hurt me."

The wolf's head had twisted around to look back at Chris, his green gaze shooting laserlike at him. He'd bent his arms so that his hands were level with his shoulders. They weren't relaxed. His fingers had sprouted claws. They punctured the plastic panels that formed a new floor above the seats. Despite Chris's weight bearing down on him, Tony's pelvis was slightly lifted. He seemed not to want pressure there, as if maybe he'd come too quickly if he got it.

Was it possible Tony had been thinking about this too?

"Can't you see I'm excited?" Tony's voice was low and rough. "I'm dripping a fucking oil slick here."

With perfect timing, Chris's sharp ears heard a droplet hit. The sound acted like a spark running up a fuse. Chris took a second to shiver before raining a storm of quick sharp smacks around Tony's ass. He kept the onslaught going for half a minute, his palm in love with Tony's resilience. When he stopped, his rear was pink all over. The blows had been forceful enough for that.

Fascinated by the effect, Chris stroked Tony's simmering glutes the same as he had after his initial strike. He hoped the spanking had felt good, that it increased Tony's awareness of this part of his body. Seeing the new marks were also fading, Chris made dents in them with his fingertips.

"God," Tony moaned, his spine twisting.

The motion sure looked like pleasure. Chris had shifted back to hit him from a better angle, and Tony's butt had lifted to meet the blows. Wanting to be sure he'd enjoyed them, Chris slipped one hand around Tony's hipbone and under him. His erection was thick and shuddering, fighting gravity with its slant. Chris ringed it snugly with thumb and fingers, pulling along its shaft to the knob.

"Shit," Tony hissed. "You're going to bring me off."

Chris wasn't ready to do that, so he released his cock. Tony wasn't looking at him anymore. Head bowed forward on his neck, he rolled his brow in small sideways motions on the floor. The pose was like the definition of surrender. Chris squeezed Tony's shoulders before drawing his hold down his sides.

The touch was enough to make the wolf shudder.

"Please—" Tony began.

"Shh," Chris cut him off firmly. He was pretty certain they both wanted him in charge. He used the knuckles and thumb of one hand to spread the cleft of Tony's clenched cheeks apart, exposing the tight creases of his anus. With his other hand he snapped the ampoule of oil, making sure the silky fluid ran to the right target.

He didn't tell Tony to relax. That seemed too soft an instruction for their current activities.

"You *will* take me," he predicted. "You can't stop me from prepping you."

His thumbs caught the lube that threatened to run astray. He pushed it over Tony's closed entrance, rubbing back and forth, letting Tony enjoy the friction on that nerve-laden area.

The wolf choked a little noise, hips shoving helplessly back toward him.

Chris decided he was ready. He pushed both thumbs inward at the same time.

Tony arched, the sound he made a sexy cross between a snarl and a groan. Chris worked his bent thumbs into and around the first stretch of his passage.

"Deeper," Tony begged.

"I don't think so," Chris growled, pulling his touch away. Swinging off him altogether, he moved on his hands and knees toward the front of the Explorer.

"Where are you going?" Tony asked.

"Wait," Chris ordered.

He kept his own supplies in the glove compartment. One in particular would prevent their scents from combining quite so much. The *Tiger!* brand condom he pulled out wasn't the most expensive the company made. Under the circumstances, Chris didn't need fancy spells to prevent conception. Ribbing was nice, though, and extra-thin latex. Hopefully, Tony would agree.

Tony had shifted partly onto his side to watch him roll the rubber on.

Chris's view of Tony's cock tantalized. The wolf was unmistakably revved up, his erection actually dark against his tanned abdomen. His balls had pulled up a little, though they still lolled between his thighs.

"I didn't tell you to move," Chris said.

Tony's eyes flared brighter. Normally, he'd have made a wiseass remark but not this time. He wriggled back onto his front instead.

His docility was exciting. Chris's heart sped up as he moved to him. Since they were there, waiting, he struck Tony's right cheek and then his left.

"Bend your legs up, wolf," he said.

Tony did. The change in position lifted his ass toward Chris. Chris bent his body around him, chest to back, pelvis to rear, hands flattened outside Tony's so he was caged. Tony's ass was hotter than normal as it cushioned his erection. The moment felt different, like they were exploring new territory. Liking that whether he should or not, Chris dragged his lengthened teeth across Tony's nape.

Tony groaned, the tease gunning his motor.

"You're mine," Chris whispered. "I won't let you get away."

Tony began to answer, but when Chris's teeth secured a stretch of skin and muscle, all he could do was moan. Chris moved one hand to his own penis, adjusting its angle to go in.

Once he was positioned, Tony's hip supplied the ideal handhold. Though he thrust with some force, he didn't meet resistance.

"God," Tony groaned once he was in all the way. His body writhed around Chris's cock in delicious slow motion. "I don't think I can breathe."

He could pant, so that wasn't a problem.

Chris tightened his grip on Tony's nape and started pounding him.

Tony cried out with pleasure. "Chris. God." His hips snapped up like they were on a hinge, allowing Chris to go deeper. "Yes. *Yes.*"

He sounded like the train that was hurtling him toward orgasm was an express. Chris shifted angles so as not to hit his prostate dead on.

"Fuck," Tony said.

Chris growled against his neck, reminding him who was boss. His assertiveness didn't anger the younger man. Tony panted harder, driving Chris's excitement to the brink. *To hell with waiting,* he thought. He'd drive them both over.

Out of nowhere, the SUV began moving.

"What the—?" Chris rose from Tony's neck to look around. Needles of hot spray were pelting the car windows. The carwash conveyor had gotten a grip on them.

"Don't stop," Tony pleaded, reaching back for his hip. "I . . . fuck . . . I tried to start the equipment when we came in. I assumed it didn't work. The computer . . . must have been booting up."

Chris didn't sense anyone outside, though the rumble of the track and the clouds of steam could have been masking them.

"There's no one," Tony said. "I swear. God, get your teeth on my neck and finish me."

Chris's adrenaline had shot into its red zone. His skin was ablaze, his fight response searching for a target. Was Tony right? Did he dare continue? His tiger made up his mind for him. It snapped him forward, clamping his jaw around Tony's nape. The possessive gesture felt so good he groaned. He drew his hips back, reveling in Tony's whine of longing . . .

Then he plunged back to screwing him like a maniac.

He should have come in seconds. His arousal and intensity of sensation were high enough. Possibly his recent stress reaction was getting in the way.

"Yes," Tony moaned. "Right there. Right *there.*"

Chris was pounding his prostate again. He hadn't intended to, but he didn't stop. He wrapped his fist around Tony's cock and pumped, figuring one of them ought to come at least. Tony let out an animal sound. The Explorer began to shudder, soapy brushes beating them from either side. Chris gasped. He was almost there. The vibrations ran up his knees and into his aching balls. Tony slammed back on him and writhed.

Christ, Chris thought, about to lose his mind. Tony groaned, his hand suddenly wrapping Chris's. He was tightening the tiger's hold on his cock, forcing it to rub the sensitive spot on its base harder. Chris felt the wolf's bulbus gland expanding. That final turn-on shattered his barriers.

He came like he meant to drown the world.

Tony went at the same time, shooting heat and wetness over their joined fingers. The roar that filled Chris's ears wasn't all from the carwash.

It echoed in his head for a while.

"Whew," Tony said, pulling carefully off of him.

Chris dropped beside him, working the condom off before shifting onto his back. His body shook from the strong climax, the sweat he was covered with beginning to cool his skin. Sanity prodded him as it did. How had this happened? They were on their way to a party—with his clan and Tony's pack. This "pit stop" was supposed to have been quick and straightforward.

"I should run myself through the carwash," he said, only half kidding.

Tony sat up. "Hold on. I have something to help with that."

He fished two towelette packets from his apparently bottomless jeans pockets.

Chris read the item he'd been handed. "'Professor Spock's Clean & Sweet Scent-Cancelling Demon Wipes.'"

"The storeowner swears they work," Tony said.

"Where do you find this stuff?"

"In places you dare not go, grasshopper."

Chris suspected that was true. He opened his towelette, sniffed . . . and smelled nothing. "They're spelled."

"That is correct. And since they work on stinky demons, de-scenting us should be no problem."

Chris unfolded the surprisingly generous towelette and began cleaning off his skin. Outside, the SUV had reached the end of the wash and was being dried by big air blowers. "I'm sorry you have to think this way for my sake."

"I don't hate it," Tony said. "It's kind of like being a spy."

Not hating it wasn't the same as being glad.

"I'm okay with it," Tony said. "Really. You make it worth my while." He stretched his arms in front of himself, wove his fingers together, and cracked his vertebrae. "You're fun when you're bossy."

"You like that, huh."

"I cannot deny I do."

"My dominant side makes me nervous sometimes," Chris confessed.

"I know." Tony's smile warmed his soft green eyes. "I'm glad you feel safe letting it out with me."

Was that why Chris did it, rather than because Tony was naturally submissive and called it out in him? The question made him uneasy. He couldn't answer it.

Tony was sorting through the pile of tossed off clothes for the ones that belonged to him. Despite his preoccupation, he caught Chris's expression.

"Oh God," he said. "Please stop that."

"Stop what?"

"Second-guessing everything we do together. I'm happy, Chris. This—" he gestured from Chris's heart to his own "—is working out for me."

If that was true, Chris was grateful. Regrettably, he couldn't help thinking Tony was painting his emotions a tad too rosy.

CHAPTER TEN

THE engagement party was in full swing by the time the private elevator let them out at Cass's super-luxe penthouse. The store her home was perched on took up a city block—plenty of room to show off what being a Maycee meant. Tony watched Chris gape at the marble-clad outer hall without letting on he'd noticed. They heard people laughing before the apartment door opened.

Nate stuck his head out of it. "What held up the two of you?"

"Traffic," Tony singsonged, giving Nate's freshly shaven cheek a gay little pat.

"Uh-huh," Nate said with both eyebrows up. Tony wasn't normally this fey. Nate and Chris exchanged soberer hetero greetings. Tony didn't tease, because he had his I-barely-know-this-tiger disguise on.

"The bartender sucks," Nate informed the cat. "Once you've had your fill of socializing, I'm sure no one would complain if you stepped in."

Tony opened his mouth to say, *Oh yeah, Chris's mango martinis are dee-licious.* He shut his jaw just in time. That was not an approved comment. At least, he didn't think it was. Chris had tended bar at Nate and Evina's engagement. If Nate remembered, wasn't Tony allowed to?

Maybe Chris's second-guessing had rubbed off on him. Having to parse every word he said for the rest of the evening suddenly seemed a drag. Also, was a party really a party if you couldn't share a single dance with your true new love?

Tony frowned at himself. He'd just had amazing sex, the sort that realigned a person's atoms and left their spine tingly. He was fine with his and Chris's arrangement. No way was he going to let a moment's doubt ruin his stellar mood.

"I'm hopping in the pool," he announced to Nate as if Chris's plans were irrelevant. "Where can I change that won't shock anyone?"

Nate laughed. "Guest bedrooms are that way. Just knock if the door is closed."

Tony sashayed off, then wondered if he should have thanked Chris for driving him. Oh screw it. Nate wasn't going to think about it one way or another. *You're in a stellar mood*, he reminded.

Selectively lying about his personal life didn't make it less awesome.

~

The wolves had a history of rooftop parties. This one at Cass's place lived up to tradition. Stripped to his red swimsuit, Tony knew he looked fine strolling onto the big terrace. He was tall but graceful, muscular but not musclebound. The air felt good on his exposed skin. The warming spell was topnotch, soft and balmy without crossing over to sweltering.

Tony wondered if Cass's father had spun it. Tony had learned from Rick that the pureblood was really juiced. If he were the enchantment's author, it might explain why the flowerbeds were blooming in midwinter.

Since he didn't want to think about Roald or their weird first meeting, he waved at the kids splashing in the pool. Maria's husband Johnny manned the barbecue, smoke from the roasting meat wafting on the breeze like incense.

Tony wasn't the only guest inhaling.

"Hel-lo, handsome," said Evina's free-spirited friend Freda. The paramedic covered her mouth when Tony turned around. "Oh, it's you. Sorry."

"Don't be sorry," he teased. "Everybody likes compliments."

She laughed good-naturedly. "Dance with me later?"

"Absolutely," he promised.

Mood buoyed, he grabbed a sunrise-orange drink from a tray—one of Chris's specials, he realized as soon as he sipped it. He must have replaced the bartender already. Determinedly avoiding looking around for him, Tony worked his way between groups of partiers toward the jazz quartet at the roof's far-end. Some of the guests looked ritzy, but most were casual. His parents were close-dancing in front of the band's low stage, still feeling the afterglow from their cruise on the submarine. Tony kissed his mother's cheek, but didn't interrupt.

"Tony," she exclaimed, catching sight of him. "You're nearly naked!"

His father whispered something in her ear and paddled her bottom. Because it was probably along the lines of *Leave the boy alone*, Tony grinned at the interplay.

The dragons liked music, and they weren't far away. They'd drawn together beneath a cluster of young maples and were peeking curiously around at everything. They'd grown fast in the last few months, closer to the size of St. Bernards now and not housecats. Since everyone trusted Tony to babysit, the trio knew him well. Auric trilled when he spotted him, his greeting joined a moment later by Scarlet and Verdi's.

Once he was close enough, they all jostled up to him.

"Hey, brats," Tony said, giving them the side slaps they liked.

Verdi burst out with a string of dragon chatter, complete with expressive wing gestures. Tony didn't know what it meant but found it amusing.

"You're totally Italian," he told the dragon, who didn't disagree. He went to his knees to stroke Verdi's muzzle with both hands. It was impossible not to smile at him. The dragons had an amazing gift for conveying affection with their eyes. Assuming Scarlet's squawk meant *me too*, he gave her a share of the petting.

A shadow came up behind him. Somewhat to his surprise, Tony recognized its shape and scent.

"They really like you," Liam said.

Tony looked up at him. The tiger's manner was tentative—and also a smidge sulky, like he wondered why Tony deserved the favor of these rare creatures. Tony's wolf wanted him on his feet to meet the potential threat, but Tony overruled its impulse. Liam was huge and a pain in the butt, but when you got down to it, he was just a confused kid. As a fellow omega, Tony understood his need for approval. Liam wanted to do what he thought would earn it, but couldn't always puzzle out what that was. It took courage for a low-ranked shifter to decide to be his own damn self and to hell with his clan's opinions.

Tony couldn't swear he'd done that a hundred percent himself.

"They're used to me," he said, maintaining a pleasant expression. "I dragon-sit sometimes."

"The red one just finished your martini."

"Crap." When he spun around to Scarlet, she blinked at him innocently. Not fooled, he took her pretty muzzle between his hands. "Drinks aren't for dragons, you little lush."

"There were only a few sips left," Liam assured him. He shifted his weight on his giant feet. "Could you . . . show me how to pet them?"

That was a concession. A guy like Liam preferred to pretend wolves—especially gay wolves—couldn't school tigers in anything.

"Sure," Tony said, working to keep his thoughts from showing. "Come down to their level and let them sniff at you."

Liam dropped to the grass a bit awkwardly. The dragons were friendly, and there wasn't much danger, certainly not with Tony to smooth the way. He'd observed the brood had good instincts about people, seeming to know their moods and intentions by reading their energy.

"Their sides are the safest place to stroke them," Tony said. "Use your palm and go head to tail, in the direction of their scales. You can use some pressure. They're too heavy and well balanced to push over."

Liam tried the technique on Verdi, who was closest and seemed the most settled. The biggest of the dragons stood patiently, gazing past Liam in apparent fascination with the bass player. The tip of his sinuous tail swished in time to the rhythm.

"He's warm," Liam said.

"They use their magic for heat, I think. They enjoy sunning, too, like cold-blooded reptiles do."

Liam accidentally bumped Verdi's wing, which caused the dragon to twitch the appendage into a tighter fold.

"They're protective of their wings," the big cat observed.

"Yes," Tony said, "and you should definitely avoid their dorsal spikes. The bigger the dragons grow, the sharper those become. You could slice a finger off on one."

Verdi made a grumbling noise in his throat.

"Just making an observation," Tony said. "I didn't say you'd do it on purpose."

Liam laughed, then looked surprised he had. "Do they understand human speech?"

Tony could not resist this opening. "They're a bit like cats. They understand instructions when they want to."

Liam smiled a little and looked down. "About before. I'm . . . sorry I gave you a hard time."

That was a nice vague statement, but Tony didn't press for more. "You're not the first to give me grief, and I doubt you'll be the last. I appreciate the apology, though. Nate and Evina are both my friends. I'd like us to get along."

Some reaction tightened Liam's face. Had Tony said the wrong thing? He must have. Liam's expression was suddenly closed down.

Tony pushed to his feet, abruptly wishing he were wearing more clothes. His mom was right. He was way too naked for some people. Liam could barely look at him. "I'm going to hit the pool. Why don't you hang with these guys a bit?"

Liam's gaze jerked to his. "They won't mind being left with me?"

"Nah. As long as you're not pushy, they like company."

"Okay," Liam said. "I'll keep an eye on them."

He seemed alarmingly serious. "Uh," Tony said. "If they're naughty or whatever, don't try to control them. They're powerful, and that's better left to Rick and Cass. Or Cass's father. He used to train dragons."

"Sure," Liam said. "Anything goes wrong, I'll find one of them."

~

Chris didn't mind playing bartender. He could people watch, and it supplied a polite excuse for not dancing with every woman who hoped to seduce him. Being a fireman and not plug ugly, he got plenty of offers. Ironically, the other tigers thought he liked mixing drinks because it made him a babe magnet.

Their misconception aside, he was so used to the tasks required he could do them on autopilot. He blended daiquiris while watching Tony introduce Liam to the dragons. Chris should have thought of that as a way to win over the grumpy cat. Who wouldn't want to make friends with magical creatures? But maybe it was better to let Tony be himself. The wolf was good with people when they gave him a chance.

"That's a true Mona Lisa smile," observed a familiar voice.

Startled, Chris stopped the blender's whir. One of the hosts from *As Luck Would Have It* had come over. His multiple viewings of their dragon special allowed him to identify her as Jin Levine. The interviewer's half elf genes made her extra pretty, though her human ones probably weren't chopped liver. Her hair and eyes were gold, her flawless skin kissed by the same 24-karat tone. Her lashes had to be false. Otherwise, they couldn't have been sooty.

"Daiquiri?" he offered. "I've made a fresh batch."

"I'd rather have your special, the mango martinis I've heard so much about."

She practically purred the words. Chris suspected she could turn reading a grocery list into a flirtation.

"Coming up," he said with a strictly professional smile.

Jin wasn't discouraged. She was a professional herself. Bending one sleek golden arm, she leaned on the bar top. If he'd been a different sort of man, he'd have admired the way she filled out her bikini. "You seem familiar. Have I seen you somewhere?"

"I'm a fireman," he said. "Sometimes we get caught on camera."

"No." Jin tapped her lips, not cooing over the fact that he battled fires. "It's something else. It'll come to me. I've got a memory like an elephant."

Chris fought a sudden chill. Unless she'd been a news junkie as a child, she was too young to remember his family tragedy.

"There isn't anything else," he said. "I'm a simple guy."

When Jin smiled, her mouth curved deeper on one side. The expression made her look unexpectedly likeable. "If there's one thing I've learned in life, it's that hardly anyone is simple."

A stir of sound and movement saved Chris from having to respond. Whatever the disturbance was it had started by the pool. A reporter down to her toes, Jin used her high-heeled sandals to peer over the party crowd.

"Oh boy," she said as if she didn't know whether to be worried or excited. "Hold onto your swizzle sticks. We've got faeries incoming."

The faeries' entrance *was* a sort of invasion. Nine purebloods in silk robes filed out through the window doors that connected the penthouse to the pool deck. Chris had never seen so many high fae in person in one place. Even from where he stood, their combined magic closed his throat. These were the beings who'd created Resurrection—possibly the actual ones, given their race's longevity. As amazing as it was to be a shifter or an elf, compared to the fae, their power was a small drop in a big bucket.

"Naughty, naughty," Jin murmured. "Cass didn't invite you to this party."

Her tone was humorous, her pretty face less so.

Feeling a sudden need to have free hands, Chris put down his drink mixing tools. "Why do you think they're here?"

"For them, I imagine." Thoroughly somber now, she tilted her head toward the young dragons.

That wasn't right. Tony's pack had risked their lives to protect the brood. No snooty faerie cabal ought to be able to sweep in and threaten them. Chris stepped out from behind the bar, his tiger's energy swelling inside him.

"Hey," Jin said, laying a cautionary hand on his arm. "Don't go all feral. I didn't say I thought the fae meant them harm."

"I need to get closer." His voice wasn't normal. His tiger had roughened it. He wasn't sure he should trust his urge to let it out . . . or if he could resist it. Obviously, he'd watched that dragon special too many times. He'd developed a sense of ownership. Knowing this was inappropriate didn't seem to matter. "Your friend Cass doesn't have to face them alone."

"She's not," Jin said, patting him. "Every wolf in this place just went to DEFCON-1, besides which Cass can handle more than people think. Look, the red dragon just flew over to help her confront them. This is politics, right here. Let the girls do their Madeleine Albright thing."

Jin seemed to know what she was talking about.

"I still want to get closer," he said gruffly. "I can't hear what they're saying from this distance."

Jin flashed a brilliant grin. "Eavesdropping is a goal I can get behind."

They shouldered through the crowd until they reached the concrete paving around the pool. Jin was right about the wolves. They'd drawn closer to the line of faeries and then fanned out, treating the purebloods as a threat that needed containing. Tony seemed to have exited the water hastily, his gorgeous underdressed body dripping from head to toe. Because those droplets were distracting, Chris yanked his gaze away. Cass and the red dragon stood nearer to the faeries than anyone. Rick's fiancée looked calm. To the sensitive eye, however, she vibrated with tension.

Rick was vibrating too . . . with watchfulness. Though he allowed his mate to face down the party crashers, only a fool would imagine he wasn't ready to defend her.

Jin crouched down by the pool coping. "Hey, kids," she murmured to the children still in the water. "Why don't you swim this way and wait?"

They were shifter kids and aware that something was happening. Without complaint, they followed her suggestion. Chris spine snapped more alert. One of the fae was speaking.

"I am Dubh," he said. "Head of the Dragon Guild."

Chris wasn't familiar with the group. Maybe the guild was big in Faerie, where little things like extinctions weren't taken seriously. He'd have thought a dragon guild protected dragons, but to go by Cass's stiff reaction, the affiliation wasn't necessarily good news.

"I am Cass," she replied. "Keeper of the Sevryn Clutch."

She inclined her head regally, more like the Snow Queen than Snow White.

Admiration sparked in him. Cass was a single half fae against nine purebloods, but she wasn't giving them an inch. Chris abruptly understood how she'd won Tony over, and why he thought his brother was lucky. The girl dragon cawed in support of her mistress, causing the Guild head to look down at the beast and smile.

The condescension in his expression set Chris's tiger teeth on edge.

"Before you put you foot in it," Cass said, "if you've come to take these dragons back to Faerie, you'll find that plan is a non-starter."

The pureblood seemed startled by her guess. "We're the Dragon Guild."

"And I'm a free citizen of Resurrection. As are my brood. The mayor himself put them on the city rolls."

Chris concluded this information was a stumper. The Guild head blinked like a man who'd lost a staring contest but wasn't ready to cede the war. "The brood will be safer in Faerie, under our protection."

"Hardly," Cass snorted. "Faerie was so unsafe, my father—your guild member—felt compelled to conceal them here. During that time, the worst threat they faced came from *your* country, from a pair of fae who cracked your Guild's secrets. The dragons' enemies had one of your magic swords. I'd say your protection hasn't been exemplary."

This reminder didn't sit well with the proud pureblood. "Are you certain you'd have done better?"

"Look around you," Cass said. "Most of these folks would lay down their lives for this brood. They protect everyone they care about—and perfect strangers too. They don't need magical swords or secret blood oaths to goose them to it. Their hearts guide them, and their sense of justice. Resurrection is so much more than a fae creation. It belongs to its people. The Sevryn clutch is going to grow up here. They're lucky this is their home."

Chris realized she'd included his tigers in the protectors she mentioned. His clan members had drawn close to the standoff too. Whatever their differences with the wolves or amongst themselves, they set them aside to stand up for these special scaly residents.

Touched and proud, a sudden burning warmed Chris's eyes.

"Do you even know what you're doing?" the Guild head demanded. "Dragons are more complicated than house cats!"

Cass was prepared for this. "We've been working with a local foundation, the Society for the Protection of Rare Creatures." She paused to smile slyly. "I hear they have a board position open. I'm sure they'd be honored if one of your members volunteered to fill it."

That she was offering him a carrot she didn't try to hide. The Guild head glanced down at the girl dragon, who tilted her head at him. Her wings were slightly lifted, their rich red color so intense, so gorgeous it was like she was showing off.

In spite of everything, the Guild head's expression softened. "They do look healthy," he admitted. "And they're certainly socialized."

The girl dragon butted his hand and crooned a sound at him.

"Fine," he conceded, obeying her demand that he pet her head. "The Guild accepts your offer, but we'll want two board seats instead of one."

"I expect they'll make room for you," Cass said.

Her tone was dry. Grimacing, the Guild head's focus shifted to the one pureblood at the party who wasn't standing in his duck line. Chris hadn't noticed the man before. His coloring was very like Cass's—a blood relation, Chris assumed. The faerie said nothing in response to the Guild head's attention, his expression as dispassionate as Rick's fiancée's.

The Guild head returned his gaze to Cass.

"You certainly are Roald's child," he said. "He was stubborn at your age too."

Chris had a feeling that was a long time ago.

"I don't believe he's outgrown it," his daughter said.

"Hmph." The Guild head peered superciliously down his nose. "I suppose you're hoping we'll award Ceallach's protector sword to him."

"That's your business."

"Your father has new commitments. He's no longer an appropriate choice. Also, you'll need two more protectors, since you have three dragons."

The Guild head obviously enjoyed dropping what seemed to be a small bombshell. Cass shut her gaping mouth and composed herself.

"Well," she said. "I trust the Guild will select candidates both the brood and I find acceptable."

This seemed to be a smart answer. Cass's father looked at his feet and smiled.

"Keeper," said the Guild head, offering her a curt bow.

"Guild head," Cass said in the same crisp tone.

Chris guessed the negotiations were over. The Guild head turned on his heel, stalking back toward the penthouse with his entourage trailing behind him.

He didn't notice the music had fallen silent until it started up. Conversations resumed, the party sounding like one again. Tony's brother moved to his future wife and hugged her. Love lit more than their faces as they held each other.

The moment seemed too private to stare at. Chris turned away, oddly uneasy. Part of him was waiting for another shoe to drop.

"Look!" cried one of the kids who was hanging on the pool edge. "The dragons are flying!"

They were—and they weren't alone. A huge gray gargoyle, as big as a delivery van, circled the night sky above the penthouse. Tony had mentioned a gargoyle with nesting rights to his brownstone's roof. Since no one seemed surprised to see this one, Chris assumed it was him. Looking much smaller by comparison, the gold and green dragons soared in the behemoth's wake. The girl dragon cawed, took a running start on the pavers, and flapped up to join them.

She and her siblings weren't flying neophytes. Incredibly swift and agile, they kept up with the gargoyle despite the difference in their wingspans. Chris's breath caught as the brood began doing loop-de-loops. They looked like leaves tumbling: green, gold, red—one after another in a synchronized aerial ballet.

How sad it would be to lose this wild beauty from the world! The fae who'd wanted to exploit these creatures to cause death were blind to their true value. The brood made everyone around them feel more alive.

The pain of his old loss stabbed his heart center. He'd have given quite a lot for his little brothers to see these amazing beings.

"They see," said a soft calm voice inches from his ear.

Chris jerked his head around. Jin stood beside him. She couldn't have spoken. The voice he'd heard was male.

"What?" she asked, her eyes widening.

Chris wagged his head. He must have imagined it.

~

Tony grinned as Grant led the dragons in their showoffy flight. What hams they were! Scarlet, in particular, was adept at waiting to pull a trick until the roof lights spotlighted her. The kids loved the spectacle—Tony too, of course. His heart leaped with excitement each time the trio tumbled and recovered.

He was glad he hadn't missed out on seeing this wild beauty. The fae who'd wanted to use the dragons for destruction had been stupid. They had so much more value than mere reservoirs of power. Cass was right about them belonging here. Resurrectioners would protect the brood—including him, proudly.

"The Guild likes to think they control Destiny," Cass's father said.

Tony jerked. He hadn't noticed Roald come up to him. The fae was unnervingly silent, not to mention unnervingly beautiful. His profile was a statue's, his slender figure somehow epitomizing grace *and* masculinity. Luckily, the pureblood's glamour was locked up tight. Tony could do without the Viagra-like effect of his faerie dust.

"Aren't you still a member of the Guild?" he asked the disquieting quiet man.

Roald smiled faintly. "I suppose I am. Perhaps I support their ends without them knowing it."

Tony shouldn't have looked straight at him. Roald's soft blue eyes dizzied him. The pureblood seemed to be examining something *inside* Tony. No wolf would have stared like that, not without intending to challenge him.

"Uh," Tony said awkwardly. "Can I get you something, sir? Maybe a burger or a drink?"

"I am well," Roald declined. "This won't be painless. Please remember you chose this the moment you first touched your brother's gauntlet and it shocked you."

"Huh?" Tony said. He remembered being zapped by Rick's brass knuckles, but not that he'd chosen anything. Mostly, he remembered being annoyed by yet more proof that Rick was the special one.

He wasn't going to get an explanation. The cryptic faerie had walked away.

Roald stopped at one of the roof's lushly green areas of grass. Mystified, Tony watched him crouch down and pat the turf like it was an animal. Then he straightened and stepped onto it. Three small cypresses grew in pots nearby. If he'd believed Cass's father was a drama hound, he'd have said the trees made a good backdrop.

"Excuse me," Roald said. "Could I have everyone's attention?"

He didn't raise his voice, nor was he someone anyone answered to. All the same, every person there stopped what they were doing and turned to him.

"What is it, Dad?" Cass asked.

He smiled with such tenderness Tony remembered faeries could be fathers too.

"Do you trust me, daughter?" he asked.

"Of course I do."

"Do you trust those men from the Dragon Guild?"

"Sort of?" she said, making it a question.

Her father smiled. "I think you and the dragons deserve better than 'sort of.' I propose that here and now, with your friends and allies to bear witness, we settle the matter of who shall carry Ceallach's sword for you."

"Can you do that, sir?" Rick asked, his arm around Cass's shoulder. Tony knew his brother well. He could tell Rick was a teensy bit wary.

"Long ago," Roald said, "when the Sevryn clutch was given into my keeping, I was entrusted with the magic that calls new protectors. Rick, your gauntlet's previous owner, who died at Ceallach's hand, called you to the position. Fortunately, the ranks of those who guard may be swelled without souls passing."

"We are the guardians!" Tony's nephew Ethan burst out without warning. Puffing out his little chest, he used the growly voice he thought made him sound adult. "We protect the dragons! We defend the innocent!"

Oh Lord, Tony thought. The five-year-old was quoting *Mini-Dragons to the Rescue.*

Super-powerful he might be, but Roald hadn't anticipated this interruption. He made Tony warm to him, at least a little, by looking as if he were about to laugh.

"That is correct, young man," he said.

Truly excited now, Ethan started to roar some more. Maria caught him first and covered up his mouth.

"Um," Cass said, looking like she wanted to laugh as well. "I assume you have a candidate in mind."

"The candidate calls himself," Roald said. "But I believe the dragons and the gauntlet agree."

Hm, Tony thought. *I wonder who he means.*

Roald looked at him and grinned.

Tony admitted it: he should have seen that coming.

"Me?" he asked, gobsmacked.

"Oh yes!" Cass exclaimed, clapping her hands together. "Tony would be perfect."

This was flattering, but Tony . . . perfect? Tony a protector like his brother? He turned to Rick, who appeared as pleased as Cass.

"If it's what you want," he said. "I'm sure you'd be great at it."

"Do you wish this, wolf?" Cass's father asked formally.

Tony suspected this wasn't a time to hem or haw. Sensing something was happening that involved them, the dragons dropped in a nimble three-stage landing to the pool deck. Verdi wore his mischievous face, the one that signaled he was about to steal a person's only pair of dress shoes and fly away with them. Auric bumped his sister's side, and—as siblings do—she bumped him back harder. The dragons were miraculous but also a handful. Was Tony ready to help his brother and Cass shoulder the responsibility?

Of course I am, he thought. *I'm already doing it.*

Nothing could have stopped him from defending them with his life. Roald just wanted to know if he'd say a couple words to make it official.

"I do wish it," he answered the pureblood.

Somewhat prosaically, Roald pulled an object from his trouser pocket. Tony expected to see brass knuckles, but Roald was balancing a silvery-gold arm cuff on the flat of his palm. Tony assumed it was the same thingamabob he'd showed him at Jin Levine's estate, just in a different shape. Stretching six inches from rim to rim, the electrum was decorated with obscure chicken-scratchy glyphs.

"This is the protector's gauntlet," Roald said quietly, every eye and ear in his audience fixed on him. "It is the symbol of a guardian's oath and his aid in fulfilling it. Place your hands atop it and allow the power of the earth and sky to consecrate your intent."

Tony felt silly, but he laid his hands on top of the cuff. Roald held it steadily, as if his arm were stone and not flesh.

"Close your eyes," he said.

Tony closed them.

He wasn't sure how Roald made it happen, but the most profound silence he'd ever encountered wrapped him up in itself.

It was like the universe hadn't formed. No stars. No planets. Just a thick breath drawn in and held. Tony's brain was blank. To be honest, he wasn't sure he existed. A rich still blackness had swallowed him. Unable to do otherwise, he waited.

The tiniest prick of light sprang to life in the vacuum.

Tony wanted to squint but he had no eyes. The light was really there. No, it was *two* lights, and they were whizzing around each other like electrons. They seemed weirdly . . . happy. Did subatomic particles experience emotion?

"It is done," said Roald's voice.

Tony's awareness snapped back so precipitously he needed to take a step to catch his balance. Roald steadied him as his eyes opened. Tony had put both hands over one of Roald's, but somehow now he was covering two. He was also touching two arm cuffs. Roald had one in each palm.

Tony looked into Roald's dreamy eyes. Starlight seemed to ray out from his pupils. The faerie's aura was a live wire that stopped just short of shocking him.

"They are twinned," Roald said.

Was that supposed to be an explanation? Then again, why would he expect faerie magic to make sense?

Roald slid one of the electrum cuffs onto Tony's wrist. Feeling dazed, Tony stroked the metal. The fit was perfect, like it had been made for him. The silvery gold was warm, the runes tingling faintly under his fingertips.

Roald lifted the second cuff so everyone could see. "Friends," he said, actually raising his voice a decibel, "as was the tradition for guards of old, when lovers fought valiantly side by side, I call Tony's mate to take up his gauntlet's twin."

Roald's warning that this wouldn't be painless rushed back to him.

Crap, Tony thought, the pureblood's meaning as plain as day.

"Sir," Rick said in a polite undertone. "You know my brother's gay, don't you?"

Rick didn't mean to be obnoxious. He was trying to spare Tony embarrassment in front of everyone he knew.

Roald pinned him with a stern gaze. "Destiny leaves no soul bereft of its complement."

"Uh," Tony put in. "Maybe you shouldn't push this."

Roald turned the same disapproving stare on him. "This isn't your choice, wolf. It belongs to another."

"But—"

"I call this wolf's mate to me," he repeated. "Do you accept the charge of defending the Sevryn brood?"

Oh God, Tony thought. He didn't know what to pray for. That Chris step up to the plate? That he stay where he was and not risk everything that mattered to him in life? He knew for sure he didn't dare turn around. His eyes would out Chris all by themselves. He held his breath, seconds ticking by.

"I accept," his lover said.

~

Chris *had* been thinking the arm cuff thing was cool for Tony. Of course he was a hero like his brother. Chris had known that all along. Liam's glower of resentment seemed a small price to pay. Yes, it would be a shame if Tony's progress winning over the tiger were undone. Really, though, Liam's envy of the omega wolf was his own issue to overcome.

And then the faerie called Tony's mate to join him.

Chris felt as if his face had frozen and at the same time gone searing hot. Tony was very carefully not turning to look at him. The wolf would protect Chris's secret no matter what it cost him.

"You know my brother's gay, don't you?" Tony's own brother asked, as if being gay meant Tony couldn't find the sort of love Rick had.

Chris *couldn't* leave Tony hanging—no more than he could have let Tony's house burn down. This was even more important. This was the measure of Chris's soul.

"I call this wolf's mate to me," Cass's father repeated. "Do you accept the charge of defending the Sevryn brood?"

"I accept," Chris said.

Incredibly, his voice was strong enough to carry. Tony turned around slowly, his green eyes blazing with emotion. For a second, Chris experienced the most extraordinary sense of liberation. Finally, he'd released his secret. Hiding what he was no longer burdened his spirit.

"Oh," he heard Tony's brother say in surprise. "Hey, that's nice."

Chris couldn't tear his gaze from Tony. Tony smiled and Chris smiled back, his eyes flaring like the wolf's.

Naturally, the moment ended before he was ready.

"Fuck no," growled one of Chris's tigers. "This is *not* okay."

Well, Chris thought. It seemed the other shoe had dropped.

CHAPTER ELEVEN

"YOU lied," Jonah said, for it was he who'd spoken. "Every word that came out of your mouth as beta was calculated to mislead us."

The clan's third-ranked tiger looked furious. Never Gandhi-like in temper, Jonah's chest had expanded so dramatically with anger he'd nearly ripped his navy and gray RFD T-shirt. Animals in the wild puffed themselves up like this. Despite the threat display, Chris felt no fear as he faced him.

No fear for his physical safety anyway.

Jonah and Liam weren't the only tigers who were offended. Syd and Vasur had crossed their arms and were staring at him with raised eyebrows. That disappointed Chris. He'd begun to hope for more from them.

Disappointed or not, he owed them a response.

"I lied to you about my personal life," he said. "Professionally, I've always been honest."

"You can't separate the two!" Jonah shouted. "If you'll lie about one thing, you'll lie about another. And no wonder you've been favoring the wolves' interests. Their omega is your butt buddy!"

"Tony is my lover," he said as calmly as he was able. "And my friend. His influence over me probably isn't any greater than Liam's over you. When the pack's interests intersect with our own, I'd be shortsighted not to support them."

Following Chris's example, Jonah lowered his voice to mere fierceness. "Not good enough," he said. "You're supposed to put us first. Hell, you're not supposed to be a cocksucker. What you sneak around doing reflects on us." His features hardened with resolve. "You're not fit to hold your position."

"No, Jonah," Evina said, stepping out of the crowd and into the fray. "Don't tear our clan apart over this."

Even now Chris couldn't tell if she'd known his secret. At least she didn't seem disgusted like the others. Nate didn't look disgusted either, though he'd stayed where he was when his wife stepped forward. He seemed disinclined to play his co-alpha card. As was the case for his fellow wolves, he watched the drama closely but didn't interfere. Tiger business was tiger business . . . until they decided otherwise. Cops were accustomed to sticking their noses wherever they thought they ought to go.

Chris wondered if Jonah understood their hosts might not let him play this out exactly as he hoped.

"*I'm* not tearing us apart," the irate tiger said. "Chris brought this on himself."

Call Chris a cynic, but he thought it would be as accurate to say Jonah's desire to move up in the clan had brought them to this point. Chris being gay or deceitful or whatever complaint Jonah wanted to assert was only the excuse. That being so, Chris didn't know how to head off the inevitable. The sense of liberation he'd felt a minute ago had been deluded. Resignation weighed him down instead.

He *knew* how this was going to end.

"You can't beat me," he said, the simplest, surest statement he knew how to make. "Whatever you believe about the righteousness of your position, you have neither the strength nor the dominance to defeat me in combat."

"Don't I?" Jonah's manner was confident. "I think we'll have to see."

"*I* challenge you, Jonah," Tony said from behind him.

Chris and Jonah let out matching gasps of astonishment, spinning to face the insane man. Tony had *not* just said that. He'd have to be stoned to even consider it.

Jonah recovered from his shock first.

"You *can't* challenge me," he sneered, his extended tiger fangs exaggerating the scorn in his expression. "You're a wolf. And an omega."

"I challenge you as the champion of my acknowledged mate, as is allowed by shifter law."

"No," Chris said, horror washing through his blood. When he'd admitted he was Tony's mate, it wasn't so this could occur.

"You're out of your fucking mind," Jonah said, which was probably what a lot of folks were thinking. Jonah was a big tiger and gamma in rank—maybe more if his ambitions had a biochemical basis. Tony looked half his size in his stupid sexy red speedo. He also looked absolutely calm.

"I'm the wolves' omega," Tony said. "That doesn't make me subordinate to you. Nate is our third, and your will bows to his."

"Shit," Chris breathed. This was not the time to rub Jonah's nose in that.

Jonah filled his big chest with air, obviously about to accept the glove Tony had thrown down.

"Stop," Evina said, her alpha power causing the command to vibrate the air.

"Evina—" Tony said.

"You shut up, too," she ordered, jabbing her mom finger straight at him. "Nobody say another word until Tony and I talk this through."

"You're not leaving me out of it," Chris said.

"Or me," Nate put in mildly.

His wife glared at all of them.

~

Adam volunteered to keep a lid on things outside while Evina led her little discussion group into the penthouse. Cass's grand Gothic living room had plenty of comfy furniture, but they were too hyped to sit. Rick would have joined them in their huddle, except he and Cass had stayed back to keep the dragons calm.

The brood seemed to think Tony was crazy too. They'd started chittering and flapping like mad things.

"You can't do this," Chris said as if he were explaining the facts of life to a two-year-old. "Jonah is twice your size."

"Not twice," Tony said, wishing everyone weren't so horrified. "Maybe a third again as big. Anyway, the bigger they are the harder they fall."

Chris didn't appreciate his humor. "What if Jonah shifts to his tiger form while you're fighting? You can't change without the moon."

"Evina can order him not to. I doubt Jonah himself would consider that anything but an appropriate handicap. You and he, on the other hand, would be sure to go tooth and claw."

"That would be an even match."

"No, it wouldn't. You'd crush him, guaranteed. How would you survive doing that after what happened to your brothers?"

Chris didn't like him bringing this up. His eyes sparked and his jaw muscles bunched.

"What happened to his brothers?" Nate asked Evina.

"His mother's boyfriend had Tomcat Syndrome and murdered them. I assume Tony is implying Chris wouldn't be comfortable killing someone in his cat form."

Chris looked at her, startled. Tony guessed he hadn't expected her to know.

"Sorry," she said. "I've been aware of your past since before I asked you to be my beta. Not about you being gay, but about your family. I uncovered it in a background check. I figured if you ever wanted to talk about it, you would."

Chris and she had been colleagues a long time. Their gazes held for a few heartbeats. Chris dropped his to the antique carpet.

"I could defeat Jonah without killing him," he said.

For Chris's sake, Tony wished he sounded a hundred percent certain.

"He'd push you," he said. "And he'd push your tiger. Challenges bring out primitive impulses in shifters. If he won't back down, he might force you to fight him to the death. Worse, if it comes to the crucial point, and you find you don't have the stomach, he could kill you."

"Oh I'd find the stomach," Chris said darkly.

He'd shoved his hands in his pockets, his body language defensive.

"Say I believe you," Tony said. "What then? How would you live with having killed your own crewmember? Your conscience would torment you. You'd always wonder what you could have done to stop the challenge from happening. I'm the catalyst in all this. You'd end up hating me."

Tony's last sentence had come out rough. Chris looked up, his orange-brown eyes burning. "Never."

Tony said nothing.

"Never," Chris repeated, then squeezed his temples between his hands. "Fuck. You couldn't challenge Liam instead? At least he's an omega."

Tony smiled gently. "Liam wasn't challenging you. Plus I kind of like that kid."

Chris shook his head. "That 'kid' thinks you're a cocksucker too."

"I am one. I just don't consider it an insult. Jonah's the manipulator. I'm willing to bet he's been planning this for a while."

This accusation surprised Evina but only for a moment. "Jonah *has* seemed like he's been taking everyone's temperature. As if he wanted to know who'd support him as beta. Crap." Her lustrous golden gaze met Tony's. Her eyes were a different color than her beta's but similarly exotic. "Maybe my crew is right about me liking you better."

Though Tony was incredibly touched, he laughed. "I'm new to your life. Our baggage is lighter. Jonah is like an annoying family member. You probably don't really want to see him hurt."

"I'd like him to get his butt kicked," she muttered, sounding pretty sincere. She frowned. "I just don't see how you'll pull it off."

"We need time to prepare," Chris said before Tony could respond. "Put Tony in training for a couple weeks. Maybe feed him up."

"No," Tony and Nate said in unison.

"No?" Evina asked her husband.

He cupped her cheek, his narrow handsome face shining with love for her. "Tony will never have a better advantage over your cat than he does right now."

"He doesn't have any advantage!" Chris exclaimed.

"I do," Tony said.

"He does," Nate agreed. "Your cat is big, and he can probably fight, but his entire career is about saving people. Tony's job is subduing them—no matter how big and fast they are or even how magical. Tony confronts beings more dominant than he is every day. Sometimes the pack is there to back him up, but sometimes we're not. He's *used* to fighting above his weight class. It's a regular thing for him."

"You've thought about this," Evina said.

"I've thought about it regarding me," Nate answered. "I think it explains why I'm dominant to your cats."

"That doesn't guarantee Tony can defeat Jonah."

Evina's anxiety was impossible to miss. Nate stroked her curly hair. "Tony has a chance to take Jonah by surprise. Also—" The wolf cracked a smile as naughty as one of Evina's cubs. "I've noticed lately Tony has been more self-assured. It's funny what knowing you're loved can do for a person."

"You knew about Chris and Tony?"

"No." Nate laughed. "I just thought Chris was crazy for not falling in love with you."

"What if . . ." Chris hesitated, and they all looked at him. "What if I step down and let Jonah be beta? He'd drop the challenge then."

This wasn't what Tony wanted. Jonah would demand he be cast out, and no other station would hire Chris if he'd simply given up. What sort of life would he have if he couldn't save people? Firefighting was more than Chris's redemption for not rescuing his brothers; it was his calling. Confounded by the possibility that he'd quit, Tony momentarily couldn't speak.

"Chris," Evina said. "The position of beta has to be earned. And you're the best man for it."

"I got us into this."

"You didn't," she said, hands planted on her hips.

"I don't think Jonah can do the job," Nate interjected. "On the surface maybe, but not in his heart. He doesn't care enough about people he doesn't like."

Evina's eyes widened. "You didn't mention you felt this way before."

Nate hitched his shoulders. "Your crew is your business. Anyway, it didn't matter until I realized he wanted to move up."

Rick stuck his head through the arch to the living room. "Adam sent me to find out if this is happening."

He looked like he wanted to say a lot more than that. Evina pursed her lips with distress. Nate squeezed her shoulder to comfort her.

"I'm up for it," Tony said. "I wouldn't have challenged him if I weren't."

"Tony," Chris said half a second before Rick chimed in with his name as well.

"I'm not a kid," Tony said to both of them. "I'm a grown man, and I know my mind."

"I won't let him kill you," Chris warned. "I don't care what it costs. I'll step in before that happens."

Since by *stepping in* he probably meant *stepping down*, Tony sincerely hoped it wouldn't come to that. "I could use a pair of pants I can fight in," he said to his brother. "The sight of my manly beauty in this swimsuit might be too much for my opponent."

"All right," Rick said.

Though he didn't laugh as he went to get them, Tony awarded him bonus points for not arguing.

~

Now that Tony had talked his way into this challenge, nervousness set in. His breath felt a little short as he stepped onto the terrace wearing Rick's black sweatpants. He hadn't bothered with a shirt. Chances were, it'd just get bloody.

"Maybe Cass could get the kids out of here," he said. "And any guests who aren't pack or clan."

"Sure," his brother said, like this was a normal way to wrap up a party.

The remaining tigers were grouped together near a flat stretch of grass—Jonah, included. The cat appeared to be in serious discussion with Cass's father. Was the pureblood a neutral party then? Tony didn't know what to make of Roald—not that it was ever easy to tell if fae were friend or foe.

Roald left Jonah and came to speak to him. The faerie's expression didn't reveal what he was thinking.

"I've taken the liberty of establishing a fighting ring for the challenge," he said, polite and businesslike. "When you and the tiger enter, its walls will activate. No one else will be able to get in."

"You mean a magical barrier," Tony said.

"Yes. What remains to decide is what will release it. The tiger has expressed a willingness that this battle be to the death, but he seems to think you might balk at that."

Tony snorted through his nose. "The tiger isn't wrong. I'd prefer a simple knockout determine victory. Or a pin, if he'll go for that. Say ten seconds with both scapulae on the ground."

"I shall present that option to him," Roald said. "Might I also suggest you allow either opponent to tap out?"

Tony looked at the impossibly handsome fae. Did everyone think he was a big pussy?

"There are those who consider surrender less onerous than death," Roald pointed out.

Tony thought the fae might be making a little funny but couldn't tell. "Fine," he said. "If either of us tap out or cry uncle, the walls should come down as well."

"Very good," Roald said. "I expect the tiger will agree. He'll like the idea of you doing that. I feel obliged to warn you, none of these stipulations prevent either of you from killing the other. As I understand it, causing an opponent's death in a dominance challenge isn't against the law."

It wasn't, which was one of the reasons shifters didn't lightly engage in them. Roald began to turn away.

"Did you know this would happen?" Tony asked. "Was that why you warned me?"

"The future isn't written until it is," Roald said over his shoulder.

Tony grimaced. He should have expected a fortune cookie answer.

Chris joined him as Roald left. Obviously upset, the cat shoveled his gold-streaked hair off his furrowed brow. "You don't have to do this."

"Pretty sure I do," Tony said.

"That magical barrier will keep me from interfering once the challenge starts."

"That's the point of it, I expect."

Chris looked extremely unhappy. "I don't want to lose you."

People were watching, but Tony clasped his face. "Please stop assuming I can't win."

Chris blew out his breath and nodded. Reluctantly, Tony dropped his hands.

"I've sparred with Jonah," Chris said almost steadily. "He drops his guard after he lands a punch. His speed is good, but sometimes his temper makes him do stupid things."

Tony hoped to avoid a boxing match. That wasn't where his strength lay. On the other hand, he didn't want Chris to worry if it turned into one.

"Good to know," he said.

Chris brow remained creased. "I love you, Tony. No one's ever done anything like this for me, but—God—I wish you weren't."

Tony grinned. "I'll be all right, *mon chat.*"

Chris cursed in response to the loathed nickname. Roald returned to them.

"Your terms have been accepted," he said. "I need to remove your gauntlet so it won't accidentally affect the outcome."

Tony held out his arm for Roald to take it off. He hadn't been wearing the thing long, but his wrist already felt naked without it. Ah well. Even if he'd known how to make the cuff change shape, he'd probably suck at sword fighting.

"I can't wish you luck," Roald said. "Coming from a pureblood, those words have power."

"Understood." Tony glanced toward the ring Roald had set up. The fae had drawn a large square outline in magic, the shimmery force clinging to grass level. Jonah stood outside the line, with Liam beside him. Two more cats were a step away from them. They might or might not approve of the challenge, but they wouldn't abandon a clan member—not when he fought an outsider. Liam tried to look tough, but to Tony's eyes he seemed conflicted. When Chris nodded at the two indeterminately aligned tigers, they nodded back. That was heartening, Tony guessed.

He sensed Rick and Nate coming up behind him. Nate was the pack member Tony trained with the most, the one who'd taught him his best tricks. Nate had a good poker face, but Tony thought he was genuinely less worried than the others. His level gaze met Tony's.

Rick could only try to look as confident.

"You ready?" his brother asked.

"I'm ready," Tony said.

~

Roald gave Jonah and Tony their final instructions outside the fighting ring.

"You understand how this works?" he asked. "You step in, the walls go up. No one else can enter from any direction. If one of you goes unconscious or is pinned for ten seconds, the spell perceives the other as the victor, and the barrier falls. The same holds true if either of you concede. Jonah, if you shift to your tiger form, the enchantment treats it as a forfeit."

"What about claws and teeth?" Jonah asked.

"They're permitted," Roald said, "since Tony can use them too. Please remove your shoes and shirt."

Jonah complied. They were both barefoot and shirtless then. There'd be no gloves for this battle, no protective headgear or timeouts. They'd fight until one of them couldn't anymore. Tony tied his sweatpants more securely at his waist. Nate had made sure Tony stretched out and warmed his muscles. Jonah rolled his neck to work out its kinks, or perhaps to draw attention to how thick it was. He punched one fist into the palm of his other hand, dancing a little on the balls of his feet.

Maybe he thought he was Sugar Ray.

"Let's get this show on the road," he said. His voice was thicker, like he was letting his tiger use his vocal chords.

Tony left the posturing to him. He stepped over the glowing line of magic without comment.

The moment Jonah joined him the walls snapped up, enclosing them in an impermeable dome of force. Tony's ears popped from a change in pressure as the sounds outside the barrier disappeared. The bubble was slightly blurry, turning the people who watched them into vague blurs of color. Inside, the air was crystalline.

Tony noticed the temperature was cooler.

Jonah grinned as Tony registered the changes. "It's just you and me, cocksucker."

"You keep calling me that," Tony said, "I'll assume you want a date."

Tony had backed up across the grass, putting distance between them. Being isolated with an opponent was kind of a luxury. On the job, he often had to consider whether a bad guy's friends might jump into a fight. Jonah didn't like his calm response. He put up his hands, and Tony followed suit.

Jonah's stance wasn't what it should have been. Like some big men did, he planted his feet too wide for good balance. His chin wasn't tucked to protect his head, and his fists were a smidge too low. He might box, but he hadn't focused on defense.

Probably he thought offense was what counted.

He *was* capable of being sneaky. He blurred forward without warning.

Tony slapped his first punch downward and parried the next two sideways. Jesus, the cat was quick. Tony unleashed a kick to Jonah's midsection, knocking him back a step. He'd struck the cat in the breadbox, but Jonah didn't seem winded.

"Dog thinks he can bite," Jonah quipped.

This time Tony sped to him. Jonah didn't block his strikes as well as Tony had blocked his. Unfortunately, Tony had less power to put behind them. Jonah barely rocked when Tony's jabs cleared an opening for a massive uppercut to his jaw.

Executing the combination had put him in arm's reach too long. Jonah backhanded him hard enough for his ears to ring, then tried to grapple him toward the ground. He couldn't throw Tony off balance the way he wanted, but the wrestling match wasn't one Tony could win if it lasted long. Jonah simply had too much brute strength. Determined to break his hold, Tony slammed his not-at-all-padded knee into the cat's family jewels.

That bent Jonah over for three seconds.

Tony shouldn't have given him even one to recover. Clearly, no quarter and no mercy was what surviving this match required. Long before Tony caught his breath, Jonah exploded from his hunker, pummeling him with such lightning quick combinations they were hard to defend against.

Sometimes imperfect form wasn't much of a handicap.

Tony's nose broke and then his left cheekbone. Knowing he had to cut this short, he tore free, leaped back, and thumped the cat's inner thigh with a powerful swinging kick. Tony's rotation added force to the impact of his lower leg, his foot now in the ideal position to hook Jonah behind the knee. Tony pulled, and the cat's feet slipped out from under him. As he fell back, Tony pounced, readying a strong rear cross for his exposed temple.

The punch never landed. Jonah whipped up both legs, feet snapping out as Tony descended. Never mind Jonah's strength, Tony's shifter-enhanced velocity ensured that his ribs would crack.

Fuck, he thought, the slam of pain impossible to breathe through. He rolled away as swiftly as he was able, aware he couldn't afford to stay where he'd been thrown. He spat out the blood that had filled his mouth from his nose breaking. His ribs weren't as quick to mend. They needed more than a couple breaths to heal enough for him to attack again.

Unsurprisingly, Jonah didn't give him time for that.

Tony couldn't move at full speed. He was still getting his feet steady under him when Jonah sped around him and launched into him from behind. Down Tony went, with the cat's weight and bulk on top of him.

His ribcage screamed at the fresh assault. Tony tried to flip Jonah off, but the tiger snaked a chokehold around his neck.

If he'd done it right, Tony would have passed out for sure. Jonah had him in an air choke rather than one that compressed the arteries and more swiftly triggered unconsciousness. Air chokes hurt like hell and could fracture the hyoid bone. What they didn't do was prevent a determined person from reacting.

Tony was determined and then some.

Jonah wasn't truly controlling him except around his neck. Despite the cat's greater size, Tony was able to shove up onto his knees. Quick as lightning, he shot out his claws, plunging them and his fingers deep into Jonah's gut.

It was a gross thing to do, but Tony didn't hesitate to dig and twist once they were in there. Blood gushed down his hands from the damage he was doing. Jonah grunted, pain loosening the vise he'd made with his bicep and forearm. Tony wrested free and staggered away from him.

"Dog," Jonah growled, on his knees, one hand clutched to his slashed stomach. "I'm going to enjoy killing you."

Okay, Tony thought. Good to know the stakes. He refrained from holding his aching ribs. They felt like they were still broken. Attacking Jonah while he was down was tempting but possibly not smart. Nate would have taken him already, he suspected. The stylish wolf was a pinpoint fighter. He'd taught Tony cruder control techniques. They didn't require Tony to be a ninja, just practiced and coolheaded. He reminded himself he'd learned some important things. Jonah was sloppy about defense, didn't have great balance, and wasn't used to being on the receiving end of pain.

Oh, and also he had fists like wrecking balls.

"Any time you want to call it quits," Tony suggested, recalling what Chris had said about the cat's temper.

Jonah peeled his lips back and bared his fangs. He was panting a little.

"I could offer to suck your cock," Tony said. "If that's an incentive."

Jonah flushed with anger, all the warning Tony got before he flung himself up and rushed forward.

Tony made sure he wasn't there to be hit. Jonah blurred at him again, and again Tony dodged. When events unfurled at super-speed, small differences in brain chemistry mattered. Maybe Jonah's perceptions were dulled by anger. Certainly, they weren't as sharp as Tony's. The cat overshot so far his shoulder bounced off the magic dome. The barrier clanged like a muffled bell.

Tony hoped the collision hurt.

"You see how this works," he said. "I can keep this up all night, making you look stupid."

Jonah sped toward him with his claws out.

Tony's ribs were now healed enough. He flipped through the air over the attacking tiger. He was where he wanted then, behind his opponent.

The tiger began to turn around . . .

Tony didn't think he'd ever moved so fast. He couldn't change, but he let his wolf's reflexes merge into his. He didn't even *think* as he shot his arms over the tiger's shoulders, grasping him by the chin with his fingers locked to form a cup. He yanked hard to tip Jonah's powerful neck backward.

The technique was based on a simple rule. Where the head went, the body followed. Tony swung his rear leg back, twisting his body in the same direction that he was pulling the cat's jaw. His rotation increased the cat's momentum. Tony dragged his forearms downward with all his strength. With his spine off kilter, Jonah's balance began to go. He toppled sideways, and Tony went with him, riding him to the ground so he could control the fall.

This was cop shit. Subdue the perp before he can pull a weapon and get him into cuffs. The cat hadn't experienced anything like it while sparring at his local gym.

Tony didn't waste the advantage. He used one bent shin to pin Jonah's neck to the grass, putting his weight behind it to increase the pain of the compression. A palm squashed flat on Jonah's face ratcheted up the discomfort and muscle strain. Then, to make sure the cat remained discouraged from struggling, he got the one arm Jonah wasn't lying on into a thumb-to-wrist twist-and-lock. That did things to a person's nerves the average person couldn't ignore.

Jonah's gasp of agony told Tony it was new to him.

"Okay," Tony said. "You're done now. I can keep pressing on your neck until you pass out, or you can cry uncle. I really don't care which."

"Fuck . . . you," Jonah gasped, still trying to wriggle free.

Tony increased the pressure on all his pressure points.

Jonah screamed at the grinding pain. Tony wished he hadn't defined a pin as shoulder blades to the ground. He'd had Jonah trapped for more than ten seconds, and he'd have liked this to be over.

He didn't kid himself that the cat was ready to surrender.

Jonah's eyes glowed through his screwed-shut lids, his energy boiling with thwarted rage. Sadly, rage wasn't all the upsurge in his energy signified.

"Fuck," Tony said, noticing a telltale distortion in Jonah's back. Muscles moved there that weren't supposed to. Despite his excruciating pain, despite the rules he'd agreed to, Jonah was trying to shift into his tiger form.

"Don't be an idiot," Tony snapped, twisting Jonah's backward facing wrist harder. "You shift, you lose the challenge. Chris keeps his position, and the instant the barrier falls, every wolf in this place attacks."

Sweat rolled down Jonah's face, all his muscles trembling with effort. "Not . . . before I rip . . . out your throat."

The cat was a damned berserker, unable to back down. Tony didn't let himself hesitate. He lifted his weight a fraction and then plunged it down on the cat's neck again. A soft cracking noise ensued. Jonah's eyes snapped open, white showing around their rims as he finally froze.

"You hear that?" Tony said, fighting an urge to wince. "That's your C5 vertebra fracturing. If you struggle with this pressure on it, you'll be too hurt to change. At the least you'll end up in a wheelchair. I wager you'd hate that worse than dying."

"You wouldn't," Jonah said, only his mouth moving.

"That's where you're wrong. I don't care about you like your beta does. I care about ending this."

Jonah panted and ground his teeth.

"Call 'out,'" Tony said, "and I'll have help for you in seconds."

The tiger wouldn't. Tony read the intransigence in his face. Hoping he didn't actually kill him, Tony set his jaw and pressed harder with his knee. At last, Jonah's eyes rolled back. The instant he was unconscious, the magical walls whooshed down like a silk curtain. Tony leaped off his opponent.

"Call an ambulance," he cried. "He needs medical attention."

Tony had forgotten about Evina's friend Freda. The paramedic rushed over with her bag and knelt beside Jonah. The tiger was still and pale.

"I broke his neck," Tony said, not sure how clearly the watchers had seen through the barrier. "He was trying to change. I didn't know how else to make him give up."

"He's not breathing," Freda said. She bent over his back to listen. "I've got no heartbeat."

Tony cursed. Shifters could heal a lot of damage, but spinal injuries were tricky. Freda whipped a collar around Jonah's neck, rolled him over very gently, and started CPR. Evina ran over to help her.

Intense emotion had caused Tony's eyes to shift. He saw Jonah with supe vision. The cat's energy had contracted to a fist-sized star in the center of his body. Tony had seen auras do this before. Not even once had it been a good sign.

He looked toward the crowd and found Roald watching the cat's aura too.

"Roald," Tony said, too wrought up to call him *sir*. The pureblood shifted his very calm gaze to him. Tony wished he could predict how the unpredictable fae would answer his request. His race had their own rules for doing or not doing magic in the Pocket. "Can you heal the injury to his spine?"

"Probably," he said. "Are you certain that's what you want? His spirit remains angry."

"Please," Tony said. "With all of us to help, we can control him until he calms down."

The fae seemed unconvinced, but he stepped to Freda's side anyway.

~

All Chris could think as he watched Tony and Jonah fight was that this was happening because of him. Though he wanted to present an unruffled front, he couldn't refrain from wrapping his arms around his ribs. Probably it was just as well. If his hands had been free, he'd have attacked someone. The pureblood, maybe. Roald had the power to end this by bringing down the ring.

Not that he would. Chris doubted a punch from a tiger would have much effect on him.

Jonah's punch had an effect on Tony. Blood sprayed from his lover's nose as Jonah's roundhouse smacked his head sideways. Tony recovered, jumped back, and responded with a kick. Overcome with anxiety, Chris shoved a thumbnail between his teeth.

A warm hand landed on Chris's arm. "This isn't your fault," Syd said. Vasur stood a little ways behind him. No one else was in Chris's immediate vicinity, tiger or otherwise. Either they sensed he needed space or were treating him like a leper.

Considering the outcome of the challenge was undecided, the show of support meant something. Chris wished he had the presence of mind to appreciate it. At the moment, the best he could do was nod.

"Jonah's been angling for this to happen for a while," Vasur said.

They hadn't seen fit to warn him. Of course, Chris hadn't acted on the warnings he'd sensed himself. Now Tony was acting instead of him.

"Jonah hasn't beaten the wolf yet," Syd said reasonably. "He's landing a few hits."

A few hits wouldn't settle this. Like everyone else, Chris was squinting to compensate for the blur of the magical barrier. No sounds passed through it, which made the fight's swift violence appear surreal. God, he hoped Tony wasn't crazy. In the list of things Tony thought Chris couldn't survive, he should have included his own death.

"Ooh," the mostly shifter crowd burst out. Jonah had gotten behind Tony for an attack, slamming him facedown onto the ground underneath his weight.

Shit, Chris thought. Were Tony's ribs broken? Before he could decide, Tony plunged a clawed hand backwards, deep into Jonah's gut.

"Ouch," Vasur said, wincing sympathetically.

As Tony wrenched away, Chris's heart was beating a mile a minute, like a jackhammer in his throat. He was going to pass out before either of the combatants.

"Keep it together, boss," Syd said.

Chris realized his claws had sprung out. This wasn't good. He was still the beta. He had to act like one. "I'm all right," he said, forcing his arms to drop and his back to straighten. "One of you stand with Liam. I don't want him to feel alone."

Syd gave him a strange look, but went off to do it. Vasur moved a step closer and crossed his fireplug arms, the pose unexpectedly protective.

"The wolf's got game," he said when Chris glanced at him. "Maybe he isn't doomed."

Chris fought an inappropriate urge to laugh. Tony would have been bowled over by his praise.

"Oh boy," Vasur said, drawing Chris's attention back to the fight.

Tony was flipping through the air over Jonah's head—something Chris hoped he wasn't doing to be flashy. Landing neatly, he grabbed Jonah's chin from behind and twisted him around. To Chris's amazement, Jonah fell like a tree. Tony got him prone and pinned so quickly the cat had no chance of escaping.

"Shit," Chris breathed, marveling at the move.

Simple though it had looked, the cat was trapped. He couldn't get out from under Tony's various presses and holds. The tiger's face was turning red from pain.

"Why aren't they ending it?" Vasur asked.

"Jonah won't call 'out,'" Chris realized, zeroing in on their moving lips. "He won't admit Tony bested him."

"Fuck," Vasur said. "He's trying to change. He's going to make the wolf kill him."

The prediction was barely out before Tony lifted and brought his weight down again. Chris couldn't swallow back a sound of distress. He was breaking the cat's neck. Jonah went limp, and the fighting ring's walls flickered. An instant later the barrier was down. Tony jumped off Jonah and called for an ambulance.

The fight was over. Tony was alive, but Chris barely registered his relief. Evina's friend Freda ran to Jonah with her paramedic gear. Chris could tell she wasn't finding signs of life.

He jogged forward to see if he could help.

"Can you heal him?" Tony was asking Cass Maycee's dad.

The fae seemed to be agreeing. He moved to Freda's side. Evina was there too. Roald knelt, laying his hands over Jonah's unpleasantly twisted neck.

"This has to be fast," the pureblood said, his hands beginning to emanate a sparkly glow. "His life force is almost gone. Please brace yourselves to control him."

Evina looked up at Chris from her kneeling position.

He knew what she was thinking. If Jonah healed and then changed, his tiger could do a lot of damage. His mental state was likely to be same as when he went unconscious.

"Do it," his alpha said.

Chris flashed into his tiger form. A second later, Vasur and Syd did the same. Chris's beast grunted at them in satisfaction. Like him, it was happy to have allies.

Jonah shifting into an enraged tiger brought him back to business.

The defeated cat scattered his healers like ninepins. They weren't hurt, but Chris wasn't sure that was deliberate. Seeing himself surrounded, Jonah snarled a threat at his three clan mates. They weren't intimidated. Bristling, crouched, Syd and Vasur edged closer.

"Think, Jonah," Evina said, still in human form and on her feet again. "I know you're disappointed you didn't win the challenge, but none of us wants to see you hurt. We want to work this out."

In spite of everything, Jonah thoroughly shocked Chris by swiping at Evina with his claws out.

The alpha jumped back too quickly for him to slash her. Nate started to move toward her protectively, but she shook her head. She must have worried her husband would further antagonize the cornered cat.

"We can work this out," she repeated. "You haven't broken the law. You're young and strong, and there's so much you can do with your life if you control your anger now."

Her implication registered with Jonah the same time it did with Chris.

Jonah wasn't going to work on her crew after this.

Probably he wasn't going to be a firefighter.

Jonah growled, backing up in a hunkered down position. Syd and Vasur padded forward to cut off his retreat. Jonah noticed them closing in. His tiger turned, gathered its great striped haunches, and bounded straight for the building's ledge.

Chris swore inside his head. He didn't know how many stories above the avenue they were, but certainly too many for the cat to survive a fall.

"Jonah, no!" Evina called.

The tiger launched himself into the air.

"Save!" Tony cried. "Save the tiger!"

Chris had no idea what he was about until three St. Bernard size streaks zoomed into the air. The green dragon was in the lead. He caught Jonah by the scruff, jerking his descent short. Verdi flapped madly to hold up the heavy cat, the burden almost too much for him. Seeing him struggling, Scarlet and Auric darted in to help. The girl dragon got the tiger by the tail. Grabbing what he could, Auric clamped his toothy muzzle around the cat's forelimb.

The sharp noises the cat let out said this was both a shock and uncomfortable.

The giant gargoyle took to the air as well, probably to ensure his protégés could manage their unbalanced load.

They managed it, more or less. They flew Jonah back above the roof, bobbled him unsteadily to the pool, then dropped him into the water with a large splash.

"Shoot," Tony said as the gargoyle landed gracefully beside him. "Sorry, Grant. I should have asked you to take care of that."

The gargoyle's goblin head grinned at him. "Dragons do good," he said in a rumbly voice. "New keeper be proud of them."

The dragons seemed proud of themselves. They squawked excitedly, scrambling around the pool where Jonah paddled in human form. He could have swum as his tiger. Chris guessed he preferred to be in a shape that allowed him to complain.

"Call them off," Jonah said. "They won't let me out of here."

Trying to kill himself and then being rescued at the last moment seemed to have sapped the cat's berserker energy. Chris went to stand by the pool to watch him wearily tread water.

"I'm bleeding," Jonah said. "Those dragon bites aren't healing."

His left arm did have a bunch of punctures from Auric's jaw.

"They saved your life," Chris reminded.

Tired or not, Jonah scowled. Scarlet did not like that. She cawed accusingly at him, then huffed a long tongue of fire.

"They're crazy," Jonah said, shrinking back in alarm.

He was one to talk, Chris thought.

~

After all that excitement, Tony's heart needed a chance to settle. Destiny didn't seem to be on board with letting him get it. Everyone except the one person he wanted with him stopped by the lounge chair he'd dropped onto beside the pool.

Rick was the first. He crouched down to pat Tony's knee and congratulate him on pulling off the fight. "Next time I won't doubt you."

"I couldn't tell you doubted me this time," Tony teased.

Nate slapped his shoulder and Evina invited him to dinner. "You and Chris," she said. "Next week. Absolutely no excuses. Nate will cook something nice."

Tony's mom and dad both hugged him.

"I'm proud of you," said his dad.

"That boy seems nice," said his mom, handing him a black T-shirt she'd found somewhere.

"He is," Tony assured her.

She opened her mouth to ask one question too many. "Grill him about his love life later," his dad advised, hugging her to his side. "After he's caught his breath."

Someone from Shifter Counseling arrived to collect Jonah. Freda had tranq'ed him as a precaution, once the dragons let him out of the pool. The tiger wasn't unconscious, but he was woozy and couldn't drive. Tony didn't think the cat was going to be charged with anything. Freda accompanied him in the ambulance. Liam looked like he wanted to go to his buddy but wasn't sure he should. A few minutes after that, Vasur, Syd and Liam left the terrace together. They were subdued but seemed okay. Tony hoped this meant they'd adjust to Jonah's expulsion from the clan.

Rick's fiancée came over then. Per usual, Cass's appearance was breathtaking.

"Cass," Tony said. "I'm so sorry we ruined your engagement party."

Snow White smiled and shook her head. "Remind me to tell you how boring my life was before I met Rick."

"That bad?"

Dimples appeared in her rosy cheeks. "A few small someones would like to see you before you go."

He thought she meant Ethan and the cubs, but when he turned in the direction she indicated, he saw the dragons clustered together near the French doors. Their mouths were agape and their eyes hopeful. Cass's dad stood with them, his hand resting casually on Auric's golden head.

The brood liked the slightly scary pureblood. Tony supposed he had to mark that as a point in Roald's favor. Rising, he glanced around the dwindling crowd. Chris stood by the shut off barbecue, packing up leftovers—probably because he hadn't felt comfortable standing around unoccupied. Tony caught his eye and waved for him to come over.

The tiger hesitated a second before he moved. As he walked toward Tony, his gaze was unusually serious. Tony realized he was self-conscious. From now on when Chris looked at him, people would be aware they were more than acquaintances.

Tony knew that would take time to get used to.

Chris stopped closer to him than he would have before. "Everything okay?"

"Yes." Tony touched his hand lightly. "Come meet the dragons officially."

Chris looked nervous but followed him. Tony went to his knees to hug each dragon first.

"You were so good tonight," he praised as they bumped up to him. "Smart and brave. I'm really proud of you."

Chris laid his hand on Tony's back.

"Want to meet your other new guardian?" Tony asked. All three dragons looked up at Chris.

"Hello," he said as if they were people. "I hope you'll like working with me too."

Auric uttered a little chirp. Scarlet edged closer and butted Chris on the thigh. Chris smiled and stroked her head. Once she'd accepted his admiration, the others crowded around as well. It wasn't long before he was on his knees, laughing and being pestered for attention.

He wore the same wondering look everyone did when interacting with the dragons for the first time, like he'd discovered Santa Claus was real.

"You're beautiful," he crooned, trying to pet them all at once. "Look at your gorgeous wings!"

"You'll want this back," Roald said quietly to Tony.

He held out the guardian cuff.

"Oh," Tony said. He took it and slid it on. "Thank you."

"I have yours as well, Mr. Savoy."

Chris looked up at him, startled. "Ah. Um, thanks."

When Chris took his bracelet, he slipped it into the pocket of his sport coat. His casualness shocked Tony. This was how he accepted a priceless mystical object? By not even putting it on?

Cass's dad seemed to find his response amusing. His ridiculously handsome mouth twitched at its corners.

Verdi distracted him from the gaffe by cracking his jaw in a noisy yawn.

Chris patted the dragon's side and smiled. "I guess it's your bedtime, huh?" He got to his feet and turned to Tony. "You ready to get out of here?"

He obviously meant together, and hopefully meant all night. That thought warmed Tony. Chris and he were officially a couple. They didn't have to hide anymore.

"You bet," he said, already planning how they could celebrate.

CHAPTER TWELVE

TONY pushed the door to his apartment open, then stopped to look back at Chris.

"Um," he said. "Don't look at the living room. The rest of the place is less of a mess."

"Still working on those dining chairs?" Chris asked, recalling his last visit.

"Those are done. I've started on a sideboard. It might have to go to eBuy. It's a little big for my space."

As he stepped into the entry, Chris wondered how he could tell. Tony's place was stuffed with stuff all over.

"That's leaving," Tony said when Chris clipped his knee on a leather-strapped pirate's chest. "I'm Special Mailing it to a mundane in Oregon."

"You sell to Outsiders?"

"You can as long as you have a permit."

Tony slapped on the hall light and then the one in his bedroom. Plaid sheets clad his unmade bed, the pillows still dented from the last time he'd slept on them. True to his claim that there was less mess here, the worn old floorboards were mostly clear. Tony crossed them and flung a window open to let in the crisp night air. The breeze was cold but felt good.

Watching him do this felt very domestic.

"If you're hungry, I've got part of a chocolate cake my parents baked in the fridge." Tony was looking at him. Chris realized he was supposed to say something.

"You okay?" Tony asked. "You look kind of . . ." He pulled an *aack* face as he trailed away.

"I think everything is hitting me at once."

"You're out," Tony said with a little smile.

"I'm out," he agreed. "And you're alive, and I'm still my clan's beta."

"A good night, everything considered."

Chris wanted to be serious a moment longer. "Thank you for asking the dragons to save Jonah."

"I knew you'd want me to. I'm just glad they succeeded. Freda said she'd make sure Jonah sticks with the counseling."

"Freda is good people."

"You and she ever—?"

"No," Chris said. "It didn't seem right to use my alpha's BFF that way."

Tony looked relieved. He scratched his cheek, which was slightly pinker than usual. His guardian cuff gleamed with the movement. Chris decided he liked the way it looked on the wolf's strong forearm.

"Speaking of the dragons," Tony said.

Chris gave him an inquiring look. Tony exhaled and dropped to the edge of his rumpled bed. Chris joined him and took his hand. Their fingers twined together in a natural easy way. His heart felt good beating slow and steady inside of him: happy *and* peaceful, he realized.

I'm content, he thought. *This is how that feels.*

"About the dragons?" he prompted.

"You didn't put on your cuff. When Cass's dad gave it to you, you stuck it in your pocket."

"I'm thinking about it before I put it on."

Chris didn't think this statement was outrageous, but Tony's jaw fell open. "Why do you have to think? You already said you'd be my co-guardian."

"I will. Ninety-nine percent probably. I admitted I was your mate when Roald asked because I would have felt like a skunk leaving you hanging. The guardian business I want to mull over."

"Don't you think the dragons are awesome?"

"Sure," Chris said. "I feel honored to be asked to protect them."

"And me? Aren't I awesome too?"

Chris laughed. Tony was kind of joking and kind of not. "You're extremely awesome."

"Then what is there to think about? Unless you think *you're* not hero material. Should I not have saved your bacon?"

Chris squeezed his hand. "I want to think because it's a big decision. I want to make it with my eyes open. I want you to know I *chose.*"

Tony considered this. "You want me to know you're certain, and that you didn't feel pressured."

"Exactly," Chris said, pleased that he'd understood.

Tony grinned. "How long is that going to take?"

"You're impossible!" Chris exclaimed, amused by his impatience.

"Yeah, but you love me anyway."

"I do." Chris stroked his fingertips down the side of Tony's face.

Tony kissed his palm and gazed into his eyes. It all felt wonderful. Heat ran through Chris, followed by a humming excitement. He curled his toes.

They could do this any time they wanted. Hold hands. Lock gazes. Even kiss in public. Everyone who mattered already knew what they were to each other.

"Would you consider selling your condo and buying Rick's place?" Tony asked.

"What?" Chris said, taken by surprise.

"Rick lives with Cass now. And I'm too much of a pack rat for us both to have our stuff here."

"Do you think your brother would sell? What about your alpha? Isn't this house kind of a pack thing?"

"Pfft." Tony waved his hand dismissively. "Adam got over Nate marrying a tiger. This isn't really a bigger deal."

Chris saw Tony believed this, and maybe it was true. He shook his head. "You wolves . . ."

"We're very forward thinking," Tony said airily.

Chris snorted. "All right. I'll—"

"—think about it," Tony finished for him.

They smiled at each other. "I love you," Chris said.

"You should," Tony teased.

"We could celebrate by having sex."

"I thought you'd never ask," his lover responded.

Tony leaned forward, and they kissed each other. Though they had exactly the same mouths and bodies as before, a sense of novelty rose in him. This was Chris's brave new world. He was gay, and happy, and Tony was right in the thick of it with him.

"Mm," Tony said. "Kissing you makes me so fricking hard."

Charmed by the claim, Chris ran his palm up Tony's thigh to check.

Tony jerked when he squeezed the big ridge between his legs. His cock was thick and long, easily standing up to the pressure he applied.

"Yup," Chris said, so happy he was almost laughing. "That is a hard hard-on."

Tony growled and kissed him more deeply. The wolf's interest was accelerating on fast forward. He yanked Chris's shirttails out of his trousers, his hands driving under it up his back. The kneading of his fingertips felt amazing. Chris squirmed and started unbuttoning his own shirt.

"God, I love watching you do that," Tony said.

Chris remembered doing it for him at the carwash. That seemed a zillion years ago—and not only because he'd been in the closet then. Tony's fight with Jonah had gotten to him, reminding him every moment they spent together should be treasured. Abruptly crazy-eager, Chris kicked off his shoes, wrestled out of his pants, and pulled Tony from the bed onto his feet.

He was so ready to ravish the sexy wolf it was not funny.

Grinning at his expression, Tony wrestled his black T-shirt over his head. Chris inhaled sharply.

Above the sweats he'd borrowed from his brother, Tony chest was bloody.

"Oh," he said, looking down at the stains. "Sorry. I'm healed. I just didn't take time to wash up before I pulled this on."

"Wait," Chris said when Tony would have kissed him again. He strode quickly to Tony's bathroom, ran a washcloth under the hot water, and wrung it out.

He brought it back to Tony, cleaning him off gently. The blood was mainly smeared on his ribs, but Chris stroked his arms and belly too. The channels inside his hipbones drew his attention like magnets. He guessed having the hollows rubbed with the cloth felt nice. Tony began to breathe faster. The front of his pants tented out fuller.

"Chris," he said, like his name really meant something.

Emotion caused Chris's eyes to flare. He tossed the washcloth toward the bathroom and reached for the drawstring of Tony's black sweatpants. The knot stymied him. Tony jiggled impatiently on his feet.

"Please hurry," he urged Chris.

Tony's words inadvertently rerouted his intent. "You should not have said that," he warned, a smile breaking out.

"Noo," Tony protested. "I had a big fight tonight. My libido is all worked up."

"You fought for *me*." Chris's grin was impossible to contain. "You deserve the best reward I can come up with."

"You're evil," Tony huffed.

This didn't deter him one bit.

~

Tony could not believe Chris was walking away from him. He wanted to make love to him, like, right then and a lot of times. Chris was already naked and hard. There was no damn reason they couldn't have at it.

Chris's fine bare ass disappeared into the bathroom while Tony gawked in amazement. The faucets squeaked, and then he heard water running into the tub. What did Tony need a bath for? Chris had just cleaned him up. Annoyed, he shoved his hand down his loosened pants. He hadn't lied about being worked up. His cock was so stiff it ached. Bothered too much by the deep-down itch, he rubbed up and down the shaft. He didn't use serious pressure. He'd rather wait for his tiger before he came. Chris didn't need to know that, however.

"I'm starting without you," he called.

Chris opened and closed a cabinet. "Don't you have bubble bath?"

"No, I don't," Tony said, miffed that he would ask. Did Chris think he was some girly queen? Then he relented. "I have bath *salts*. In the towel closet."

"Got 'em!"

The scent of lime and spice exploded into the air. Tony released his cock so he could fold his arms. Chris wasn't earning his forgiveness that easy.

"Come on," the tiger coaxed. "It's not as fun if I sit in this thing alone."

Chris was taking the bath too? That *would* make it more interesting. Tony dropped his pants without more ado.

He found Chris lolling in the clawfoot tub.

"Wow," Tony said, admiring the yummy picture his big naked body made.

His muscled arms were stretched along the rim, one long leg crooked up there as well. The richly scented water wasn't high enough to cover his erection. That was on full display, thrusting up from his groin all flushed and pulsing and delicious. Water glistened on the cat's smooth skin, or maybe it was sweat. Chris rubbed one hand over his own chest hair.

"Uh," Tony said, feeling like he was being hypnotized. Chris's pecs were solid and inviting, his nipples beaded like pencil erasers. The cat's hand drifted lower, over his six-pack abs and navel. Long strong fingers combed into the widening swath of his pubic hair. Chris's updrawn thigh sprawled wider as his wandering hand cupped and lifted his heavy sac. Tony gulped audibly. Chris's thumb cruised over the wet curve of one testicle, causing Tony's balls to jerk in sympathy.

"Don't just stand there," Chris teased, his eyes aglow with lust and humor. "The water's nice and hot."

Tony bet it was. "Shit," he breathed, realizing what was missing. "Hold that thought a sec."

Praying his neighbors weren't peeking in, he zipped naked to the kitchen, returning with two lit votive candles in slightly dusty cut glass holders.

"Aww," Chris said, seeing what he'd brought.

He was almost laughing, but Tony could tell he was also touched. Thinking a moment, he set the candles on the sink. If he put them too near bath, they were liable to get splashed out.

Chris swished his fingers through the steaming water. "I'm still waiting," he reminded.

Tony knelt beside the tub to give him a long deep kiss. Bracing one hand on Chris's bicep, he cradled the back of his head with the other. Chris's hand touched his chest and petted. They made low hungry noises as their tongues slid along each other.

When Tony pulled back at last, both their eyes opened languorously.

"Get in here," Chris whispered.

Tony swung in with his back to Chris. The tub was full enough to shut off the tap, the water silky from the oiled salts that had dispersed in it. They were big men, and it took a bit of negotiation for them to get comfortable. Tony sighed as his head settled into the perfect spot on Chris's broad shoulder.

"Good," Chris said, skating his hand over Tony's chest.

Chris's dick was pressed behind Tony's buttocks, thick and hard and hot enough to make him shiver.

"Do me," Tony said, needing that ferociously. "I want your hand on my cock."

"You don't want to be teased some more?"

"Nuh-uh." He took Chris's hand from the pectoral it was circling, dragging it toward the part of him that most desired to be held by it. Chris resisted just enough to make Tony use his strength.

Tony had a feeling they both got a thrill from that.

"Fuck," Chris breathed as Tony wrapped his hand around his very firm erection. Tony kept his grip over Chris's, forcing it up and pulling it down while his pelvis rocked his shaft through their tightly joined fingers. The oil in the water made the tiger's fist squeeze over him sleekly, beads of excitement at the tip of his cock lubing it even more. Waves of pleasure chased each other warmly along his nerves. Tony's eyes drifted shut, his head rolling against Chris's strong shoulder.

"Let go of my hand," Chris said, hushed and husky. "I know what you like by now."

He did . . . and what he didn't know, he figured out enjoyably. Tony released his hand and gripped Chris's knees instead. He needed something to hold onto. Chris put his second hand to work on Tony's cock, pulling one fist up him and then the other, making sure his fingers contracted as each stroke reached his swollen crown. Though the head of his penis was sensitive, Tony was too aroused for the extra pressure to be anything but welcome.

He groaned when Chris started swiping faster. Chris's tugs pulled sensations from deep within his groin, making his entire body feel like it was coiling up to come. Chris nearly sent him over when he nipped his bunched shoulder.

He was excited too. His tiger fangs were down.

"What me inside of you when you go?"

"Yes," Tony moaned. "Please."

Chris helped him lift and slide onto him. Water wasn't lube, but this water was slick enough. Chris's throbbing length went in with the exact amount of stretch and rub Tony was craving.

"God, that's hot," he said, squirming as Chris filled him. He understood what people meant when they talked about being impaled. Chris's knob hit his prostate and stayed there. The pulsing pressure intensified his awareness of the erotically charged gland.

Tony's hands clamped hard on the cat's kneecaps.

"Good?" Chris asked hoarsely beside his ear.

A tortured groan was the only answer he could supply.

"Okay then," Chris chuckled.

He returned his hands to Tony's thudding shaft. Without preamble, he jacked him at shifter speed, pulling one silky wet tight fist in a blur after the other. Tony gasped for air as his nerves all went nuclear. There was no holding back under that barrage. He ejaculated in a long concentrated burst, his pleasure made ecstatic by Chris's skill.

The only drawback was that it was over.

"More?" Chris suggested, his hard cock jerking inside of him. His breath was chopped by excitement, his heart pounding.

Driving Tony to climax had made him want his own.

"Yes," Tony said. "Fuck me, Chris. Push me forward and get me good."

Chris growled, a brief flash of light indicating his eyes had flared. With a bit of wriggling, he got his knees down into the tub, pushing Tony up by the ass until his arms braced him on the rim. Water sloshed, but their bodies stayed connected.

Tony pressed his cheek to his bent forearms so he could look back at Chris.

Chris's irises smoldered with orange fire. His chest was up, his hands free to roam Tony's back muscles. Tony arched to give the tiger's cock unrestricted access. Chris's eyes nearly closed with bliss, palms sliding down Tony's sides to his hips. The hold he got on them was steely. Tony's groin re-heated with interest.

"You ready?" his tiger lover growled.

"Oh yes," Tony said sincerely.

Chris knew exactly how hard to go to make Tony feel overwhelmed. Surrender was what he wanted, the sense that he was completely in Chris's power. He never felt threatened when Chris took over. Being with him, even in secret, had increased his sense of security, his trust in himself for picking a good man. Nate's words came back to him.

It's funny what knowing you're loved can do for a person.

Chris's groin slapped his, his fingers steering him securely. Tony bit his lip with pleasure, his head flung back helplessly. Chris knew the signs that he was close to getting off and found them inspiring. He groaned as his own end raced nearer. Unable not to, his thrusts sped up.

Tony braced, his strength heightening the impact of Chris's drives.

"Tony," Chris moaned, jamming in and holding. "Tony . . ."

He went, flooding Tony's ass with heat. Tony thought it was over, but suddenly Chris snarled and started up again. This time he fucked him like an animal: ruthless and abandoned. His hips twisted as he pumped, desperate to give and get more and more sensation. Half a minute hadn't passed before he reached under Tony to jack his cock. Tony sucked in a breath, not having realized how close he was to going over a second time. Chris's longest finger found Tony's bulbus and rubbed it. The gland went buzzy and flashed hot.

Tony came so hard he literally saw stars.

Chris cried out and poured into him, the spasms of ejaculation deliciously drawn out. Tony's climax was longer too. When it ended he was too wrung out to move.

Chris's big chest rested on his back, his panting ringing in the tiled room. The floor was a candlelit expanse of water, splashed from the tub by their crazed screw fest.

"Oh man," Chris said in dismay. "We're gonna flood your basement."

"'s okay." Because it was what he could reach, Tony patted his ear weakly. "I installed a backup drain in the floor. The water should be gone in a few minutes."

"Good thinking," Chris said, relaxing on top of him.

"Just another reason to buy Rick's place: easy access to a boyfriend who's handy."

Chris kissed the back of his neck. His lips curved like he was smiling.

"I don't need a bribe," he said, "but you are very persuasive."

Some time passed before their strength recovered enough to clamber out of the tub, dry each other off, and totter to Tony's bed. Chris flopped onto it on his back. Looking like he knew he belonged, he patted the mattress beside him.

Tony quite enjoyed climbing up and snuggling into him, especially since they were both naked. His head settled on Chris's chest, his ear pressed to his heartbeat. The cat was warm and relaxed. His long fingers stroked Tony's drying hair.

"Oh hey," he said like he'd just remembered something. He rolled slightly and reached sideways.

Chris had tossed his jacket onto a nearby chair—one of the harp-back dining seats Tony had refurbished. Snagging the garment by the arm, he dug into its pocket and pulled out the dragon cuff.

Tony watched it glint as Chris tilted it. The scratchy runes were as mysterious as ever. Was he going to wear it, or was he still thinking?

"I feel like I should make a speech," Chris said. "A magic promise or whatever."

"The cuff is already yours. If it weren't, it would be zapping you."

"So I just put it on?"

"If you're ready. Or you could let me help."

Chris's lips twitched with suppressed amusement. He handed the cuff to him, then held out his arm. Tony's pulse beat faster. Ignoring his nerves, he sat up without a fuss and slid the band over Chris's hand. Part of him was tempted to make a joke about being engaged, but that seemed presumptuous.

Once the cuff was on, Chris turned his arm back and forth to consider it. His fit as well as Tony's.

"We're the guardians," he growled, imitating Tony's nephew.

Tony laughed. Chris's gaze lifted to his and stayed. "My cuff is humming."

"Mine too."

They both wore them on their right wrist. Chris clasped Tony's forearm so that the gleaming bands of metal were pressed together. A flush of warmth joined the low vibration. Tony's soul went still with awe. This man was the other half of him—twinned to him just like the electrum cuffs.

"We're a team now," Chris said quietly, seeming to feel the moment too. "We'll protect the dragons, and we'll stand by each other."

"We'll love each other."

"We will," Chris agreed. "And, by the way, you're an excellent partner already."

Tony grinned. This was totally like an engagement. Chris touched Tony's face, kissed him gently on the lips, and sat back. He seemed less dozy than before. "What sort of cake did you say you had in your fridge?"

"Chocolate."

Chris contemplated this. "Your parents spoil you."

"Like crazy." Tony's grin reached epic proportions. "If you stick with me, they'll spoil you too."

"Well," Chris said, his eyebrows arching higher. "I guess I'll have to then."

CHAPTER
THIRTEEN

CHRIS wasn't an idiot. He knew the only things preventing him from committing completely to Tony were his own issues. These last few months as a couple had been great. Tony alone would have made his days a joy, but Tony came with perks.

Chris and Nate got along already, due to the wolf marrying Evina. Once Nate's pack wrapped their heads around Chris's existence in Tony's life, they treated him with interest, consideration, and—soon enough—affection. They didn't tease Chris like they did Tony, but doing that to his lover was kind of irresistible.

He and Tony lived together now. Rick had sold Chris his apartment with a minimum of haggling. *Treat my brother like he's special* was the only demand he made.

Chris became so cozy with the wolves he had to remind himself not to neglect his tigers. Setting aside his discomfort over the pool hall's associations, he hired a retired firefighter to reopen and manage it. Once a month, he and the cats—including Evina—took over the back room for poker night. Jonah's replacement, a young cat everyone called Twink because of his amazing balance, lost his whole first paycheck. Deciding that wouldn't foster good crew relations, Evina restricted them to playing for pennies from then on.

The evening Syd suggested Tony might like to join them—and Liam seconded—Chris nearly fell off his chair.

"Ask him to bring that chocolate cake his folks make," Vasur added, having sampled it when Chris brought a piece to work. "That bad boy is excellent."

So the clan and the pack began to twine together, asking after each other and getting familiar with their assorted personalities. It wasn't the case that no one ever butted heads, but only in normal ways. The fire crew seemed happier —possibly to their own surprise. Overall, Chris's life was running with supernatural smoothness.

Every morning he got to wake up and be himself. Every day he performed the job he was born to do. Every night he crawled into bed with the man he loved.

And then there were the dragons.

The Society for the Protection of Rare Creatures took the news that Tony and Chris were guardians with barely a batted eye. The Dragon Guild wasn't as agreeable. They'd wanted to fill the posts themselves. Even so, they came around. Every few weeks the SPORC folks, the two Guild members on their board, and Cass's father put Rick, Cass, Tony, and Chris through an intensive training day.

They worked on communicating with the brood, learned dragon history, and practiced sword fighting. Getting their protector gauntlets to change shape on demand was tricky, but they were all improving. The dragons viewing everything as a game made the lessons enjoyable. Chris knew none of the caretakers minded the time required.

"It's like joining the National Guard," Tony said. "It's serious but it's fun."

Tony made Chris proud to be his lover.

Tony deserved a partner who held back nothing.

The corner Chris couldn't quite commit was why he was at Rykers Maximum Security today, handing a tan-uniformed red-eyed guard his watch, wallet, and house keys. The Monk demons who ran the prison were pale-skinned and slightly built. They rarely spoke—hence the name they went by in the Pocket. Monks were longtime residents who specialized in keeping locked-up things secure. A metal sign bolted to the wall promised Chris his belongings would be returned. He was scanned all over for hidden spells, which made him glad he'd given his dragon cuff to Tony for safekeeping.

When the demon was satisfied he wasn't here to break convicts out, he was given a metal-cased palm computer that issued instructions in a machine voice—perhaps from some other demon typing them. Whatever the voice's source, it directed him through another secure door and down a corridor big enough for an eighteen-wheeler to drive along. The size of the passage made Chris wonder what other creatures Rykers housed.

He'd have to ask Tony later. Thus far, he hadn't encountered another soul.

"You have reached the visitors facility," the palm unit informed him. "Please wait while we activate the entrance."

Until the door was activated, it was invisible. When the illusion that hid it fell, the entrance emerged from the gray cinderblock as heavy riveted steel. A buzz and a click announced its lock being sprung. Chris inhaled and then blew out his breath. He thought he was ready for this but couldn't predict exactly what *this* would be. Truthfully, he wasn't sure what he hoped to accomplish. After all these years, what was he going to prove?

That you can face him, he thought. *That you're willing to.*

He stepped through the opening.

A dim room lay behind it, furnished with a single chair, a carrel desk, plus the magic-proof glass so popular for prison visits on TV shows. Chris pulled out the plastic chair and sat. As he did, the opposite half of the room lit up. The chair on that side held a large male shifter in an orange jumpsuit. For the first few seconds, he seemed a complete stranger. Gray laced his hair, and he was bulky from weightlifting. The terms of his sentence must have prohibited him from changing. More than one bone had been broken in his face—in inmate fights, Chris assumed—without healing completely. Though no longer handsome, Chris could tell the cat used to be. Unexpectedly, he was taller than Chris recalled.

Then Chris recognized his eyes. They were dark brown and not quite *right*, as if the brain behind them were interpreting the world in askew ways. Chris was looking at Mark Naegel: his mother's one-time boyfriend, his brothers' murderer.

"Chris," Naegel said, which struck him as so strange a shudder ran down his spine.

Thirty years later, the tiger remembered him. Then again, Naegel's normal life ended back when he knew Chris. Probably everything surrounding those events was etched in his memory.

"Why are you here?" Naegel asked, rationally enough.

Why was he there? "I needed to see you," Chris answered.

"Did you get religion or something? Did you come here to forgive me?"

"Do you need me to?" Chris asked curiously.

Naegel gave him his off-kilter stare. His fingers rubbed back and forth along the edge of his carrel desk. "I'd have killed you too if you'd been there that night."

Chris didn't doubt he'd have tried. His tone was so matter-of-fact. "Are you sorry you killed my brothers?"

If Naegel was sorry, it wasn't in his eyes. In truth, he seemed to have trouble understanding what Chris had asked, as if *life is sacred* was in some language he didn't speak. Was he a killer because he'd been born with a few bad genes? Or was he one because he'd let those genes control him?

"I'm sorry your mother committed suicide," Naegel finally said. "She was a hot piece of ass."

He didn't seem to be saying this to make Chris angry. No doubt he'd have liked it if she'd been available for conjugal visits. That his mother *wouldn't* have visited the man who'd slaughtered her children didn't compute for him.

Realization clicked inside Chris. The ghosts he'd been fighting weren't real. He'd invented them in his head. Certainly, they weren't residing in this prison.

Chris scraped back his chair and rose.

"Will you come again?" Naegel asked. His face was lifted, his strange dark eyes hopeful. He'd shamed his clan and his family by turning killer. Chris doubted he got many visitors.

"No," he said. "We're not really anything to each other. You probably only want to see me because you're bored."

Naegel sat back without disputing this. Chris sensed his emotionless eyes tracking him as he departed.

The dark gaze felt like it followed him up the vast gray hall, prickling his hackles in icy waves. That was impossible, of course. Only Chris's memories pursued him.

At the security post, he turned in his palm computer and was given back his belongings. The silent Monk demon pointed the way to the outside door. Chris hadn't forgotten how to find it, but he was grateful to be dismissed even so.

A final pair of guards buzzed him through the last exit. Then he was in the fresh air again. Rykers had no yard. Prisoners exercised within its walls. Chris had the sunny April sky to himself as he strode along an asphalt path to the parking lot. The spring day was warm enough to chase the chill from his soul. Every step he took was lighter, every swing of his arms more free. By the time he reached his slightly dirty white Explorer, he felt like he'd regained a self he'd forgotten he could be.

Tony waited for him in the front seat. He unlocked the door to let Chris in.

"That was quick," he said, tilting his head to consider him. "You look better, like you found what you were looking for."

Chris slid behind the wheel and shut the door behind him. "I think I did. Naegel was . . . different."

"Different as in changed or different than you remembered?"

"Different than I remembered, but also—" Chris pressed a fist to his lips and thought. "He's different than normal people, like important pieces are missing from his brain. Maybe he hid that better when he was younger. All I know is if I were that off, someone would have noticed by now. Hell, I'd have noticed myself."

Tony's mouth slanted. "I could say 'I told you so,' but I'm far too mature."

Chris wagged his head in amusement and dug out his car keys.

"You okay to drive?" Tony asked.

"I'm good," Chris assured him. "I just want to get home and enjoy the rest of our day off."

Tony nodded. He was unusually quiet as Chris headed back to town. Normally he'd talk about work or friends or some fun thing he'd like them to do. Chris wondered if Tony had expected this confrontation to be more momentous.

Frowning, he rubbed one finger across his lips. He'd thanked Tony for coming with him already, and the wolf had waved it off as nothing. He'd said he was glad Chris wanted his company. Maybe Chris should take him out for a nice dinner. Right then, he preferred staying home and hanging out together, but if Tony needed to mark Chris conquering this hurdle . . .

Chris opened his mouth to speak, then had an epiphany.

Tony didn't need to mark the changes Chris had made inside himself. Chris was the one who wanted to test his readiness for the next level.

Butterflies fluttered in his stomach—part nerves but part excitement too. He glanced quickly at Tony.

"So," he said. "You probably know Resurrection has liberal marriage laws."

Tony's eyes widened. "Right," he said almost casually. "Because we have a lot of species and cultures here."

"So we, um, could think about doing that."

His butterflies did backflips in the heartbeats before Tony twisted toward him on the seat and grinned. His hand came up to stroke Chris's jaw. "Any time you want, lover."

God, it was awesome that Tony was so sure. And maybe Chris was sure too. Maybe he wouldn't have to think long at all.

"July is my favorite month," he announced impulsively.

Tony rubbed Chris's leg, which he'd been jiggling nervously. Instantly calm, Chris covered his hand and squeezed. Tony looked at him with love shining in his gaze.

"July is green like your eyes," Chris blurted.

Tony laughed, more than love warming his beautiful irises. "Why don't we go home," he suggested, "and think about July together?

# # #

ABOUT THE AUTHOR

EMMA Holly is the award winning, *USA Today* bestselling author of more than thirty romantic books, featuring vampires, demons, faeries and just plain extraordinary ordinary folks. She loves the hot stuff, both to read and to write!

If you'd like to discover what else she's written, please visit her website at http://www.emmaholly.com.

Emma runs monthly contests and sends out newsletters that often include coupons for ebooks. To receive them, go to her contest page.

Thanks so much for reading this book! If you enjoyed it, please consider leaving a review.

PROLOGUE

HIDDEN DRAGONS

The Last Dragon

THE great bronze dragon circled the red desert, leathery wings spread to block the stars. Her name was T'Fain, and her sinuous, whipping tail was longer than her body—though that was long enough. Twenty grown men could stand on her dorsal ridge, assuming they had the stones. Black spines as sharp as razors thrust from her supple back, each worth more than a king's ransom to poachers. No armor known could withstand the piercing power of these spikes. When crushed to powder for a tincture, they counteracted illness and poisons. The dragon's tail was another marvel. If severed, it—and all her limbs—would regenerate.

Then there was the fiery breath *draconem magister* could produce. If used in conjunction with certain spells, water could not quench these flames, only magic of equal strength. What they touched would burn up in instants or smolder on for days—a gruesome passing, by all reports. Though dragons didn't possess the level of sentience of man or fae, their minds were wonders too, capable of executing complex strategies without oversight. Understandably, the beasts had played a role in all the realm of Faerie's important wars.

What few understood was that *draconem's* greatest value lay in its loyalty. The phrase "faithful as a dragon" was not empty. Where dragons loved, they loved with all their hearts. They would not betray their masters or let them come to harm. Many dragon keepers claimed to love their beasts better than their wives.

Despite being a woman, this was a sentiment Queen Joscela understood perfectly.

At a signal from its trainer, the dragon she watched tonight dropped silently to the arid plain. The fact that T'Fain was the last of her kind lent her grace poignancy. Puffs of dry dust burst up—first from the deadly back claws and then the front. The huge scaled body dwarfed the man who'd called her, but the fae was in no danger. The beast hunkered before him as obediently as a dog, glowing ruby eyes fixed lovingly on the being who'd imprinted her as a hatchling. She lowered her scaly head to bring her gaze level with the man's.

The dragon could not anticipate the sacrifice that would be asked of her.

The dragon master was aware. As a member of the secretive Dragon Guild, his family's bloodline was as pure—if not as royal—as Joscela's. At the moment, his face was masklike, his movements stiff and self-conscious. Dressed in fireproof leather from hood to breastplate to hip-high boots, he stretched a gloved hand to rub the dragon between her eyes. T'Fain let out a *chirr* of pleasure, wisps of steam trailing from her nostrils. The trainer stepped back, his attention shifting toward the king to whom his family owed allegiance.

King Manfred was the fae of the hour—of the century, to hear him. Hundreds stood behind him in quiet ranks, soldiers for the most part. As if these troops weren't enough for his dignity, a traveling throne splendidly supported his royal butt. Elevated on a platform set on the sand, the seat glistered with electrum and precious jewels. For five decades, ever since this last dragon had been hatched, Manfred had badgered the High Fae Council over how he thought the precious resource should be employed. Finally he'd won his way. As regally as if *he'd* trained the dragon, Manfred nodded toward his sworn man.

Queen Joscela watched all this from above, from the deck of her floating ship. Magic and not hot air buoyed the vehicle's black and tan striped balloon. Keeping her company at the rail were her personal guards, her hand servants, and her most trusted advisers. Though this was an important night, no wine casks had been opened. She most definitely hadn't triumphed in the long debate with the High Council. This, however, didn't mean she was willing to miss the show.

Those royals who felt a similar reluctance bobbed in the airspace above the plain, each elaborate vessel declaring the uniqueness of its sponsor. Here was a ship that resembled a daffodil, there one entirely formed of gears. All were lit by torches or faerie lights, but not all were festive. Some of Joscela's peers had sided with Manfred and some with her. She consoled herself that few would actually delight in the pompous bastard's ascendency.

Of course they'd abandon her quick enough, now that his star had eclipsed hers.

"If Manfred's head swells any bigger, it will explode."

This comment came from her Minister of Plots. Ceallach stood closest to her shoulder, a smooth and handsome male who'd been her lover for many years. He served in both capacities very well.

"We should be so lucky," she murmured back.

"It's not too late to arrange for a hell dimension door to open and swallow him."

The plain below was dotted with portals, this being the best place in Faerie for forming them. Most were invisible, created too long ago and used to seldom to be active. Others were so popular they had duplicates throughout the realms. These glimmered on the edge of vision, ghost doors to alien existences. Despite their proximity, it was too late to shove Manfred through one—as they both were aware. Joscela's opposition to her rival's plan had been too public and impassioned. Should any ill befall the ruler, suspicion would fall on her.

She touched Ceallach's hand in thanks for his support. "With the way my luck's run lately, we'd send him to a bunny realm."

She sounded bitter. Ceallach squeezed her fingers.

She appreciated that, though her hatred for the puffed-up sovereign knotted darkly inside of her. *I won't let resentment consume me*, she swore. Manfred didn't deserve any more victories.

A stir rippled through the crowd at her vessel's rail.

"Oh joy," Ceallach said. "The idiot is rising to make his speech."

Manfred was a handsome faerie: black-haired, black-garbed, with flashing silver eyes and a sensual mouth. His greater than normal height—further raised by the throne's platform—commanded attention. Then again, if he hadn't known how to present himself, he couldn't have bested her.

"Countrymen," he began in a resonant spell-enhanced voice. "Neighbors and fellow fae. Tonight is a momentous occasion, one many of us fought long and hard to bring about. Tonight we undo the narrow-mindedness of our forefathers, who saw only the backwardness of the human realm and not its value. They closed the door between our worlds, but tonight we re-open it. Those who were stranded among the humans can now come home. Those who wish to visit the human world will have that option. The reason for this is simple. Tonight we do more than our ancestors ever could. Tonight we create a Pocket behind the portal, half fae and half mortal—a place of stability, immune to the magical anarchy that threatens our less fortunate regions. Plodding though they are, humans anchor reality, a service the wise among us know we can no longer live without. I do not exaggerate when I say the Pocket is our future."

"Well, it's certainly his future," Ceallach observed dryly. "And that of anyone who likes conditions exactly as they are."

Joscela pressed her lips together but did not speak. They'd talked of this before. Ceallach knew she agreed with him. The dragon master must have believed Manfred's argument. No matter if he were Manfred's vassal, she couldn't see him going along with this otherwise.

A gust of wind buffeted her ship, forcing her to grip the rail or be knocked off balance. Ceallach's arm came protectively around her back.

Because flashing one's wings in public was bad form, hers were flawlessly spell-folded beneath her gown. Ceallach knew they were there. His bicep tightened, reminding her of the pleasure of having him stroke them. His fingers were capable of great delicacy, his tall body fair and hard. Joscela shuddered at the memory of many intimacies.

"Cease," she whispered as his hand squeezed her waist. She didn't need the distraction. Events were progressing down on the plain. Manfred's cupbearer jogged across the sand toward the dragon master, a ceremonial chest tucked beneath his arm like a suckling pig. Going down on one knee, the youth extended it toward the man.

Not wanting to miss a detail, Joscela whispered an invocation to extend the focus of her vision. The magic snapped into place with spyglass clarity, bringing the scene closer. A muscle ticked in the keeper's jaw as he stared at the cupbearer's offering. The chest was electrum and heavily enchanted, the alloy of gold and silver good for retaining spells. When the keeper opened the flowery lid, slender beams of light spoked out.

Involuntary gasps broke out as people identified the object the beams came from. Nestled within the padded red velvet was a quartz crystal sphere. Joscela would have given her right arm—at least temporarily—for ten minutes alone with it. That clear orb contained the blueprint for the proposed Pocket: the magical rules by which it would be governed, its capacity for expansion. As Manfred's staunchest opposition, Joscela hadn't been invited to participate in planning. He and his cronies wanted to stack the new territory's deck in their own favor, to suit their own agendas. Though this was to be expected, the exclusion offended her more than any of Manfred's slights.

To ignore the genius of a mind like hers was criminal.

Manfred was too enamored with his grand experiment to consider how dangerous humans were. The race seemed weak and easily dazzled compared to fae, but their very susceptibility to fae glamour seduced their superiors. Mixed blood children brought shame to proud families—nor were Joscela's concerns theoretical. Just as fae had been trapped beyond the Veil when it dropped, humans had been trapped here. Her sensibilities rebelled at the results. Pure humans could be useful, but halves? And quarters? They were a mockery of what fae were supposed to be, always causing trouble or getting into it.

As a wise fae once said, a little power is a dangerous thing.

The dragon master removed the crystal from its nest of velvet.

The dragon nosed it, smart enough to be curious. Joscela wondered how the keeper felt to stand so close to the ancient beast. She'd never had a dragon. Once every queen possessed one, but their number had dwindled by the era in which she'd assumed the throne. Some compared the creatures to dolphins in intelligence, others to small children. Though they couldn't speak, they understood commands. Crucial to tonight's proceedings was the magic that packed each cell of their huge bodies. Pure magic. Old magic. The very magic the one-time gods used to form fae reality. Never mind combatting poison or piercing good armor, the spell power within one dragon could create or destroy worlds.

Compared to that, burning enemy villages couldn't measure up. Every hatchling was a weapon someone, someday wouldn't be able to resist deploying.

Though the dragon's playful nudge nearly pushed him over, the dragon master didn't scold or shove her off. Perhaps he couldn't bear to with so little time remaining. He braced his back leg instead, closed his eyes, and composed himself.

As if sensing the seriousness of the situation, T'Fain settled back onto her forelimbs. Her keeper held the sphere between them. As he connected his mind to it, the crystal began to glow. The detail Manfred and his cohorts had encoded into the quartz soon poured into him. The keeper's eyes moved behind their lids. Unlike inferior races, pureblood fae could grasp immense amounts of knowledge, each bit as clear and accurate as the rest. This dragon master's lineage endowed him with yet another skill: the ability to communicate with his charge telepathically.

The dragon's wings twitched as the river of information hit her awareness. Fortunately, like her keeper, she could hold it. Comprehension wasn't needed, only accepting what was sent. The beast seemed to be doing exactly that. Her upper and lower lids closed over her ruby eyes.

At last the transfer was complete. The keeper set the empty crystal on the cracked sand, then gently clasped the dragon's cart-size muzzle. The creature blinked as if emerging from a dream.

"Be," the keeper said softly in High Fae. "Be what I have shown you."

He let go and stepped back. T'Fain shook her body and raised her wings, not for flight but in display. The keeper retreated faster. Despite her misgivings, Joscela couldn't deny a thrill. It wasn't every day one witnessed new realities being born. The dragon tilted her great bronze head as if listening to faint music. Joscela's heart thumped behind her ribs. If she'd been in the beast's position, she'd have been screaming or belching flame. The dragon didn't seem upset, merely attentive. The keeper turned and ran.

Joscela wasn't prepared. Possibly no one was.

Like a star exploding, a blinding brilliance replaced the bronze dragon. The power blasted Joscela's hair back, and her ship jerked to the end of its anchor line. She couldn't tell if the tether snapped, because her senses were overwhelmed. Lightning swallowed the world around her, rainbow sparks dancing in the white. Her ears rang with alien chords. The air was so thick with power it felt like feathers against her skin.

He's killed us, she thought. *The dragon keeper wanted us all to die.*

Even as this possibility arose, the sight-stealing radiance ebbed. Her vessel was still aloft, still anchored, though she'd been knocked onto her ass on the wooden deck. Everyone around her had, from what she could see through her watering eyes.

Ignoring the disarray of her long silk gown, she stumbled to the railing to see what had transpired below. The scene she discovered made her smile unexpectedly. Manfred's fancy throne had toppled over with him in it. He didn't appear hurt, but half a dozen shaky soldiers vied comically with each other to help him up. Everywhere she looked, fae pushed dazedly to their feet. The dragon was gone. Her death had produced that great white light.

Joscela focused on the spot where T'Fain had been standing. Beside her, Ceallach pulled himself up as well.

"Look," he said, a note of grudging awe in his voice. "The new portal is forming."

She'd already seen what caught his attention. The opening was round or would be when it finished coalescing. Years might pass before the doorway was mature enough to use. For now, streaks of green and brown and blue swirled like clouds within the aperture. Though she'd had no part in its design, she understood what was happening. The essence of the realm of Faerie was outfolding into the human world, blending with it to form a combined reality bubble. Silver glimmered and then disappeared at the top of the portal's ring—a pair of dragon wings taking shape, she thought.

"The sacrifice succeeded," she observed, though this was obvious.

"The dragon master should find that some comfort."

"That presumes comfort matters. The last living reason for his bloodline's existence was just wiped out. The protectors among the Guild can hire out as mercenaries. Gods know what purpose he and his kin will find."

Ceallach put his hand on her arm, and they gazed at the man together. The dragon's trainer had run as far as he could from the explosion. Now he stood on the sand, a solitary figure looking grimly back toward the forming door. Char marks streaked his face and leathers, as if he alone had passed through real fire. The soot obscured his expression, but still . . .

"Shouldn't he be more devastated?" she asked Ceallach quietly.

When she glanced at her companion, one corner of his mouth tugged up. His intensely blue eyes met hers, and the grin deepened. "I believe he should, my queen."

Joscela's heart skipped a beat. "Perhaps the rumors are true."

"Perhaps they are."

Though willing to believe almost anything of her kind, Joscela had discounted the whispers as wishful conspiracy theories. If they were true, however . . . If more dragon eggs existed, hidden away by the fae whose calling it had always been to train them . . .

If that were true, all might not be lost. Joscela could transform her present disgrace into victory. She could undo everything Manfred had accomplished.

As to that, she could undo him.

The increasing warmth at her side told her Ceallach had shifted closer.

Unwilling to risk any associate but him hearing, she spoke in a spell-hushed voice. "We must discover everything we can about this dragon master."

"Yes, my queen," Ceallach agreed in the same fashion.

He laid his hand over hers on the silver rail. They were royals—cool thinking and strategic. It wasn't their way to let their emotions run rampant. Nonetheless, both their palms were damp with excitement.

"We'll have our work cut out for us," she said, meaning the caution for herself as much as her confidante. "The Dragon Guild is as good at keeping secrets as the nobility."

"Better." Ceallach flashed a wolfish grin. "Nobles come and go. Dragon masters have survived whoever sat on the high throne. If someone held back a clutch, it won't be discovered easily."

Joscela longed to grin in return. She could always count on Ceallach relishing a challenge. Instead, she returned her gaze to the chaotic scene below, her expression carefully composed to queenly placidity.

"Good thing we have forever to rewrite destiny," she observed.

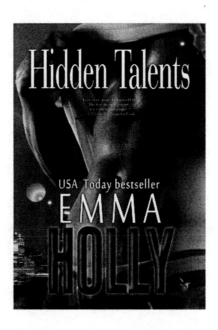

WEREWOLF cop Adam Santini is sworn to protect and serve all the supes in Resurrection, NY—including unsuspecting human Talents who wander in from Outside.

Telekinetic Ari is hot on the trail of a mysterious crime boss who wants to exploit her gift for his own evil ends, a mission that puts her on a collision course with the hottest cop in the RPD.

Adam wants the crime boss too, but mostly he wants Ari. She seems to be the mate he's been yearning for all his life, though getting a former street kid into bed with the Law could be his toughest case to date.

"Hidden Talents is the perfect package of supes, romance, mystery and HEA!"—**Paperback Dolls**

available in ebook and print

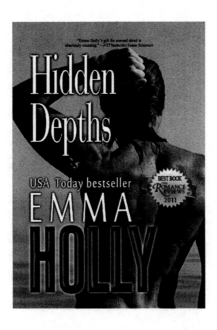

JAMES and Olivia Forster have been happily married for many years. A harmless kink here or there spices up their love life, but they can't imagine the kinks they'll encounter while sneaking off to their beach house for a long hot weekend.

Anso Vitul has ruled the wereseals for one short month. He hardly needs his authority questioned because he's going crazy from mating heat. Anso's best friend and male lover Ty offers to help him find the human mate his genes are seeking.

To Ty's amazement, Anso's quest leads him claim not one partner but a pair. Ty would object, except he too finds the Forsters hopelessly attractive.

"The most captivating and titillating story I have read in some time . . . Flaming hot . . . even under water"—**Tara's Blog**

available in ebook and print

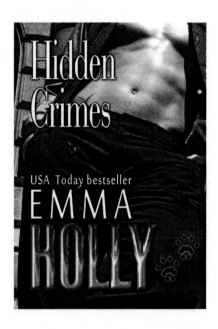

CATS and dogs shouldn't fall in love. Like any wolf, detective Nate Rivera knows this. He can't help it if the tigress he's been trading quips with at the supermarket is the most alluring woman he's ever met—sassy too, which suits him down to his designer boots.

Evina Mohajit is aware their flirtation can't lead to more. Still, she relishes trading banter with the hot werewolf. This hardworking single mom hasn't felt so female since her twins' baby daddy left to start his new family. Plus, as a station chief in Resurrection's Fire Department, she understands the demands of a dangerous job.

Their will-they-or-won't-they tango could go on forever if it weren't for the mortal peril the city's shifter children fall into. To save them, Nate and Evina must team up, a choice that ignites the sparks smoldering between them . . .

"Weaving the police procedural with her inventive love scenes [made] this book one I could not put down."—**The Romance Reviews**

available in ebook and print

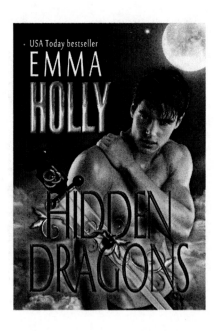

DO you believe in dragons? Werewolf cop Rick Lupone would say no . . . until a dying faerie tells him the fate of his city depends on him. If he can't protect a mysterious woman in peril, everything may be lost. The only discovery more shocking is that the woman he's meant to save is his high school crush, Cass Maycee.

Half fae Cass didn't earn her Snow White nickname by chance. All her life, her refusal to abuse fae glamour kept men like Rick at arm's length. Now something new is waking up inside her, a secret heritage her pureblood father kept her in the dark about. Letting it out might kill her, but keeping it hidden is no longer an option. The dragons' ancient enemies are moving. If they find the prize before Rick and Cass, the supe-friendly city of Resurrection just might go up in flames.

"[Hidden Dragons] kept me completely enthralled . . . sexy & erotic"
—Platinum Reviews

available in ebook and print

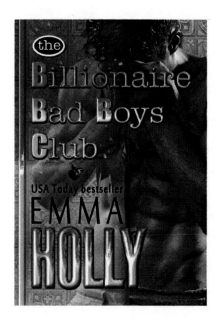

SELF-made billionaires Zane and Trey have been a club of two since they were eighteen. They've done everything together: play football, fall in love, even get smacked around by their dads. The only thing they haven't tried is seducing the same woman. When they set their sights on sexy chef Rebecca, these bad boys just might have met their match!

"This book is a mesmerizing, beautiful and oh-my-gods-hot work of art!"
—**BittenByLove** 5-hearts review

available in ebook and print

CPSIA information can be obtained at www.ICGtesting.com
Printed in the USA
LVOW10s2014180614

390653LV00030B/1571/P